Bree wanted Jorie's answer but she didn't remember the question. Music was so easy but this...this was so hard to follow, to make sense of. Her climax was unbearably close. What words could even matter? But she needed more than Jorie's touch. "Please tell me you love me!"

Jorie ceased all movement and Bree could only hear her pounding heart, like timpani in her ears. "Don't—don't stop!"

Jorie's fingers surged into her, deep and hard. Bree cried out as orgasm raced over her like a waterfall, churning her heart and body from passion to vibrant, searing ecstasy.

It was several minutes before Bree recalled where she was, and that the friendly passion they'd agreed to share wasn't supposed to include a profession of love.

Maybe Next Time

BY
KARIN KALLMAKER

Bella
BOOKS

2003

Bella Books, Inc.
P.O. Box 10543
Tallahassee, FL 32302

Printed in the United States of America on acid-free paper
First Edition

Editors: Kelly Smith and Greg Herren
Cover designer: Bonnie Liss (Phoenix Graphics)

ISBN 1-931513-26-0

For Maria, Past, Present and Future
Falling in Love Again...Can't Help It
In Memory of IZ

A baker's dozen

About the Author

Karin Kallmaker was born in 1960 and raised by her loving, middle-class parents in California's Central Valley. The physician's Statement of Live Birth plainly declares, "Sex: Female" and "Cry: Lusty." Both are still true.

From a normal childhood and equally unremarkable public school adolescence, she went on to obtain an ordinary Bachelor's degree from the California State University at Sacramento. At the age of 16, eyes wide open, she fell into the arms of her first and only sweetheart.

Ten years later, after seeing the film *Desert Hearts*, her sweetheart descended on the Berkeley Public Library determined to find some of "those" books. "Rule, Jane" led to "Lesbianism — Fiction" and then on to book after self-affirming book by and about lesbians. These books were the encouragement Karin needed to forget the so-called "mainstream" and spin her first romance for lesbians. That manuscript became her first novel, *In Every Port*. She now lives in the San Francisco Bay Area with that very same sweetheart; she is a one-woman woman. The happily-ever-after couple became Mom and Moogie to Kelson in 1995 and Eleanor in 1997. They celebrate their twenty-seventh anniversary in 2004.

Karin also writes as Laura Adams, her science fiction and fantasy persona.

Hawaiian Words and Phrases
Used in This Book

A'la: Lava that has cooled to jagged, glassy rock

Ahe Honi: Literally, "Breeze Kiss." As a song title,
   the kiss of the breeze.

'Ai: Food

Alania: Undulating ocean surface, without obvious swells or breaks

Anake: Aunt

Aniani: A light, gentle breeze without certain direction

ao pua'a: Mist that surrounds mountain tops

'Epa: Traitor; on who violates kapu or guest rights

Ha'ihai: A hunter, particularly of prey that evades capture

Heiau: A sacred place closed to all but native Hawaiians and celebrants

Honu, honumaoli: Sea turtle, Giant tortoise

Hupo haole: Stupid or foolish white person or mainlander

Kapa: Weaving from native bark; also labia

Kapu: Taboos and laws

Keiki: Child

Kihei: A dress knotted over one shoulder, leaving the other bare

Kolohe: Evil

Kuamo'o: A path frequently taken and generally known

Lehua: Honored woman, particularly an elder

Limu: Moss

Lolelua: Fickle and unreliable

Maʻehaʻeha: Near twilight

Maʻeleʻele: Benumbed, usually in a pleasant state, as in love. Also bewildered.

Makani: A sharp, landward wind

Makawela: Outcasts, those who violated a taboo

Manu: Any creature with wings

Milimili keiki: Beloved, treasured child

Muumuu: Traditional Hawaiian dress with a wide variety of styling from informal to ceremonial

ʻOhana: Family of blood or choice. *ʻOhana* is the first priority of traditional Hawaiian culture.

Pakaha: Small minty herb

Paniolo: Cowboys of the Waimea Valley

Pahoehoe: Lava that has cooled to a flat, smooth surface, usually opaque and dull

Pia: Beer

Pilikia: Trouble, unrest

Pule: Prayer or blessing

Tutu: Grandmother

ʻUhane: Sad, slow or funereal

Uhaua: Testicles

Wiwoʻole: Courage, boldness

Kuamoʻo

(The Frequented Path)

CHAPTER ONE

"Ms. Starling, you've got six claim checks, but I've only got five bags. What's missing?"

Bree stared fixedly at the skycap but could still see the bag in question out of the corner of her eye, circling on the baggage claim conveyor. The violin case was soon going to be the only unclaimed item.

Walk away, she told herself. It's that easy.

She'd never checked her instrument through the regular baggage service before, but this time she had hoped for fate's intervention. Luggage went missing all the time. Items could be crushed beyond recognition. But the violin had survived. Even the fates wouldn't take pity on her, not that there was any reason that they should.

She could have left it behind, she told herself. It would be as easy as, say, leaving her skin behind.

"Oh." The round face split into a wide smile. "The violin, of course. I'll take good care of it."

He held it out, but she gestured at the cart. She would not touch it herself. If she didn't touch it she could pretend the pain wasn't there.

The skycap escorted her to the rental kiosk, then waited while a utilitarian white sedan was brought around. It wasn't until after she had tipped him and settled into the car that she realized he had set the violin case on the passenger seat. He'd even fixed the seatbelt around it.

The car was an inferno in spite of the air conditioner on full blast. She shrugged off the jacket that had kept the airplane's chill at bay and sat for a moment in the swelter. Her back broke into a sweat against the hot seat. It was one of the most alive sensations she'd felt in a very long time. It was not particularly welcome.

Her sunglasses were nowhere to be found. The glare was so bright she had to close her eyes halfway, leaving her no strength or inclination to look at the violin. She didn't have to look at it. She had other things to worry about.

She turned south onto the Queen Kaahumanu Highway and idly punched on the radio. She quickly switched away from music, searching out news. Voices drowned out the crooning of the violin. She didn't really listen, but the cadence was a kind of white noise.

Rock, island, punk, country, rock, classical.

No, she thought. Not that.

She swerved into a dead end near a new subdivision and marina at Wawahiwaa Point. It was the fourteenth minute of the Tallis Fantasia. The bass line rose, in came the viola. She could see Osawa's upraised hand, signaling her...

She was out of the car, standing in the dirt, with no recollection of having opened the door. The voice of her own violin poured over her body like lava. When she forgot her injury she called it Stupid Pain. When others forgot she called it Thoughtless Pain. She had nearly as many words for pain as her ancestors did for the wind, but there was no word for this agony, to hear the way it had been...

4

When the final note faded under the roar of a rising aircraft, she felt the tears on her cheeks and tasted iron in her mouth. The radio spilled out voices now, in measured tones.

"And welcome back to those of you listening today to the KUOH tribute on this fortieth birthday of the internationally known local girl made good, Sabrina Starling. That was the Fantasia on a theme by Thomas Tallis, composed by Ralph Vaughan Williams, and recorded with the Stuttgarter Kammerorchester under the direction of..."

Bree backed away from the car, and only stopped when she stumbled. She'd reached the lava field. The voice was very far away. Soon there would be music, more unbearable music.

Dr. Sheridan told her to lose herself in the physical world when her head felt as if it would burst open from the waves of remembered music. All the gods, she wasn't prepared for this trip, what would be required of her, how she would have to act. Not here, not with all the pain that had made the journey with her.

"Happy birthday," she muttered. Forty was even less fun than thirty-nine had been. That the day was the thirty-third anniversary of her arrival on the island was completely unimportant, at least right now.

Look around. White car, black lava, blue sky, brown dirt. Any detail will do, Dr. Sheridan had said. She inhaled deeply and opened her eyes wide, trying to dampen the inner anguish with her external senses. The late afternoon air was heavy, damp, and stank of jet fuel. But underneath were the sea, the mountains, and the undeniable, almost electrical smell of sunlight on the lava field.

The air traffic above her quieted and the sound of her name unwillingly drew her attention back to the car.

"...Starling's considerable and diverse body of work speaks for her past accomplishments. Though she hasn't performed in public since a mainland concert two years ago..."

She forced air into her lungs, consciously making herself breathe. The sparkles behind her eyes gradually faded away. Look at anything but the violin, she told herself.

5

Beyond the black rubble was the orange-gold sun, arcing downward toward the *alania* sea, smooth, without swells or breaks. The breeze blowing in was as soft as the touch of a petal to her burning cheeks. She turned from the ocean to gaze at green-crusted Mauna Kea. The peak, 13,000 feet above her, was wreathed in *ao pua'a*. The mist clung in defiance of what had been a warm day, and the singing blue sky was deepening into evening.

The breathtaking splendor was merely an average afternoon for the Kona coast. Tomorrow would be just like it. Yesterday probably had been.

Anake Lani hadn't seen yesterday's sun, nor the one before. Aunt Lani was gone. She wasn't even Bree's real aunt, and so couldn't join the hosts of Bree's ancestors. If Aunt Lani's voice could have joined them Bree might almost welcome their words, but she suspected she'd gone so far from them that even Aunt Lani could not have brought her back.

The cooling evening breeze swept over her again, briefly lifting her short black hair from her neck. There was music from the car, but it fell to such low tones she wasn't able to identify the piece. A small mercy, one she could barely appreciate.

She could sit here, just like this, for a week. She knew she was expected, but now that she was here, she did not know if she was strong enough to drive to Aunt Lani's house and not find her there.

There is nothing you can't do, Bree, Aunt Lani said, from the past.

Perhaps it had been true then, but it was a lie now. There was so much she could no longer do. Her left hand twitched and she recognized the urge. A crystal theme rose over the rumble of a launch leaving the marina, a line from the Goldberg Variations. It set off the recording in her head where every sterling note vibrated. Her left index finger twitched — it remembered. She tried to coil her hand as if it caressed the neck of her instrument, but it didn't obey her.

In paradise, standing on the shore of the fire and ocean that had made the land, she'd hoped for more healing than this.

More music from the faraway radio flooded her with memories of concert halls and endless airplane flights, theaters and practice rooms, rolling back in time. The past had lost none of its sharpness. The memory of the violin Aunt Lani had found for her and the music she had wrung from it was as clear in her mind as the passionate, soul-burning Bach that had soared from the Stradivarius. The music of a child was as vibrantly painful as all of the music that she would never play again.

"I suppose you're Sabrina." The other girl shrugged her hair over one shoulder.

Bree held out her hand.

Hands remained firmly on slender hips, then all Bree saw was a swish of long black hair disappearing into the house.

"Jorie, you can find a kind word." Her new aunt bustled up, carrying the largest of Bree's suitcases.

Bree was deeply aware of Jorie's flounce into the kitchen. When she saw the small bedroom with the new twin bed installed on the far side she understood.

She had nothing of value, so unpacking took little time. Just clothes, unimportant things. She'd never need the socks, it was warm and sticky. Moist air would warp strings anyway. Just as well.

It took her only the rest of the afternoon to like Laniakilani Elenola Pukui as much as she could like any grownup stranger. Aunt Lani sang while she did everything. Funny songs about grass shacks and crab bakes, and others in Hawaiian that sounded like poetry, though Aunt Lani said they were mostly about grass shacks and crab bakes. Some were about living close to their ancestors. Aunt Lani said she would explain about that later, when Bree had had a chance to meet a few of her own.

Jorie, Marjorie Kelekia Pukui, was another matter, but Bree was used to hostility. Dee had been hostile. The last of her father's three wives, Dee hadn't liked Bree — the product of marriage two — at all.

Bree tried not to think about Dee. Daddy had thought it funny that their names rhymed. If there was a word for how she felt about Dee, she didn't know it. She couldn't play it. So she didn't feel it. She held it in. Los Angeles was far away and the things she hadn't been able to bring with her seemed like they belonged in Australia. She'd been having a long, no good day for months.

"You'll be glad it's summer." Aunt Lani handed her a heaping plate of white fish stewed in tomatoes and pineapple. "Jorie and you can get to know each other."

Jorie had no enthusiasm for it, and after dinner ran out to play with her friends. Bree trailed after her, pretending to study the lush green leaves and vibrant blooming flowers that carpeted Aunt Lani's front yard. They reminded her of Schumann.

"Ignore her," Jorie ordered from halfway up the odd tree that sent roots down from limbs to forms dozens of new trunks. "She's only six and she's not even related to me."

Bree might have told them it was her seventh birthday, but she didn't. She couldn't play it, so what was the point?

She came in after dark when Aunt Lani called, had a bath, was read to and tucked into her new bed. The sheets smelled like the ocean that she could hear from what seemed a long way off.

"Welcome to your *'ohana*," Aunt Lani said, after she kissed Bree's forehead. "You will feel better soon."

Feeling better wasn't something she had any strength for. The days limped by. Jorie hated her. None of the kids had any use for her. She didn't talk much, to begin with, and they all chattered so freely. They all knew Hawaiian and lapsed into it when she was around. She didn't know what *hupo haole* meant, but it couldn't be a compliment. They would gather on the fallen log at the top of the hill and tell stories, using their hands as they spoke of Pele and Kamehameha and Captain Cook. Bree watched from a distance, waiting for when Momi would sing. It was something.

Aunt Lani was nicer than Dee ever had been, Bree appreciated that. Sometimes, if she didn't look right at her, Bree could almost imagine Aunt Lani was her mother. She moved like mommy had, quick and light.

"Do you think you could cut up the oranges?" Aunt Lani gestured at the peeled fruit and the paring knife that lay next to them.

Bree nodded, but hesitated. She wasn't allowed to use knives. Mr. Proctor, her old music teacher, had told her never to touch one. Never.

"Go on. There is nothing you can't do, Bree."

She swallowed hard and didn't know what to do.

Aunt Lani glanced at her as she stirred together macaroni salad. "What are you thinking, *keiki*?"

Bree picked up the knife in her right hand, holding the handle between her fingertips and thumb.

"That's not how you hold it, to begin with. Let me show you how."

Aunt Lani wrapped her fist around the handle. Not like a bow, then. "The trick is to keep your other hand away from the tip of the knife while you slice. I just need chunks, like that."

The job was quickly done. Bree washed her hands while Aunt Lani went back to the macaroni salad. Bree liked the macaroni salad Aunt Lani made. Jorie was out playing, but Bree really didn't mind helping. Sometimes Aunt Lani sang and when she wasn't singing she had the radio playing whatever the small local station felt like that day.

"Only two more gallons to go." Aunt Lani scooped finished salad into an old plastic tub. The tub threatened to skitter off the counter, so Bree held it in place. "I like a good party, but I don't know what I was thinking when I said I'd bring the salad. I had planned to spend the afternoon finishing the last of that commission."

Some noodles missed and Bree quickly scooped them off the counter with her finger and popped them into her mouth. She liked the artwork that Aunt Lani did, made up of pottery and her own knitted pieces, stained and soaked and spattered with colors. They sang when they were done, in a way.

"You have to wash your hands again if you want to help." After Bree finished at the sink Aunt Lani observed, "That didn't take nearly long enough."

Bree turned her hands back and front to show she had gotten them clean. She'd even used soap.

"Whatever happened to your fingers, *keiki*?" Aunt Lani took Bree's hands in her own, then looked hard at the calluses on Bree's left fingertips. "How did you get these marks?"

She shrugged. They were going away, slowly.

"Hmm. I remember your father writing you had music lessons in that last Christmas card — too young if you ask me. Your fingers might never be the same."

Bree pulled her hands away. Mr. Proctor had said she would never want her fingers to go back the way they had been. Aunt Lani was looking at her very seriously. Bree wondered what she was supposed to say.

Aunt Lani turned to the bubbling pot of macaroni. "If you decide to say something let me know so I can pay attention. I wouldn't want to miss it."

Bree wondered if she was being teased. Grownups liked to do that. Dee had always said she was teasing when she said something that hurt. Aunt Lani didn't hurt, she just didn't understand.

Bree went out to the garage to get another jug of mayonnaise. When she came back Aunt Lani had turned on the radio.

Neither an island ballad nor a mainland hit, she knew the music right away: Symphony Number Four in B-flat Major, Opus 60 by Ludwig van Beethoven as conducted by Leonard Bernstein with the New York Philharmonic Orchestra. It had been one of daddy's birthday presents to her last year. Because of the tempo, she could tell the Bernstein from the others she had in her collection. Her records had been too heavy to bring with her. Aunt Lani didn't own a phonograph anyway.

After a minute, Aunt Lani took the jug out of her hand and Bree put her arms around the radio. She listened.

"...Musette for Strings, opus fifty-eight. Next we'll turn to an unaccompanied transcription of the Adagio by Samuel Barber..."

Grace, from the fates or the gods, from anywhere — all Bree wanted was grace and mercy. She didn't deserve it, she reminded herself. Maybe, once, long ago, she'd been touched by it, but not since...not since San Francisco. Stumbling, she made her way to the car, slapping at the radio before the Adagio cut her soul to ribbons. There was a second of silence, but before she could relax, relentless memory surged again.

"I don't get to go?" Jorie snapped her mouth shut, then opened it again. "But mom!"

"I thought you would like a sleepover at Momi's instead."

"But I like music. Too." Her gaze flickered to Bree.

"Since when have you liked any music besides those Beatles?" Aunt Lani pulled her *muumuu* over her head. Bree loved the elegant stitching around the collar that Aunt Lani had done herself. Aunt Lani looked like a princess in it.

She glanced down at her own striped pants. She knew what *hupo haole* meant now, and the Los Angeles bought pants did make her look like a stupid mainlander, a foolish white girl, even though her skin was only a little lighter than Jorie's.

"She's just a kid. I like it more."

"Bree is older than both of us when it comes to music."

"Mom!" Jorie gave the word five beats. "She's not even '*ohana*."

"Marjorie! You will never say that again!"

Bree stepped back. She'd never heard Aunt Lani raise her voice before. It was her fault. Now Jorie would hate her for always.

"You know what I mean." Jorie stared at her feet.

"Yes, I do. Be glad I'm still going to let you go to Momi's after that remark."

"Okay."

Bree decided it was a good time to go to the bathroom. She managed not to get in Jorie's way until Jorie had clambered out of the car at Momi's, a duffel bag over one shoulder.

Aunt Lani's station wagon was hot, though the sun was near setting. "It's not going to have any classical music, Bree. I don't want you to be disappointed. But your mother was my dearest friend in life, and she loved her island music heritage, so I think you will like it, too. After her parents and granny died, music was all she had. It was her granny who taught her to sing."

11

Bree had heard all this before, except the part about her grandmother. She didn't know anything about her mother's family. Her father hadn't wanted to talk about it, and she could even now only barely remember her mother. She could remember her mother's laugh. She remembered playing a game where mommy wrapped her long, beautiful hair around Bree's waist while Bree yelled, "Rapunzel, let down your hair!"

And the song about the turtles, she'd never forget that. She didn't forget music.

Aunt Lani was quiet for a while, and Bree hummed the gentle lullaby. *Honu, grandmother of the waves, your shell like a star in the sea, flying honu take me away, to where my true love will always be.*

She still missed mommy and she couldn't even think about daddy without feeling like she'd cry. The night mommy went away in the ambulance Bree had sung it to herself. She'd kept on singing it to herself every night since mommy couldn't anymore. Dee hadn't liked it, though, so she'd stopped doing it so anyone else could hear.

After daddy's funeral no one could decide where Bree would live. Tbe documents said who got daddy's money, and her half-brother, apparently, got most of it. Sean was twenty-five and didn't need a baby around, especially one with a noisy violin. She'd heard him and Dee talking about her. She didn't know what a caterwaul was but it couldn't be a compliment, no more than *hupo haole* was. Bree had something called a trust and trustees and Dee really hated them because there wasn't a sum lump or something like that.

She didn't understand things like antibiotic and embolus, but she'd learned to spell them. Infection took mommy and embolus took daddy. People called them surprises, but not the kind like a birthday party. She'd played songs that made her feel better because she was so alone, but Dee hadn't liked the music as much after daddy died. There hadn't been any music after awhile. Not until Aunt Lani had turned on her radio.

"We'll sit on the ground, too. I brought blankets. It'll be so pleasant near the water. As long as you're not expecting an orchestra."

Bree shook her head. She was not expecting anything like when daddy had taken her along on a business trip last year just so she could hear the Chicago Symphony Orchestra. Dee had hated that she had gotten to go. But she would never forget her first vision of the hall — the soaring ceiling, the rows and rows and rows of seats, the balconies, the stage filled with music stands and waiting instruments. She had held her breath as much as she could. Aunt Lani had told her the island of Hawaii did not have a concert hall even half that size.

"The *heiau* is a sacred place, so just watch what I do and you will learn. I don't think there will be any other children, but you never know. We won't be inside the real temple, but between it and the beach. I hope you like it."

Bree didn't care about the details. It was music and performed live. She would hear instruments singing. The radio was good, but it wasn't the same.

She held tight to Aunt Lani's hand and then snuggled close after the blanket was spread out. There wasn't a real stage, but a cleared area with a rough awning over it. The drums and microphone said that was where she should keep looking for the music to start. There was a small guitar resting on a stand there, its strings covered just below the tuning keys by a steel bar. She wondered what that would sound like. *Portamento*, perhaps? Would it give the guitar *legato*, like a trombone?

She noticed the man as soon as she settled into place. He was enormous. His legs were like the banyan tree in Aunt Lani's yard. He was so large he might have been two trees in one. His laugh carried as he talked. At no particular point in time that she could see he heaved himself to his feet, without stopping his conversation, and went to the microphone. Then she saw that he was carrying a four-string guitar, very small. It looked so tiny against his huge chest it might have been a necklace. Aunt Lani had explained about ukuleles, so that was probably what it was.

He spoke for a time about the *heiau* and the plight of the native Hawaiians, caught between the bitter loss of community in the past and the unavoidable, modern future, a tiny cluster of gods-made islands in the shadows of superpowers. All the while his fingers strummed the ukulele softly, making it sing so sweetly that Bree found her mother's song rising in her too, and she wanted to sing with him, because maybe he would know about the silence inside her. When he spoke in Hawaiian she almost felt she could understand because the ukulele translated the words.

The concert was long and mostly in Hawaiian. Sometimes the music was so low that the sound of the ocean behind them became part of it. Other parts were loud enough to send sea birds cawing overhead. The moon rose and the walls of stacked rock that framed the *heiau* gleamed in the silver light. Her shoulder blades itched all at once and something whispered to her. It was so gentle that the silence almost covered it up. *Milimili keiki*...it could have been the waves rustling onto the sand.

When it was over Aunt Lani took Bree by the hand and led her toward the awning. They waited for a long time, but finally the singer, looming like a giant — Bree wasn't afraid — noticed them.

He greeted Aunt Lani by name, with a kiss on her cheek, and they spoke of family. Bree only saw the ukulele resting on the stool near the microphone.

"This is the newest member of my *'ohana*," Aunt Lani said. "She's Ienipa's child and came to me because her father passed on in the spring. He had no family and her...guardians thought Sabrina belonged with Ienipa's people."

"And you're all Ienipa had." The singer smiled down at Bree, then his smile faded. He gave her a long, piercing look. Bree thought about words she might say, that he might understand. But before she could find them he nodded. "Go ahead." He did not call her *keiki*.

She left Aunt Lani's side to pick up the ukulele. She heard someone say something sharp to her, but the giant, the one who gave her such a moment, shushed the protest.

She could not hold it the way he did — her hands didn't know his way. Instead, she tucked it under her chin and plucked the strings with her right hand. She heard the notes, then let her left hand curl around the neck so her fingers could press down on the strings. She closed her eyes. *Pizzicato* would work with this instrument, but none of the melodies she knew fit strings so strangely tuned.

She remembered his sad song of the warrior's lost bride, and she picked it out to learn the way of the ukulele.

Her voice...she could feel her voice coming out, even with this strange instrument. She learned the resonance of the strings and their response to the pressure of her fingertips. Middle C was here on a violin, but there on a ukulele. Her fingers would remember now. The ukulele wanted to sing. The melodies she knew began to flow.

At some point she was aware that a large, infinitely gentle hand was resting on the top of her head as she played.

"You don't have to come with us, Jorie. We're just driving into town for a bit."

Bree was surprised when Jorie got in the front seat next to her. It was the last day of summer and Jorie's friends probably had plans. "I got nothing better to do."

Aunt Lani's big station wagon chugged into Kona proper, squeaking to a stop near the farmer's market.

"Ah, mom, are we just getting vegetables?" Jorie slumped in the seat.

"Not just that. You staying or coming?"

Bree liked Jorie's sandals. She thought it would be nice to be eight, to have long legs and hair that seemed to float even when there was no breeze. She followed Aunt Lani into a store. The smell — the sharp mix of musty paper, mineral oil and resin — took her breath away.

She stood staring while Aunt Lani talked to the man behind the counter.

"I can't afford a really good one," Aunt Lani was saying. "She's had some lessons and seems awfully good for a child."

Their voices faded to a rustling background. Bree could only see that behind the man, in a locked case, were violins. From a factory, but that didn't matter. Violins.

He was holding one out. Holding it out to her.

"Do you know how to tune it, little sister? I can do..."

"Her father told me she liked music..."

15

Her fingers sounded the strings and turned the tuning pegs. She tightened the bow.

"...Advise you to keep it cheap right off, because kids change their minds..."

Bow met strings, brushing notes into the air.

"...This is so boring..."

She closed her eyes and found her voice in the violin.

Vivaldi seized her. She'd been working on the piece when her father had died. Winter, sawing, piercing, swirling cold of ice and snow, jabbing pain and exultation, fierce spirals of tone and rhythm...Vivaldi, goodbye, grieving. Vivaldi...Dee hated Vivaldi.

She opened her eyes when she finished. Aunt Lani looked as if she might cry. The man behind the counter was sitting down, his mouth slack. Jorie blinked at her.

"I had lessons three times a week and on Thursdays Mr. Proctor said I couldn't practice, I had to let it alone for the whole day." Bree ran out of breath. "I like Vivaldi and Mozart. Mr. Proctor said that I should leave Bach out for now, but I practiced it on the sly because Dad liked the Goldbergs and I could do the opening to the first one even though it takes a bigger hand to make some of the combinations and my arm gets tired of bowing on the longer pieces and my calluses will come back I suppose and I should start doing the exercises for my arms and shoulders again..."

Bree shook herself out of the past, away from the day when she had reclaimed her voice. Aunt Lani had had only instinct to go on, but she'd known Bree wasn't complete. She cared enough for her best friend's daughter that she'd found what was missing.

The violin on the passenger seat called to her from its case. It cost infinitely more than the one Aunt Lani had bought on credit that day, but it was still only practice quality. The beautiful, luminous Guarneri was in the care of her agent, and another more expensive still was in a secured, insured, climate-controlled storage vault. Not that she would ever touch either of them again. She could hardly bear to subject this less powerful instrument to her clumsy fumblings. Like the others, it wanted to sing, but she could no longer help.

16

The Queen Kaahumanu Highway had a posted speed limit of fifty-five. The two-lane ribbon could take her between the extreme northern and southern points of the island. The reality of the speed limit, however, was that she could only move as fast as the car in front of her. In Beijing she would have swung out into the opposing lane and used the sidewalk at the corner. The entire traffic structure of Beijing presumed that one would do so — timidity wreaked havoc. But she was on island time now. Today there was sun. Tomorrow there was sun. Next week, for a change, there would be sun. There was always later.

Island time was ideal since she didn't want to get where she was going.

Kona had grown. A multiplex sat next to a Kmart off the highway. Not far beyond she passed a Wal-Mart and then a Borders. It was all so commercial, and not just for the tourists. What the residents seemed to want had changed as well.

Impulse made her turn left at the Mamalahoa Highway when she should have continued south to Keauhou. The long grade was no problem for her rental car, but it had certainly taxed Aunt Lani's station wagon.

"No sense in having it boil over. I allowed time." Aunt Lani turned off the engine. Bree could hear its unhappy hiss. The early September Friday was one of the hottest she'd experienced so far. She was glad she wasn't sitting in a classroom, though she liked her new school.

"Are we on a volcano now?"

"All of the island was made by volcanoes. The people are used to fire and ocean. It made the land."

Bree looked down the mountain at the tiny town they lived in, spread across the foot of the mountain. Houses dotted the shoreline, and fingers of roads wove across what she thought of as the mountain's

17

knees. They were at the hip level, now, to cross the island to Hilo on the other side. Aunt Lani had made them an appointment to talk to a professor of music at the University of Hawaii. Bree wasn't sure she understood why, but she'd brought her violin. Even though it didn't have the same voice as the one her father had bought her, she was learning to let it speak through her.

They continued the journey once the radiator stopped hissing. Aunt Lani told her about the Waimea Valley and the culture of the *paniolos*, the Hawaiian cowboys. Bree was skeptical about John Wayne in Hawaii. Then she saw the cows. She could understand that where there were cows, there were most likely cowboys. They passed riding stables and a ranch. It was almost cold.

Bree was trying to accept that Hawaii was not what she had expected. Dee had told her she'd live on a beach and spend every day swimming. In no time she'd look just like all the other brown Hawaiians. Well, there were schools in Hawaii, and plenty of kids who thought she was strange, just like in Los Angeles. Though she looked more like Jorie and her friends from all the summer sun, Bree still didn't feel like them. She was *haole*, and even worse, a mainlander.

She was used to feeling different, though. It didn't bother her, not much. Not everyone had a violin for a best friend.

The red roofs on the scattered buildings of the University of Hawaii at Hilo reminded Bree of the fuchsias on Aunt Lani's deck. Everyone seemed so tall. She had to half skip to keep up with Aunt Lani.

It was cold inside the music department office and Bree thought some of the cold came from the woman who sat at the desk. She gave Bree an icy look, then fixed on the violin case Bree carried.

"You made this appointment so a child could audition for the department head?"

"It's not an audition." Aunt Lani was very calm and Bree decided not to be afraid. "I am hoping to get guidance for Sabrina's talent."

The woman sniffed. "It's highly irregular. I doubt Professor Stockwell will agree, appointment or not."

"It was a very long drive to get here."

Bree could tell the woman didn't care about that. She gave the two of them another freezing look and left the room. When she returned her eyes were like rocks.

Aunt Lani argued and Bree could tell Aunt Lani was very angry. She hid behind her, wondering what was at stake. She clutched her violin. She'd be okay if she had one. She'd been sad but okay when daddy died because she'd had the beautiful violin he'd given her for her fifth birthday. It had only been nearly unbearable after Dee had sold it.

Aunt Lani bustled her out of the building, walking twice as fast as when they'd arrived. They left the red roofs behind. Aunt Lani's mouth was set into a hard, straight line.

They stopped a short while later in what looked like just another parking lot. Aunt Lani urged her out of the car. Bree followed, hearing an unusually deep thrumming sound.

There were a couple dozen stone steps to climb. She kept a grip on her violin case, thinking she should have probably left it in the car. The air was getting damp and the booming roar was growing louder.

Aunt Lani was standing at a railing, taking big, deep breaths.

It was a waterfall.

Bree'd never seen one before. She'd never felt one before, through her feet. She'd never *heard* one before.

Rainbows shimmered in the mist. The falling river waters were churned to white.

It was so beautiful.

"Play something for me, Bree, for the rainbows." Aunt Lani didn't sound like herself.

Bach was like falling water and unrestrained power. Bach was geometries, Mr. Proctor had said, the kind that unlocked the secrets of the universe. She played what she could of the first Goldberg, then the easier pieces adapted from the Well Tempered Clavier. Her fingers grew damp on the strings. It changed the sound, made it more resonant but flat. She turned to the simple melody she remembered from the gentle giant's concert.

When the last note fell out over the rainbows, Aunt Lani finally turned away from the beauty of the waterfall, her face wet. "Thank you, Bree. You've given me great comfort."

Bree went to settle her violin in the case when she saw money in it. Quarters, perhaps four or five dollars' worth, from the busload of tourists who had come and gone.

"Aunt Lani, look!" She had always been used to having her own pocket money and now she knew how to get some. "I could get everybody those cookies at the farmer's market."

Aunt Lani helped her gather the coins up, but her face was back in firm, hard lines. "Oh, Ienipa," she whispered. "I can't let this road have her, too."

Bree knew that Ienipa was Jennifer in Hawaiian, her mother's name, but the rest she didn't understand.

"How tired are your fingers, *keiki*? Could you play me another piece, the best you've ever played?"

"I would try. The strings are wet, but the car should dry them again."

They drove back to the university, and Aunt Lani walked her slowly and calmly back to the hallway outside the icy woman's office.

"Your best, Bree. This is a big building. Wake up the *manu* nesting under the roof."

It was a cold building, so Bree decided on the Vivaldi Winter again. She had better control of herself than she'd had at the music store. Her fingers were well warmed. She let the brittle wind skitter down the hallways, pushing ice into the stairwells and under doors. Her voice, through the violin, brought winter to rooms that had never known the drift of snow.

She let her bow go silent and felt goosepimples on her bare legs.

Applause startled her. Doors had opened. The icy woman was glaring at her. But other people — they were all grown-ups — stood round her in a circle, and they clapped.

"It's not an audition," Aunt Lani said to the woman. "I need guidance."

"I didn't understand," a man said. Bree turned toward the voice and thought the bony, tall man looked kind for someone as old as Aunt Lani or her father. He was probably even forty. "Let's have that appointment, shall we?"

20

If she didn't turn around soon Bree knew she would end up in Waimea, four thousand feet above sea level and far from where she was supposed to be. Jorie was expecting her. Jorie was having to do it all by herself. All the gods knew that Jorie was strong, but it wasn't fair that she should have to go through this alone.

Even with the prod of guilt, Bree found it hard to turn the car around. She didn't want to go to Aunt Lani's, not with memory chasing her like this.

Memory should always be summer, Aunt Lani said from the past.

Endless vistas of mountain and ocean spread out before her as she drove toward the sea again. Her memories were winter without a hope of spring. She'd lived with the gray of pain for so long that green felt unreal. Green was a completely different kind of pain, one she didn't have a word for yet. Dizzied, she pulled off the road at the overlook where she had stopped with Aunt Lani on their way to Hilo that long-ago day.

She rested at Mauna Kea's knees and didn't fight the pull of that particular tide. That day had been the beginning of her musical career. Professor Stockwell had been the final word on who taught her what and when, had provided access to better and better instruments, and been the guiding force in the choice of conservatory when no one in the islands could teach her more.

With Aunt Lani, he had protected her from maturing too soon, as a child and as a musician. She had never resented that, but she knew now she could never have those years again. There were things she might have done had she known when it would all end. There were things she would have never done, too.

She had no doubt that Professor Stockwell knew of her situation. She knew there was no way she could find the strength to visit him. What could she say? She was all out of words and the only reliable voice she had ever had was silent.

The last time she had seen him she had brought him to Tokyo for the — no. No, if she thought about that she would remember the

21

Concerto in E. She didn't need more music in her head right now. She could hardly breathe for the cacophony. No, she thought. I don't want to go there. No more memories. No more music.

Not even the turtle lullaby could touch her any longer.

Aunt Lani was gone. Aunt Lani had only wanted her to have a real childhood, the one her mother had never had. She hadn't wanted Sabrina to follow in Jennifer's footsteps. She tried to spare Bree the path of early fame, easy money, then the chill of not knowing who you really were, what you were made of, or who your ancestors were when life became hard.

Bree whispered into the coiling breeze, "I didn't escape it, though you tried." It had all been too easy. Until it got hard.

No more memories, she thought. I can't bear it.

All memories, joyous or painful, every step, every turn, all led to this place of perpetual pain.

Her left hand twitched — even in pain it remembered the music.

Because of the pain it also remembered Diana.

CHAPTER 2

The golden-orange sunset was so vivid it made her eyes water. The landscaped roadway swam in front of her. Blinking back tears caused the scene to change, and she could easily recall the way this intersection had been when she was a teenager. No mega-bookstore, no gigantic retail outlet. Memory merged with the present and Bree bit back a gasp.

They had torn down the roller rink. Sometime in the last several years the place where she had tried the hardest to be like other kids had been wiped away.

She turned into the manicured parking lot. Even that was changed — no potholes and mudsinks. She had learned to like Pez and Pixie Stix at the roller rink, because they were cool. Later, she'd tried smoking cigarettes and pot at the rink, because they were cool.

Tobacco made her stomach sour and left her fingertips dry. Pot just made her slow. So she'd given them up. Another lesson that part of her was just not bitchin' and never would be. Still, she had paraded new fashions under Jorie's tutelage. She had tried so hard.

Even there, she had only been reminded that she was different. She'd been fifteen when she'd begun to realize that it wasn't just the violin that set her apart.

She turned off the engine and put her head on the steering wheel. Jorie needed her right now. Jorie needed her *'ohana*. A wonderful word, Bree had come to understand. Not just family, but those you loved best. *'Ohana* was what you said it was. Aunt Lani had wanted them to become like sisters, but it had never worked. Jorie was a year older, a year cooler, a year smarter, a year more gorgeous...

"Where did those come from?" Jorie dumped the dry laundry on her bed.

Bree blushed as she struggled into the ridiculous training bra Aunt Lani suggested she wear when she'd turned eleven. It was a lot tighter than it had been six months ago. "Where do you think?"

"You're going to have boys after you."

Bree hated the thought. Boys smelled and she had yet to meet one who could say Mozart, let alone stop talking about his surfboard long enough to spell it. She hid her vexation at the way her boobs overflowed the cups and turned her back on Jorie. She didn't want Jorie to look. She reached for one of her bigger shirts.

"Wait," Jorie said. "Here."

Bree had to turn. Her face flamed. Jorie was holding out one of her bras.

"Don't look like that. Tell Mom you need new ones. I bet mine fits." Jorie sighed. "You're going to be stacked. I'll be this flat all my life, just like mom."

The bra did fit much better, but the cups were still a little too small. She was reaching for the shirt again when Jorie again said, "Here."

"I couldn't." It was one of Jorie's favorite shirts, one that made her look like she was in high school.

"I think you need some new clothes. Tell Mom to spend some of that trust money. You still look like a mainlander." Jorie grinned as she went back to folding laundry.

The grin didn't take all the sting out of the remark, but Bree knew Jorie no longer meant it to hurt, at least when they were by themselves. Her friends might, especially Cici, who could be a bitch. She slipped into the brilliant orange top and swept her hair in front of her right shoulder. It hid some of the bulges.

Jorie was staring at her chest and Bree wanted to turn her back again. "You look like Marilyn Monroe."

"I'm not blond." Bree could feel another blush starting in her cheeks.

"Okay, from the neck down. You want some advice?"

Bree waited. Jorie's advice had saved her from making a fool of herself many times, but she didn't want to ask for it outright. It was pathetic, still needing advice to fit in. She didn't know the talk, all the ways to be cool. She spent too much time with her violin to learn. It wasn't something she regretted. Okay, sometimes she did. Like when they were going skating.

"Boys think they can touch anything. You want one to leave you alone, you just tell him you'll put his *uhaua* in a blender."

Bree laughed. "I'll try to remember."

She helped Jorie finish folding the clothes from the line, then they went out to the front porch to wait for Momi. Her mom was driving them to the rink.

Aunt Lani looked up from her knitting. After a pause she said, "Let's go shopping tomorrow, Bree. I hadn't realized."

Was everyone looking at her chest? In that shirt maybe they would. She wasn't sure she liked it now.

Momi's mom's Corolla veered into the driveway. It was too late to take off Jorie's shirt. It didn't make her Jorie. Great, another reason for everyone to think she was a freak.

Bree's eyes swam with the past. She could smell the popcorn and hear the relentless turn of wheels on the smooth wooden floor. Hot dogs with warm relish and paper plates heaped with macaroni salad — it all came back. Circling the floor, wondering who was watching, who was looking, who was trying to get up the nerve to ask you if you wanted an Icee Pop or a Coke float, or to hold hands during a mirrorball skate. Maybe, if the manager wasn't there, they would play real rock and roll.

She had hated the rink sometimes, but she'd liked it, too. Jorie had looked out for her, though when she was with her friends Jorie could be as mean as they were. Year after year, Saturday night after Saturday night, around in circles like a fugue that never ended. Jorie was the melody and she was merely counterpoint.

"Fuck!" Bree rubbed her elbow while she glared at the smooth floor.

"Just get up," Momi advised as she glided by.

Bree heard Cici snicker as she skated past. A cluster of boys zoomed around her, their skates sounding like the drone of airplanes.

Jorie came to a perfect stop in front of her and planted the side of one skate against Bree's foot. "You really shouldn't be doing this," she advised as she pulled Bree upright. "What'll happen if you break a wrist?"

"I know," Bree muttered. She quickly let go of Jorie's hand even though she didn't want to. "It's just this once. It is a party."

"You know," Jorie added with a common flash of forbearance and bitterness, "the only reason all these people came to my sweet sixteen was to hear you play." She flipped her feathery black hair over one shoulder and skated off before Bree could protest that the kids were here because Jorie was one of the most popular girls in sophomore class. Even the juniors let Jorie hang out with them. But she did see Jorie's point — the parents weren't lingering because they wanted to watch the skating.

Part of her wanted to tell Jorie that it wasn't so easy being Sabrina Starling. She really wasn't supposed to skate. She didn't cut up fruit or anything else anymore. Performance pressure never let up, even at a birthday party. She practiced six days out of seven. When she went on a trip for a recital she still had to make up all her classes. Nobody let her slide because Aunt Lani wouldn't let them.

She couldn't complain because she wouldn't have it any other way. The sacrifices meant nothing because she was nothing without a violin. Even now she could feel it waiting for her with Aunt Lani.

She decided on one more lap, just to show she wasn't afraid of breaking a wrist. Maybe, she thought, she wouldn't play today. She'd save the piece for home, just for the three of them. Except she knew it wouldn't work — Jorie had never responded to her music with more than a bored sigh. She wanted Jorie to hear the piece, and the only way to ensure that was to play it here.

She didn't know why it mattered so much. She thought about Jorie all the time, though. She wondered if Jorie liked her shirt. She wondered if Jorie would notice it was tight. Jorie had told her these jeans were what everyone was wearing, but she never said if Bree looked good in them. What did it matter what Jorie thought? It just did, she told herself. It just did.

She watched Jorie skate, following her slowly around the oval. Jorie was laughing at something Cici said, then she put one hand on Cici's shoulder.

She hated Cici.

What was wrong with her? Jorie had always been beautiful, and she looked great in hip huggers and the skates made her legs seem a thousand miles long. She skated and ran track and she had great muscles in her butt.

Bree watched Jorie's butt muscles moving like the tide over sand, so smooth and rippling, and told herself it was envy. Her own butt would never be that firm, that shapely. No one would ever look at her and think, "Nice ass."

Ass — good god, she was staring at Jorie's ass. Not butt. What boys meant when they said that a particular girl could shake her ass.

It wasn't like she hadn't seen it, naked and clothed, every day for the last eight-plus years. Why was Jorie's ass different today?

It wasn't. She realized Jorie was the same as always.

27

She couldn't breathe.

She skated around and around, watching Jorie's ass. Part of her was terrified and the part that wasn't didn't know what she could possibly be afraid of. She knew she had that feeling. It was the feeling that meant she would have to do something about it tonight, in the dark, in the quiet, and hope that when her legs thrashed and she stifled a moan she didn't wake Jorie.

The feeling was strong and harsh, delirious and dangerous, and watching Jorie's ass only made it worse.

Boys talked about horny, boys talked about doing it, getting off, jerking off, porking, fucking, turning on, feeling up. None of those words were anything like the way she felt. No one would understand.

Time for cake, time to stand somewhere near Jorie and not think about why she wanted Jorie to notice her shirt and jeans. Her hair would never float, never lightly curl the way Jorie's did. Jorie had said it would probably look good short, but Bree thought being the only girl with short hair would just make her more of a nerd.

Bree watched Jorie take a deep, deep breath, watched her mouth form an "O" to blow out the candles. Maybe Jorie would look at her. She wanted to see Jorie's eyes, study the liquid brown that sometimes shimmered with laughter.

When Jorie did look Bree didn't know what to do. She watched Jorie's eyes darken slightly, resigned.

I want her to love me, Bree thought, I want her to love me, like in bed. Oh my fucking god, I'm in love with her.

Aunt Lani nudged her with her violin case. She hadn't tuned, she hadn't loosened up. Everyone was looking. Momi was rolling her eyes. Jorie was smiling, but it was a false smile. It was Jorie's party. It ought to be about her, Bree realized. But it was obvious that whatever most of the kids thought, the grownups were expecting Bree to play. She always played at parties. Her gift belonged to her 'ohana as much as herself — giving it away only made it stronger.

Recitals were easy. Lessons and practice, endless, repetitive scales were a welcome honing of her skills. It was all happiness, all bliss. Perfection was hers to reach for. The violin asked and she played. Why was playing for Jorie so hard?

It wasn't Jorie's party any more. It was a Sabrina Starling performance. She'd been pretty insensitive for a long time. No wonder Jorie hated her. Jorie would never love her. Not like that. Jorie wasn't like that. Jorie was good and pure....

She tuned, not looking at Jorie, but feeling the restless air from the kids. The music on the loudspeaker was shut off and everyone who was skating slowly came to a stop.

The violin slipped under her chin and her bow arm flexed as she snapped out the fingers on her left hand. If they laughed she would be humiliated. But she couldn't have stopped if she had wanted to. The violin had her now.

Carefully, heart pounding, she let the first line of the melody soar out. There could be nothing tentative about it. For Jorie, her favorite song, "Stairway to Heaven." After the first recitation of the striking melody line she bridged to the Fantasia in F-minor, and strove to bring out the classical patterns that progressed just as the modern piece did. When the music began to dance and climb toward its climax she forgot about the rink, and the grownups, and the kids. It was just the violin. The violin let her head fill with Jorie and from there she could weave any dream. From the Fantasia back to the rock melody, slowing finally, and fading away.

Applause, she had learned, was hard to gauge. The adults clapped enthusiastically, but she could have played "Happy Birthday" and they would have done the same. The other kids — they didn't know anything about music, only what they liked. They had no idea why they liked it, that Led Zeppelin wrote their music on the shoulders of giants.

But it still hurt, it still felt like a knife when she heard Cici say to Jorie, "Way to ruin a good song."

Jorie came around from behind the table. Remembering the moment it seemed to Bree that the world took a deep breath right along with her.

Maybe, after all these years, she — and the world — had never exhaled.

Jorie said, "Thank you, Bree. That was great."

And kissed her.

A sweet kiss on her cheek, that's all it was. A sweet kiss...

Bree would have liked to stay in that memory for a long, long time. It was innocent. It was natural, it seemed the most normal thing in the world, to appreciate how beautiful Jorie was. To want her. Dr. Sheridan said it was okay to remember that her life hadn't always been full of pain. She'd said Bree was learning to divert her mind from negative patterns. Was it better to obsess about what you loved or what you hated? Wasn't obsession the same either way?

None of that mattered. She wanted to stay in this particular past because it was before Diana.

She stopped at the farmer's market to buy sunglasses. At least the market was still there, even if it, too, seemed to sell more packaged goods than fresh produce. But the mound of pineapples made her stop in mid-step. She inhaled deeply. Truly fresh pineapple...it had been a very long time. She almost bought some but Jorie would be inundated with gifts of food.

Walking around Kona would have been more nostalgic if it hadn't changed so much. There had always been tourist restaurants and shops, but the sidewalks were dotted with hawkers wanting everyone to buy their excursion trips from them. She skirted them and ducked into a garish T-shirt shop.

Sunglasses were a prominent item. The purchase took no time at all and she found herself meandering through the marketplace to the seawalk. It was just to test the sunglasses in the glare of *ma'eha'eha*, the impending twilight.

The golden disk was slipping beyond the world's edge. Her eyes watered again, but it wasn't because the sunglasses were inadequate. Fifteen, and in love with Jorie, sixteen, and in love with Jorie...time had seemed to change nothing.

She had told herself it was just Jorie. Anyone would love Jorie. It didn't mean Bree was...that way. It was just Jorie she loved.

She snaked a fingertip under her glasses to wipe away the tear. A smile trembled on her lips, as wan as the last of the sun's glow. It was funny to think there had been a time in her life when she hadn't accepted she was gay, had thought it was how she felt about Jorie that defined her. Never mind the fact that she'd never wanted to let a boy anywhere near her.

The smile grew as she let the sun kiss her face with the last of its rays. The tickle in her stomach told her she still responded to that moment in her past, at her first competition, when she had had an inkling of what women would mean to her.

Mr. Proctor had picked her up at the airport in Los Angeles in what Bree swore had to be the same ancient Volvo he'd driven nine years ago. He talked mostly of how he'd have known Bree anywhere, though he hadn't seen her in more than a decade.

"Our first stop is the vault where the instrument you're borrowing is kept. You'll need to get comfortable with it."

"It's in a vault?" Bree's memories of L.A. were dim, but the sky was orange and she didn't remember it that way. Perhaps it was just that she was used to pure blue. She pushed away the thought of home. This would be her longest trip away from Aunt Lani, but she was nearly seventeen. She was old enough. Ten years and over seven thousand hours of practice — she was old enough.

"It's a Guarneri owned by a bank and on loan to the insurance company that sponsors the Philharmonic." He detailed who knew a friend of a former student whose uncle knew a director at the insurance company. "I know I don't have to tell you to take care of it."

"Of course." She wasn't intimidated by the value of the violin, but by its power and voice. When it spoke to her she wasn't sure if she could control it. She'd never held an instrument so aged.

"I just can't get over how you've grown up. You look like a real native."

The remark, though she sensed it was a compliment, left her irked by conflicting emotions. She was half Hawaiian so how else was she supposed to look? But at home she was considered *haole*. Jorie's friends never let her forget it. Her best friend, her violin, cared only that she was a musician.

The chilled interior of the bank was a long way from the island breezes she'd left behind. They were met by two businessmen looking bored with their errand. They both had to sign in to use the key they had brought, and an attendant with a measured gait led them past locked grilles to the vault's deepest chamber. The chill deepened. Keys were turned and the attendant carried the large box into a side room. Bree waited with Mr. Proctor until the two men emerged, one carrying a violin case and a long leather tube that must hold the bow.

Her fingertips itched and she gripped her hands behind her to keep from reaching for both items. A bow as well — that was a relief. The one she had was made of synthetic resin and had twice slipped in her grasp.

The attendant put the box back into place and the shorter of the two men reclaimed the key.

Bree signed a slip of paper stating that she had been given the eighteenth-century Guarneri violin and not nearly so old bow as a loan for the next four days. After she gave one of the men his pen back she said, "I suppose I should see if there's really a violin in there."

They gave her the case. She set it gently on the table and fumbled with the latches. She raised the lid as gently as she would a blanket from a sleeping baby's face.

The violin was so similar to the one her father had bought her that it might have been the same instrument, but she knew it was not. There was a streak in the wood on the neck that set it apart. She would have to learn this violin anew.

She brushed the strings with her index finger. Poor thing, it was so out of tune.

She ignored the impatient cough as she lifted the instrument gingerly from the case. She approximated the tuning as precisely as her ear could manage, testing each peg to make sure it would hold the string. This beautiful creature had been well cared for. The bow had been maintained as well — the tension was still very high.

The tuning would need to be improved, she thought. It had a slightly gypsy quality to it, and she smiled, because the violin wanted to laugh about that. She brushed the strings with the bow, loving the rakish skirl. The violin suggested a Polovtsian dance, all firelight and fortune tellers.

The instrument had a magnificent voice, resonant and rich. The vibrant rhythm bounced off the cold marble walls and Bree glanced up as she played to see that the attendant looked shocked, but he was smiling.

It was over too soon and now she heard an impatient shuffle behind her. She was still laughing with the violin when she said, "I think this will do."

The man with the key said coolly, "I would think so."

Bree realized then that people probably didn't play violins in banks very often. She set the Guarneri carefully in the case and risked a glance at the other man. With relief she saw the glimmer of a smile. He understood, maybe.

"My dear child." Mr. Proctor's voice shook slightly. "You have worked so very hard."

She double-checked the latches before she picked up the case. She had learned that no one else understood that the violin played her, and not the other way around. When she held the instrument its voice spoke through her.

They all went upstairs and the businessmen melted away while Mr. Proctor led her toward the parking garage.

"Look around you, Sabrina. There will be a day when some of these people will tell their friends that they heard you playing in a bank."

"How could they possibly remember?" She glanced around and saw that there *were* surreptitious looks following her. "Maybe they think I've got a machine gun in here."

He chuckled, but added, "Everyone who sees you will remember you."

Not at all sure that was a good thing, Bree had walked out of the bank and not thought about home — not much, anyway — for the next three days. The qualifications and quarter-final rounds went well for her, and Mr. Proctor and his wife kept her distracted in the evenings with sightseeing and a trip to the movies. She was too tense to identify with any of the young people portrayed in *Fame*, but maybe she'd see the movie again when it made its way to the Big Island. She was a little over-rehearsed and listened to Mr. Proctor's advice about resting. Bree was surprised when she glided into the finals, but Mr. Proctor said he'd never doubted it.

Mrs. Proctor had insisted on taking in the waist of Bree's dress for the final day, and adding make-up to Bree's eyes. "The judges are biased toward conservatory students, so let's help them think you're a little older than you are," she'd said.

Bree felt strange in make-up. Jorie always looked so good in it. Just a little lip gloss made her seem like a star. Bree felt as if the make-up was sitting on top of her skin, not really a part of her. Her eyes looked strange. Mrs. Proctor said they were exotic. Wasn't the competition about music and not how she looked?

Competitors were sequestered in what someone called the Green Room though the walls were beige. No one spoke to anyone else. Bree caught several of the others studying her, though, and she sensed hostility. As the day progressed and the tension increased, she fought back the urge to cry because she missed Aunt Lani and felt very alone. She filled her mind with Jorie, too. Jorie would never cry because someone looked at her crossly. Jorie could do anything, could handle any situation.

Her shoulder blades began to itch. It was a hot sensation, one she'd had before but had never felt so strongly. It was as if a chorus began speaking to her, a buzz of courage and strength. *Wiwo'ole*, they seemed to hum. Ancestors? That was absurd. She was *haole*. Half her ancestors were mainlanders who'd never stopped their pursuit of money long enough to sink their toes into sand.

In this place, though, she felt so far from her *'ohana* that maybe what was in her of the People needed to be stronger. Maybe here was where she needed her ancestors and their *wiwo'ole*. She sat up straight. Her shoulders still felt hot, but the voices subsided to a faint ripple that was slowly lost as she considered the task that lay ahead of her. She let the Schumann *Études de Concert composées d'après des caprices de Paganini* fill her mind. There was a lot of Paganini being performed today, but the Schumann was hers alone. Everyone had agreed that the third caprice seemed as if it had been written for her with its lively tempo that faded into an intensely romantic conclusion.

One by one other names were called. When there were only three of them left, a blond girl who looked twenty or more sat down next to her. "You okay?"

Bree nodded. She was no longer intimidated that the other finalists were all conservatory students two to four years older than she was. She allowed herself a quick look at the other girl. "I'll be fine."

"I don't doubt it." The girl laughed and held out her hand. "Anna Burley. I'll come in twelfth out of twelve."

Bree had to smile back as she shook Anna's hand. An unsettling tingle ran up her arm. Anna had a warm smile. "What makes you say that?"

"I've never made it to any finals before and I was playing so far above my head yesterday I thought my nose would bleed." The smile took on an intriguing sideways look. Bree was reminded of when Jorie was teasing her.

"I think anyone could win except maybe me," Bree admitted. "I'm too young. This was really just for practice."

Bree jumped as the other musician, a boy maybe two years older, kicked a chair.

Anna chortled. "If I could practice like you I'd have first chair anywhere I wanted."

"I didn't mean it that way."

"Of course not." Anna went on smiling at her and Bree didn't know where to look. She abruptly realized how full Anna's lips seemed. She wondered what it would be like to kiss them.

She swallowed hard. She didn't need this distraction. She wasn't like that. She just loved Jorie. If not for Jorie of course she'd be dating boys. Wouldn't she?

She went on looking at Anna, who chattered and smiled and sat closer.

The boy was called next. He looked funereal when he left. The minutes ticked by. Anna giggled a lot.

When the assistant stuck her head in and told Anna she had five minutes, Bree felt a surge of pure panic. She was going to be last. The judges were all bludgeoned with violins by now.

Anna opened her case. "We both have a Guarneri." She lifted it out, tilting the strings toward Bree.

Unable to resist, Bree got up to examine the instrument more closely. She opened her case as well and they studied them side-by-side. Bree stated the obvious. "They're beautiful."

"Yeah." Anna caressed the strings on hers carefully. The tuning sounded perfect to Bree's ear. "I should be loosening up."

"You haven't got long," Bree agreed.

Anna wasn't smiling when she gave Bree a long, steady look. "You make beautiful music. I'm glad you're last so I can hear you again."

Bree thought later she was the one who moved, the one who shifted just enough to make it seem perfectly natural that Anna would kiss her. It was very soft, that kiss, very sweet.

"I could make out with you all day," Anna murmured when their lips parted.

Bree didn't know what to say so she kissed Anna again, and this kiss was not soft and not sweet. Anna's tongue was in her mouth and she tightened her arms around Anna's body. Anna was a girl. All the gods having no mercy on her, Anna felt perfect to hold, perfect to smell, perfect to want. She knew the word for girls who like girls. It was harsh and awkward. The other choice was ugly and clinical. She wasn't one of those. She was Joriesexual, and that was all she was. But she liked this kiss. She liked the way Anna felt against her.

Bree would have gone on to another kiss and another, might have let her hands wander from Anna's waist, but Anna pulled away finally.

"I'm glad I'm playing a romantic piece." She smiled into Bree's eyes. "Thank you."

Bree hadn't found a single thing to say before Anna was gone.

Her turn came in a blur. Her ancestors were humming *wiwo'ole*. Every lesson, every note, every minute of practice...they all came together like concrete, a foundation that let her carry her bow and violin onto the darkened stage. There was a flash of fear, but her ancestors began to sing.

She kissed the violin quickly, between the tuning pegs, and gave her hair one last toss behind her shoulder. She usually tied it back, but Mrs. Proctor thought it was nicer loose.

She was never alone when she had a violin in her hands. She let the music swell between them and became a channel for the violin's beauty. All that voice, the resonance and power poured into the wood by an 18th-century genius, soared into the hall by the gift of Bree's fingertips and bowing arm. The violin was a living thing, filled with the magic of its creator and the constant care and affection of each person who had played or maintained it. She was just a technician, freeing all that magnificence. She was the violin's tool.

She gave the judges a precise, almost clinical performance of the first piece, but by the third she had forgotten about the judges. She was the music, it was her. She was the violin. They were bound.

She was a musician. She was other things, too. The shivering silence when she was done overflowed with wisdom she did not yet understand. She was a musician, she was *haole*, she was Hawaiian, a mainlander, an islander, the daughter of a businessman and a singer. She was a woman and she liked girls...the list was long and it swirled like an arpeggio, different notes for different pieces of herself. The arpeggio became a chord and for a shining moment she understood all mysteries and magic, all wonder and music.

Bree wiped away the tears and let the cool evening breeze cool the salt on her cheeks. When she'd played she'd had answers. She'd always known that if she felt confused or afraid, playing would sort it out. Every violin she'd ever held had that power.

Her left wrist was throbbing. The Schumann, oh that beautiful Schumann, another piece she would never play again. She wanted to let the pain have her, to fall to her knees and sob while the ocean lapped at the rocks below her. There was no healing here, only memories of all her mistakes. There had been so many.

Listen to your ancestors and you can never go wrong, Aunt Lani said from the past.

I know you would never hurt me, Diana said from the past.

What good are ancestors to you? You have that damned violin, Jorie said, also from the past.

No, please, she did not want to go there...not to that memory. Jorie...

"I heard you came in second." Jorie pulled the headphones down around her neck. Her trigonometry homework was spread across the bed.

Bree set her violin case in its usual corner and dropped the duffel bag in the middle of the floor. "Yeah. It was a lot of fun. I'd forgotten how ugly the sky in Los Angeles is." She would never forget Anna kissing her, though. They hadn't been alone again, but Anna had winked at Bree when she'd gone to the stage to get her certificate for twelfth place. When Bree had gone up for her second place trophy she'd known the whistle mingled with applause was Anna's, too.

"Mainland." Jorie shrugged. "Anyone else your age there?"

Bree hid her annoyance at the way Jorie made her sound like a juvenile, decades removed, though Jorie was only fifteen months older. "Just me. The rest were all conservatory students."

"You're gonna be one of those next year. Next year you'll win."

"Maybe. Second place prize money was okay. It got paid to my trust, though. I was hoping I'd be able to get a car for the summer."

Jorie snorted. "Yeah, right. You know how that argument will go. I've *got* enough money — "

" — But you don't have a job to pay the insurance and you can't get a job right now because — "

" — Studies are too important."

They grinned at each other and Bree stood there, unpleasantly aware that being away for a week hadn't made it any easier to be around Jorie. The tight, spaghetti-strapped tank top, the cutoffs, the dusty sandal dangling from her toes... There was Mendelssohn that was a

38

little Jorie, there was Tchaikovsky and Chopin. They were inadequate, though, because nothing could capture how Bree felt about her.

She was staring at Jorie's breasts. It had taken her a whole fifteen seconds to be right back where she had been. Realizing that maybe girls did it for her hadn't changed how much she felt for Jorie. "I know I smell banana bread."

"Mom was up mashing bananas and coconut at first light." Jorie shrugged. "I guess she missed you."

It was said with a smile, and Bree wanted so much to ask the next question, but she had no courage for it. Jorie could destroy her with a laugh. If Jorie knew how Bree felt she'd be repelled, worse — pitying.

Remembering Anna's kiss made her hot between her legs, hot in her nipples, hot at the back of her neck. Looking at Jorie brought everything to a boiling point.

The banana bread had all the good things of home and *'ohana* baked into it. Bree finished her third slice and her recitation of events in Los Angeles. She left out the kiss.

"You were well taken care of, then?" Aunt Lani's gaze was searching. "I wish I could bring myself to trust airplanes."

"Really," Bree said. "Mrs. Proctor was like a mother hen. She made me wear eyeliner."

"How did it look?" Jorie was staring at Bree's eyes and Bree fought back a blush as she shrugged.

"I don't know. I thought it was a bit much, I guess."

"Yeah, I never wear it. But I guess for stage it would look nice." Jorie reached for the last slice of banana bread.

"Hey, that's mine." Bree's protest was only token. She was stuffed.

"Loser." Jorie spread it with mango marmalade and bit into it with a defiant smirk.

"Mr. Proctor says I didn't win because they really don't want it to be a prodigy's competition. I was too young to win, though several judges made a point of telling me that I was excellent and they look forward to my future career."

"You didn't go to win." Aunt Lani nodded thanks as Bree began stacking dinner plates. "You went for the experience."

"I know, but after I heard the others I thought I might." The experience had been useful, there was no doubt about that. She felt different now, but how different was scary. She liked girls.

"Still thinking you're that good, eh?" Jorie grinned at her as she picked up the empty soup tureen.

Bree stuck her tongue out in reply. "I've been assured that self-confidence is important to my success."

"Sure, one girl's self-confidence is another's bragging, isn't that right, Mom? Geez, the lecture I got the other day when I said I thought my hair was perfect."

They banged into the kitchen with the dishes and Bree began scraping. Jorie did have perfect hair.

"Perfect hair doesn't last forever. Music does, either a recording or just in our hearts."

"I know." Jorie flipped on the faucet to fill the dishtub.

Bree didn't know if it was her heightened feelings about Jorie that let her see how hurt Jorie was. Aunt Lani looked a little weary. It must have been quite a fight. She had no idea what she could say to make it better. It had always puzzled her that she never balked at Aunt Lani's mothering and Jorie did. She had never wanted to be Aunt Lani's real daughter. Her memories of her own mother were just present enough not to want her replaced by anyone else. Maybe that was the difference. Aunt Lani was 'ohana by choice. And Aunt Lani, out of everyone Bree had met, seemed to understand best what the violin meant to her.

As she dried the rinsed dishes she remembered the brief advice Mr. Proctor had given her as they had driven to the competition the first day.

"Most people don't understand," he'd said, "and they never will. Your gift will change lives, but those who love you best may be jealous or tired of feeling like your music always comes first. Or they'll treat you like glass and never see that you're real. Seeing yourself through their images of you can be a prison. You have to see yourself for what you are — a musician, even a genius, and a person, and a young woman. Not just one, but all. How much of each at any given time changes except when you're on stage. Tune yourself as you do your instrument for every situation you meet. It's much harder than it sounds."

It was a hard word to think about, genius. Some of the judges had told her to keep working on her genius. She didn't know if she was one. The violin seemed to do all the work. She touched it and felt helpless to do anything but play. How was she supposed to square genius with drying dishes and being in love and pimples on her butt? Tuning herself the way she did a violin — it didn't make sense. There was only one way to tune a violin.

Chores finished, Jorie announced that she was going to a party to plan the senior graduation dance, and Bree wished she was nearly eighteen and Jorie, and didn't have to worry about actualizing her genius, whatever the hell that meant. She would be eighteen eventually, of course, but never soon enough.

Going to conservatory early meant she would never be a senior, either. She'd passed the equivalency to graduate easily, but sometimes she could see the tradeoffs so clearly. She longed to get to conservatory, but she was missing out on her senior year. Jorie was experiencing things Bree would never fully understand.

She watched Jorie bolt out the door in response to a horn and felt the familiar sense of being an outsider as "Stayin' Alive" faded into the distance.

"I saw Dee. After the finals. She was there with husband number three, fourteen, I'm not sure. I don't know how she even knew I would be there." The only good thing about Jorie leaving was that she could now talk to Aunt Lani about the things that were bothering her.

The click of Aunt Lani's thin knitting needles never slowed. She was working in purples and greens today with fine silks. "Did she have anything to say for herself?"

Bree shrugged. Dee had been effusively affectionate, but it wasn't as if Bree believed a word of it. "You'd think it hadn't been nearly ten years since she packed me on a plane and forgot about me."

"What did your father see in her?"

"Same thing her current husband sees, probably." She mimed boobs the size of Montana in front of her chest. "She was all phony and sweet, and hoped I knew she'd done the right thing, sending me to my mother's people."

"After she took the only thing that mattered to you away." Aunt Lani let the anger show the way she never had when Bree was a child.

"She probably put the money she got for it up her nose. I don't know," Bree admitted as she flung herself into her favorite chair. "She was a lot like I remembered. I have to ask...you don't talk about my mother much. Was she like Dee?" She couldn't quite bring herself to use the word "bimbo," not about her mother.

Aunt Lani looked at her over her glasses, clearly undecided. Then she gave a little nod. "Your mother had her shortcomings. She had such a beautiful singing voice, and she was lovely to look at. She could be warm and generous. She was my best friend. You know that she walked out on a singing engagement when Jorie's father drowned, of course. She kept me together."

Bree knew all of that, but had never heard Aunt Lani choosing her words with such care. "I hear a but in there."

"She desperately needed to be told she was good and would do almost anything for anyone's approval. Probably because she had lost her parents so young and her voice was the only thing she felt anyone could like about her. She had problems with drinking at times. It was sad to watch someone so talented not believe in it. You're not at all like her that way. You're like your father, who knew who he was and was very sure of himself at his business. He was good for your mother though he was so much older and I think she was good for him. He'd been a widower a very long time. She stopped drinking when she met him. She was ecstatic to have you, and I know she dreamed of a large family, the family she never had. It was such a shock, such a shame..."

Bree felt the familiar, gentle tightening of grief. It was called an opportunistic infection now, resistant to antibiotics. Young, strong women weren't supposed to die from pneumonia, even in the mid-1960s. "All my father's money didn't do a bit of good. Whyever did he marry Dee, then, and just a year later?"

"Maybe because she was nothing like Ienipa. Or your mother left

42

such a large hole in his life he filled it as quickly as he could. People do funny things when they're grieving."

"Maybe." Bree heard the lilting cadence of the turtle lullaby. She felt warm and her shoulder blades itched, reminding her of that sensation at the competition. "Do ancestors really talk?"

"Why? Have you heard from yours, finally?"

"*Wiwo'ole* is courage, right? I felt like voices were helping me before the competition."

"That would be your ancestors, then."

Bree chewed on her lower lip. "People don't just hear voices."

"Why not?" Aunt Lani snipped through her yarn and tied it off.

"I'm not really Hawaiian. I mean I wasn't born here. I've never felt like I belonged." Bree hurried on, hoping she wasn't hurting Aunt Lani's feelings. "I mean, I belong with my *'ohana*. But I've never felt like I belonged to the islands."

Bree didn't know what to make of what might have been the glimmer of tears in Aunt Lani's eyes. "Fair enough. In some ways your gift has made you part of a different world. But hearing your ancestors isn't about how Hawaiian you are. It's about who you are, all of you. I know plenty with no mixed blood who don't hear a peep. Their souls aren't open to it."

"I've always heard Mama. I told you about that."

"*Milimili keiki* — her beloved child. You were always that."

Aunt Lani seemed content that Bree had told everything about her trip, and Bree almost headed for bed then. It was late by L.A. time. "There was something else. Serious. I've never kept anything from you."

Aunt Lani sorted another skein of silks across her lap. "So what was this so-serious thing that happened?"

Bree sat up, needing to see Aunt Lani's eyes. She would never tell Aunt Lani that she was in love with Jorie — she would never tell Jorie that either. They would both think it was sick. Or mistaken friendship. But maybe if she told Aunt Lani about liking girls she wouldn't feel so confused. "It's about sex."

Aunt Lani's hands stilled. "Then it was a good thing we had that little talk before you left, wasn't it?"

"Yes, though, well, I guess I could say it was irrelevant. It just didn't apply." Bree had squirmed when Aunt Lani had talked about a variety of topics, including how boys would not die from an erection. She'd also explained about how older men could seem very attractive and kind and that Bree was far too young to consider any kind of intimacy. But Aunt Lani was a realist and the condom in Bree's wallet was meant to remind her that first and foremost, Aunt Lani wanted her to respect herself.

"I don't understand, *keiki*."

"I kissed a girl. I mean, well, she kissed me."

"And that felt right to you?"

Bree nodded fervently.

"I meant what I said about you being too young for any kind of physical intimacy." Aunt Lani sipped her coffee. "I guess not having the fear of getting pregnant might make that seem less risky, but it's not."

"That wasn't it. I was scared to death. But I wanted to. Because she was a girl. Well, not exactly a girl. She was a conservatory student and we were waiting by ourselves. We were last and it sort of, well, it happened. Just before the finals."

"Did she know how old you were?" Aunt Lani looked angry, but not furious.

Bree shrugged and waited.

After a long moment with her eyes closed, Aunt Lani looked directly at Bree. "Our ancestors don't judge us by what feels good to us and hurts no one. I know you must have lots of feelings right now. I had them at your age. I'm only going to ask you not to do anything rash, or assume that this one kiss dictates your life."

"I don't think it does, but, well, it was sort of...nice."

Aunt Lani picked up her knitting with a snort. "I will tell you a secret about girls kissing girls. I wasn't much younger than you are now when I kissed your mother." Bree's shocked gasp brought a smile to Aunt Lani's mouth. "We were both bragging about being good kissers and so we decided to prove it. Boys weren't safe to practice on. But it didn't mean any more than that. We laughed about it."

Bree knew in her heart kissing Anna had meant more than practice.

44

She wasn't sure she could make Aunt Lani understand, and maybe she didn't want to. She would die if Aunt Lani knew how she felt about Jorie.

"Bree, dear, if you really do...prefer another girl it would be another kind of isolation. That's the only thing that frightens me. You're already an island of your own. This would make it worse."

Bree didn't have an answer to that. She couldn't change how she felt. Aunt Lani's hands weren't as steady as usual with the needles. "Are you saying if I want to belong I should like boys, lots and lots of boys?"

Aunt Lani looked horrified, then she responded to Bree's teasing grin. "Heavens, no, and you know it. Pretending to be something you're not can never last a lifetime. I'm glad you told me, *keiki*. I will try not to assume things, then. Don't listen to those *pule* addicts who have forsaken our ancestors to run around judging the rest of us."

It was a good change of topic. Her knitting needles clicked furiously. "I think about those mainland idiots last year trying to make it against the law to be a homosexual and a teacher. Ridiculous! When we were still the People, a man and a man or a woman and a woman, it just was. It's not good or bad. Better to judge a person by the way they treat their *'ohana*, by things that really matter. I don't care how many men Dottie Tomia has, she's there every day at noon to fix her mother lunch." She put down her knitting long enough to turn on the radio next to her chair.

Bree immediately recognized the voice — the singer who had so long ago put his hand on her head in what she now knew was a blessing.

"Listen to your ancestors, Bree, and be true to your *'ohana*, and nothing you ever do can be bad..."

The sky had embraced the night and even the waves crashing on the sea wall seemed drowsy. Bree turned from its beauty, chastising herself for useless maundering when Jorie, all the *'ohana* she had, needed her. She couldn't even stick to that part of it. Her ancestors knew she'd stopped listening to them long ago.

If she'd listened...

She massaged her wrist as she walked back to her rental car.

CHAPTER THREE

Keauhou nestled at the shore of what had been the violent collision of lava from Mauna Kea and Mauna Loa. Forever-frozen rock poured thousands of feet toward the sea, covered by an endless fall of foliage that proved the tenacity of nature. The beaches were short and coarse by Hawaiian standards, but Kilauea still bubbled not far to the south, adding to the landmass of the island. This island was an adolescent. As with all teenagers, Bree thought, anything could happen.

She chose Alii Drive over the faster highway, watching tourists. Aunt Lani was gone and Jorie was still at home. She was hours late now. Her wrist was killing her, and the ibuprofen she'd downed hadn't kicked in yet. She let the nightlights of the restaurants and souvenir shops dazzle her eyes. She needed to get home.

She'd been away so long. Jorie would have changed. This time would be different. This Jorie was grieving for her mother. She was not the Jorie who had said yes, one night, who had said yes only a few others. The first should have never happened. None of them should have ever happened.

What was wrong with her, Bree suddenly thought. Why was she lost in the past? Jorie needs you, she told herself. You need to be there for her now. You are 'ohana. Let the past go. The future matters so much more than the past.

But it wasn't easy to let the past go, driving in the dark. She passed Ka'ai Road and it was enough to call up that night, when everything between Jorie and her had changed.

Bree had still found it a thrill to drive by herself. She turned up Ka'ai Road, glad of the new station wagon's more powerful engine. Not that the vehicle was new, but it was a fair improvement over the old one. It got them wherever more reliably and had automatic transmission as a bonus. With the back seats down it held Aunt Lani's larger pieces with ease.

She got to run this errand because Jorie was at a midsummer party thrown by one of her co-workers at the new department store. A job at last, and almost enough money for insurance and a car of her own. The experience would be good, Jorie'd argued, and besides, she needed extra cash for college. Aunt Lani had grudgingly agreed, especially when it was clear that Jorie had no intention of taking summer courses to get a head start on her freshman year.

Bree realized quickly that parking was going to be a problem. Cars were crammed on every available inch of grass and roadway. She edged slowly through the bottleneck and continued to Ginger Munson's house with Aunt Lani's loan of blankets and pillows for houseguests. She visited with the mainlanders for a while, even though she would have preferred being introduced as Aunt Lani's 'ohana instead of Sabrina Starling. As soon as it was polite she began the treacherous journey back down the clogged road.

In the dark she might not have taken notice of two figures in a struggle, might even have assumed it was mutual and gone on her way. Her shoulder blades itched. She looked, focused.

It was Jorie. Jorie and some guy. Jorie stumbled on her way into the house, followed closely by the boy she had just shoved off of her.

Bree wondered what to do. Jorie didn't want her new friends to meet her. Jorie didn't want to have to explain that, no, they weren't really related, and yes, Bree really was Sabrina Starling.

Face it, she told herself. Probably no one at that party has even heard of Sabrina Starling as anything but some prodigy freak. Ginger Munson's guests had never heard of her. It had been a bit of a relief. Ginger had tried to explain, and Bree hated that. She was well aware that no one could be told someone was well-known. She already had some understanding of the vagaries of fame.

The heat between her shoulder blades increased. She wasn't sure at all she believed it was her ancestors. What she knew then was that Jorie was in trouble and she didn't have a choice about what she did.

There was nowhere to park so she blocked the road. Maybe someone would call the cops. It might be a good idea.

No one noticed her opening the front door.

Jorie was downing a glass full of amber liquid and laughing. Nothing was wrong after all.

Her shoulders burned, still.

Then Jorie moved, her steps overly cautious. Bree quickly assessed the rest of the party and realized with a sharp pang of instinctive fear that Jorie was one of perhaps three girls there with twenty or so boys. Not boys, men. One of the other girls was in a clinch with her skirt all the way up. The other wasn't far from it. The bedroom door was open and Bree didn't want to look.

Cursing Jorie for an idiot, she never thought twice. She intercepted the beer a boy was handing to Jorie to replace the glass she'd just emptied. "It's time to go home."

"Heya, Bree!" Jorie's smile was bright, her eyes watery. No doubt the room was spinning. "Hava drink."

"It's time to go home," she repeated. "Where's your purse?"

"It's early, honey," the man said.

Bree turned on him with all the ferocity she could manage. "She's going home!"

When she had Jorie in the car she realized she ought to have been afraid. The guy had to have been twenty-one or more and he easily outweighed both of them. Maybe he'd been too drunk to realize what he could have done instead of letting them go.

Having no idea she knew how, Bree reversed back up the drive to Ginger Munson's and calmly asked her to call the cops, saying the drive was blocked. Then she waited, only venturing back down once she saw a flashing light. The party was being broken up and she saw at least one of the other girls walk off on her own.

She realized then she was shaking.

"Where're we going?"

She wanted to punch Jorie, she was that scared. "What were you thinking? Are you willing to do anything to be popular?"

"What'd I do?"

Bree gritted her teeth and realized that if she took Jorie home now Aunt Lani would know she'd gotten falling-down drunk. There was no way Aunt Lani wasn't going to know Jorie had been drinking. The trick would be to hide just how much.

She got coffee to go at the Burger Hut and overrode Jorie's protests. "I hate coffee."

"Drink it. And if you think you're going to puke tell me and you can do it outside."

They coasted into the parking lot at the roller rink. Bree was hoping to go unnoticed as she slipped inside. She hated lying to Aunt Lani. The roller rink sounded so innocent. "We'll just be here an hour or two. She said the party fizzled out after a while."

"Thank you for letting me know. You got the things to Ginger's okay?"

"Yeah, just fine. The party was below that, that's where I ran into Jorie. They were blocking the road so Ginger called Five-Oh." A lot of the truth was better than none.

Jorie was a little more lucid when she got back to the car. "Why did you stop here, Beena?"

The grammar school nickname rankled. They were not kids

50

anymore. "You need to get sober."

"I don't understand."

"Who did you know at that party?"

"Ray. I work with Ray."

"Look at me." Aunt Lani always said there was no way to tell someone the truth without looking them in the eye.

Jorie turned her head like the car was rocking. "What?"

"There were a bunch of guys and only a couple of girls. What do you think you were there for?"

"To have a good time?" Jorie looked genuinely puzzled.

"You were gonna get raped, you idiot!" Bree was breathing hard.

"Was not. I know how to say no."

"Those guys weren't taking no for an answer. They were watching other guys make their move. It was sick." She wanted to kick them all off the nearest cliff.

Jorie tried to sit up but slumped again. "You don't know anything about it. You've never even been to a party."

True, the reception after the competition hadn't exactly been a party, but dangerous was dangerous. "If they're all like that I don't want to go."

"You're just jealous guys like me."

"You're drunk," Bree said bitterly. "They wouldn't have liked you tomorrow." She had no real concept of how bad it would have been. Illicit looks through a neighbor dad's *Playboy* hadn't been that educational. The pictures had left her palms damp, though.

"Nothing would've happened. I'd have said no. I don't screw just anybody."

She pushed away the knowledge that Jorie had screwed some boy at some point. That made Bree a pathetic virgin, wanting what she couldn't have. But that didn't matter right now. Jorie didn't believe she'd been in danger. Tomorrow Jorie would light into her about ruining the evening. Bree didn't think she could take being told, again, how she just didn't understand anything.

She grabbed Jorie's forearm and squeezed.

"Let go!"

"Make me."

Jorie made a few ineffectual attempts. "Doesn't mean anything. I don't want to hurt you."

With a flash of desperation, Bree flung herself across the car, pinning Jorie in place. "You think you can push me off?"

"Get off!" Jorie gave her a hard push, but Bree had no trouble staying on top of her. "I said get off!"

"You can't even get me off of you, and those guys were twice my size."

"What are you gonna do, rape me? Is that what you want to do, huh?" Jorie caught Bree in the ribs with a fist and Bree trapped her arm.

"I'm just trying to prove a point. You're drunk and you can't defend yourself."

The truth of her own words silenced Bree for a moment. She could feel Jorie's body heat seeping through her thin blouse. If she wanted to she could touch Jorie anywhere. She could take a kiss, even. Maybe Jorie wouldn't remember tomorrow.

Shaken, she let go and backed across to the driver's door. How could a guy do something like that? She didn't get it. Nothing would work for her unless she was wanted, and Jorie didn't want her.

"Whoever that guy was, he was going to fuck you and then I think he planned to share. Were you willing to do it with all of them just so they'd like you?"

Jorie swallowed hard. "I'm not like you, Bree. I've never been like you."

"What's that supposed to mean?"

"You don't need anybody. You just need that damned violin."

"You think it's easy being me?"

"You think it's easy being me? Look at me!" Jorie's face was flushed in the flickering parking lot light. "My hips are too big, my legs are too short, and all I've got for assets are my butt and my hair. Half the time the only reason any boy tries to be my friend is to feel me up and the other half is to get introduced to you."

"Me?"

"Sabrina Starling, the wonder of the Big Island. You get notices in the newspaper and half the island's got a scrapbook on you. And you have a trust fund. Plus you're skinny and you don't even have to work at it, and you still have big tits, and I don't know any guy who doesn't want to get in your pants."

"That's not true. Boys never notice me."

"You mean you never notice them. You've got that damned violin. I hate that thing!"

Bree had thought Jorie's worst weapon was her deprecating laugh, but those words sliced into her brain and kept echoing. She struggled to breathe and finally said, "Let's go home." *I hate that thing!*

"I'm sorry, I didn't mean it."

"Yes, you did."

"I didn't. I'm just sick, okay. I hurt all over and I don't know why. I have to pee."

With a resigned sigh, and feeling as if she was bleeding somewhere deep in her gut, Bree helped Jorie inside the rink to the bathroom. She got a couple of hot dogs, too, and Jorie managed to get one down.

Back in the car, Jorie put her head back weakly. "I think I'll live."

"Lani's going to know you were drinking."

Jorie nodded. "Yeah, I'm busted. Okay. Thanks."

It was probably all the thanks she would get. Bree didn't know if Jorie would hate her tomorrow. Maybe she already did. *I hate that thing!*

Maybe she always had.

Aunt Lani gave Jorie a hard look. "Tomorrow your head will pay you back for being so foolish."

"I know, mom."

"I'll get her into bed," Bree murmured. "I'm tired, too, so I'll be there if she needs anything."

"Thanks for being so responsible, Bree."

Great, Bree thought, another reason for Jorie to resent me.

Jorie didn't say anything while Bree helped her get her clothes off.

She turned her back as Jorie pulled on an old T-shirt, then stumbled into bed.

Bree felt as if she was the one who had been drinking as she sat down on Jorie's bed and patted her back. She'd had no idea Jorie felt so bad about herself. Jorie was lovely and popular, and she was smart when she wanted to be. "Jorie?"

"What?"

"I think you're beautiful."

"Yeah, what does that get me?"

Okay, Bree thought, what did you think she would say? "I mean it. I wish I was more like you."

Jorie rolled over onto her stomach. "If you had my head right now you wouldn't."

"Is it bad?"

"Just woozy. Not the on-the-way-to-getting-plastered woozy. This is definitely the on-the-way-to-getting-sober woozy, which is worse."

"I wouldn't know. I'm sorry — I didn't mean that like it sounded."

Jorie pulled herself up on her elbows. "Have you ever made a mistake? Ever?"

"Of course I have."

"Name one."

Bree couldn't come up with anything major. "I spend so much time practicing I don't have time for trouble, I guess." She was glad, too, that Aunt Lani had told her about her mother's struggle with alcohol. It made her wary. She was aware right now that being woozy would give her the courage to do what she was longing to do, to lean over Jorie and kiss her. It was something a good girl wouldn't do, but Bree was getting tired of being good. "But I'm not perfect."

She couldn't see Jorie's eyes very well. She only had her voice to go on. "I think you are."

Bree shook her head. She felt all nerves and heartbeat. "So I can play the violin — "

"More than play it. Your world revolves around that violin." *I hate that thing!*

Bree started to protest but when the ground trembles it's an earthquake. "Maybe for the most part. But there are other things to want from life." Like Jorie's lips against hers.

Jorie put her forearm across her eyes. "Yeah, like what?"

"Two good curls in an afternoon of surfing. Just two." Bree tried to find something to make Jorie laugh. "No pimples on my butt."

Jorie's quiet snicker was reward enough. "Dream on. What would a *haole* like you know about a good curl, anyway?"

It was so casually said, but Bree reeled from the blow. After all these years. She swallowed around a huge knot in her throat. "That's what I am? A *haole* mainlander?"

Tears were falling before she made it to her own bed in the opposite corner.

"Hey, where'd you go?"

The tears were thick, like lava. She felt as if her hands were burning as she wiped them away. She curled up facing the wall.

She didn't realize Jorie had followed her across the room until her bed moved. Jorie's hip was against Bree's turned back. "I'm sorry. I didn't mean it that way. I was just teasing — like we always have."

"I don't think I can pretend it doesn't hurt anymore," Bree said miserably.

"I didn't mean to hurt you."

"You can." Bree rolled onto her back and wished she could see Jorie's eyes. "You can hurt me so easily." She wanted to say it, to explain it. Jorie would run.

Oh, all the gods, was that Jorie's hand on her hip? "I guess I was thinking so much about growing up that I forgot you were, too. Even though it seems like you were born grown up."

Bree shook her head. It was Jorie's hand. It moved slightly, drifted toward her waist. She wanted to strip her shirt off, she wanted Jorie's hands on her breasts. She shuddered with the effort to hold back a moan.

"Don't cry, I'm sorry," Jorie said softly.

No, no, Bree thought. She can't lie down. We're not kids anymore.

Jorie was stretched alongside her, one arm over Bree's stomach while her head rested on Bree's shoulder. "I really am sorry. I don't hate your violin. When you play you make me think about things."

Through lips stiff with the desire to turn her head, to kiss Jorie's mouth, to taste Jorie's neck, Bree managed to say, "Like what?"

Jorie was quiet so long Bree had thought she had fallen asleep. "Don't laugh."

"I won't."

"The one you've been working on lately. That rhapsody thing?"

"The Rachmaninoff." Jorie's Rachmaninoff.

"Yeah. It makes me think of sea spray. The way the wave rises up and drops separate in the air and they blow into your face when the wind is just right."

"Oh." Bree had not thought of it like that. But she could see it the way Jorie did. Hear it that way, too. "That's a very nice image."

"I really don't hate it."

"Okay."

Jorie kissed her.

Maybe Jorie was aiming for her cheek.

Maybe Jorie was saying goodnight.

Maybe it didn't mean anything.

Maybe it meant more than music.

Bree kissed Jorie back.

Jorie's hand tightened on her waist. Bree moaned and then she felt Jorie's tongue through their parted lips.

Jorie was drunk, she told herself, and knew she was drunk on the moment, too. The world was spinning around the bed, everything else a vortex of emptiness. All that mattered, all that existed was on the bed, flowing from Jorie's kiss and the touch of her fingertips on Bree's ribs.

She couldn't breathe, she couldn't think, she could only respond, could only moan, wanted nothing more than for the kiss to go on until morning, until night. A neverending kiss, a neverending symphony, that would be what made her happy. This was genius, this heart pounding passion. She'd been made for this, made for Jorie's kiss.

Jorie breathed out her name when their mouths parted. Then, "I don't believe it."

They kissed again and again. Bree's mind cascaded with music that

56

had always meant Jorie to her. They kissed through the English Suite, with its measured perfection, through the rising passion of the overture to Sleeping Beauty, and through the opening strains of Bolero. Bolero rose, gave way to Schönberg. A kiss was not enough. Atonal scales tore away the flow of passion and insisted on more physical rhythms.

Her hips moved against Jorie. She wanted to say something, ask for something, but she didn't know any music that spoke this harsh and needy language.

"Take off your shirt."

Bree was too stunned to do anything more than comply. She pulled it over her head, then Jorie's hands were around her back, unhooking her bra. Jorie wanted her. Jorie was drunk. She wanted Jorie. Jorie would find out that she loved her, desperately. Tomorrow would ruin everything.

Tomorrow ceased to matter when Jorie's mouth found her nipple.

Years of fantasy, years of wanting, years of wondering what it would feel like to have Jorie touch her like that — none of it even came close to the sweep of pleasure that rolled over her body. Her hips shivered and she clutched Jorie to her, liking it, wanting more. Anna, had she tried, could have never made her feel like this.

Jorie raised her head with a little gasp. "I'm sorry, I don't know why...oh."

Bree's hands swept up Jorie's back, then down again to seize the hem of her T-shirt. The quiver that shook Jorie's shoulders was not fear, Bree could sense that much. Her cramped bed in their tiny, shared room bore no resemblance to her fantasies of luxurious hotel suites, whirlpool baths and fireplaces. There was no graceful way to move to a comfortable position for what she wanted to do.

She still managed to get Jorie's back to the wall, and when Jorie's hand touched her cheek she felt a deep sense of peace. This was right.

Her mouth closed around Jorie's small, erect nipple and her tongue had never felt such a thing before. It was so sweet, so intense. Was it supposed to be like this? As if her teeth, her tongue, her lips were all connected to the throb between her legs? It was nothing like what she thought sex would be. It was so much better.

Jorie shifted her position slightly and Bree realized her thigh was between Jorie's legs. It changed everything, as if the tempo doubled back on itself. Boys had words for it, snatch, cunt, getting some pussy. The words seemed dirty and what she felt seemed so right and clean. But she wanted to touch Jorie there, wanted to feel if Jorie was wet with that wonderful stuff that she knew was between her own legs now, a river of it.

She moved against Jorie, who moaned quietly in response. "Please."

Bree didn't know what it meant, whispered like that, like a secret. She ran the back of her hand down Jorie's abdomen. A pulse was beating high in her ears as she felt the soft cotton of Jorie's panties, then the bristle of hair underneath them.

Jorie's legs opened more and Bree found the courage to turn her hand and let her fingertips touch Jorie. The panties were wet and Bree swallowed hard, knowing she wanted to do the thing she'd read about. There were more dirty words for it, and all of them made it seem like a sin and a crime and something perverted and vile, as if she shouldn't want to and if she liked it then she was filth.

She wanted to so much. In that instant it made sense that she wanted to, but couldn't, because Jorie wasn't that kind of girl. Jorie wouldn't, couldn't like it if Bree's mouth was down there. Her fingers slipped past the elastic at Jorie's hips instead.

She found sweetness beyond imagination and with a hard, tight knot in her stomach she slid through Jorie's wet. She found the spot she had to trust would please Jorie. She stroked it and a spasm shook through Jorie's legs. Her hips came up and Bree's fingers were abruptly inside her, where she had never thought Jorie would let her go. She pulled her fingers out, but Jorie's hips followed her. She went in again and realized she couldn't avoid the words now. She was fucking Jorie and nothing, nothing would ever convince her it was wrong.

She held onto Jorie, her thigh behind her hand, moving against Jorie, holding back her gasps, wondering what would happen next, what could possibly end something so beautiful.

Jorie threw her head back. Her body was rigid as she made a stifled sound in the back of her throat that Bree knew she would never forget.

Her fingers could feel Jorie surrounding them, trying to hold them deep and tight.

Passionate whispers surrounded her. "Oh, god, oh Bree...oh my god...oh my..."

Bree was suddenly embarrassed. She didn't know if Jorie would want her to take her fingers out now. She didn't know if Jorie would also be embarrassed, wouldn't want Bree to look at her. But she couldn't take her gaze from Jorie's tightly closed eyes, her lips slightly apart as she panted. It was the most breathtaking thing she had ever seen.

Finally, she felt Jorie relax and she gently freed her hand from between Jorie's tightly clenched thighs. Her fingers were covered with Jorie's wet. She swallowed again. Jorie would think she was a pervert — but she couldn't help herself. She closed her eyes to taste her fingers and began to shake because she did want to put her mouth on Jorie and fill her mouth with this indescribable sweetness. She shook because there was no music she knew that could be this and she had not realized there were mysteries beyond music.

Hardly knowing how she dared, she opened her eyes to seek out Jorie's gaze.

Jorie was asleep.

In sleep she was all softness and everything that could be beauty. Bree kissed the side of her mouth, letting her wet fingers slide down her own body to ease off her shorts, to touch herself, mingling her wet with Jorie's. Her head was nestled under Jorie's chin as she brought herself to her own moment of ecstasy. As she rested her head on Jorie's shoulder she was aware that their hair mingled on the pillow. It would be a long, long time before anything seemed so sensual again.

Bree drove past the left turn that would take her away from the new subdivisions and up the old lane toward Aunt Lani's house. Her head was swirling with memories. She could not go home with her mind overrun by that night and the night that had followed, when

Jorie had been everything. They'd had five nights in twenty-three years. None of the tomorrows had been welcome.

She knew all the words now, could use them in casual conversation. Could even say, with a sophisticated smirk, "Sure I went down on her the second time around, she wanted me to." Had even, once upon a time, said, "Being someone's first, well, you know how that goes. She wanted everything and I got nothing."

She pushed away the recollection of knowing laughs of agreement. She'd never said they'd been each other's first, never explained that the first girl she'd fucked was the only girl she'd ever loved. At the time it had been true, too.

She had to pull into the fast food parking lot then.

Tears came, as hot as they always were, shaking out of her.

She'd joked about that first time with Jorie at the poker game. The game where she'd let Stacy take her to bed after. The game where she'd realized Diana was dangerously alluring. Where she'd seen Diana with Pam and seen what she could have had with Jorie, but had never had the courage to ask Jorie for...a life together. Diana and Pam had it.

A poker game, so innocent on the surface. Life was a game, and so was love. Wanting Diana's love had seemed like a game until it wasn't anymore.

She'd told Dr. Sheridan about Dee's abandonment, her father's death, Aunt Lani's kindness, Jorie's beauty, even that she never felt she played the violin, that in the utmost experience of her gift, the violin played her. But she hadn't said a word about Diana.

She wrapped her arms around the steering wheel and held it tight, trying not to lose herself to the wide-open ocean of black that spread past the shore. Her shoulder blades were hot with the voices of her ancestors, but she shut them out and cried, knowing she was lost, and lost forever.

CHAPTER FOUR

Her headlights swept over the front of the house. She could only hope her puffy eyes were mistaken for tears of grief. In a way, they were, tears for what she'd lost that she could never have back. But they weren't tears for Aunt Lani, not yet. That tidal wave was still offshore.

Someone moved at the kitchen window and Bree wondered if it was Jorie, her hair back in a braid, looking twenty, the way she always looked twenty, every time Bree had seen her in the years since she'd left Aunt Lani's for the conservatory in Vancouver. The first ten years they'd just missed each other, busy lives and schedules being convenient excuses. Aunt Lani had seemed to understand, too, though Bree had never told her that she and Jorie had...done what they'd done. Jorie had told Aunt Lani something, though. Maybe Aunt Lani had known it was something Bree could not be comforted about.

What had they been doing, dabbling at sex and never talking about love? Bree hadn't wanted to think about how hard it must have been on Aunt Lani, to love them both and know neither of them was happy apart, nor happy together.

She had thought she would hate leaving the island, but in truth she had been excited for the music she would learn, for the knowledge she would gain. She had known since she was four, at least, that the violin was her life. It was sharply painful to leave Aunt Lani's home, but she had no other choice. She wanted no other choice.

She knew now she'd also been running away, and running as far as she could go. That she had been swept into a life most people would envy, a life that had been free of regrets for a very long time, didn't change the fact that it had been an escape.

No matter where she went she could not escape the bewilderment in Jorie's eyes. Jorie had never understood her, and she could not expect this visit home to be any different. They would fight as they always did.

She would not hope, not plan for, not think about the other thing that happened when she went home — wanting Jorie so badly she could not think. She would not fantasize about going to bed with Jorie, not this trip, but she would stop remembering the times when they actually had. They would fight regardless, why make it worse with false hope beforehand?

She told herself fiercely that she did not love Jorie anymore. It had been twenty-three years since their first night. During those years she'd had her share of affairs.

Her mind turned to Diana and she did not want to think about her at all. Not her stricken face, not Pam, not any of it. She didn't want to think.

As she drove up the driveway her headlights shone on the kitchen window like twin spots, illuminating the square of light as if it were a stage. Would Jorie be listening to music, would she be singing like Aunt Lani always did?

The figure in the window went still, then broke for the door. A silhouette of slender darkness came out onto the porch, out of the glare of the lights. This time, however, the figure was staying, waiting, welcoming. But, for as long as it took Bree to breathe past the pain, it could have been like that night, their second night together, when Jorie had been running away.

After sleeping most of the night against Jorie's motionless warmth, Bree had woken alone. The memory of the night before had washed over her with piercing heat. It was like Bartok stabbing and she could not breathe.

The sensation eased and she turned her head to look at Jorie's empty bed. It was early, yet. Then she heard the sound of retching from the bathroom. Poor Jorie, she thought.

Aunt Lani was unsympathetic. It was hard to watch them go on being mad at each other over little things. Bree brought Jorie cold washcloths and otherwise left Jorie alone while Aunt Lani went about her morning cooking, none too quietly.

Bree had a strong urge to tell Aunt Lani. But it wasn't just her secret. She and Jorie should tell her together. Jorie would come with her when Bree went to conservatory. Jorie didn't have to worry about college. They would be together. Why couldn't they be?

After lunch Bree retired to Aunt Lani's workshop in the back garden to practice. She preferred the small and very crowded room in the house where Aunt Lani kept her fabrics, but she was certain that today of all days Jorie did not want to hear the violin start up. The workshop, though it had more open air than she liked for practice, would do.

She ran scales while she emptied her mind. It was hard not to think about the night before. Hard not to remember Jorie's silk on her fingers and the exploding welcome she had felt inside herself. They loved each other.

Hard not to think about it, but not impossible, though. Scale after scale, technique after technique, all the while thinking about nothing, which was the only way to get through it. Her mind was literally a blank as the fingers of her left hand found the notes and the arc of her right arm brought them into being.

Thirty-five minutes later she turned to something for pleasure, at last, and didn't hesitate when the "Stairway to Heaven" piece came back to her. She improved on it as she played — she knew more than she'd known then. For Jorie, for loving her so much, for the wet and the kisses and the stunning heat of her body. Now her mind could enjoy the music, shape it, work with the violin's power to create beauty.

She felt less uptight when she was done, though she wanted to run back to the house and see if Jorie was any better. She just wanted to hold her. It was easy to admit today that she wanted to be with her again, too.

Instead she turned to her assigned pieces. Professor Stockwell wanted to hear her again next week, which meant driving over to Hilo. Another reason to get a car of her own, she reasoned, but she knew Aunt Lani planned to drive her, as always. Maybe she and Jorie could go together. Maybe they could stop somewhere, overnight. The thought of going to a motel together, to be together like the adults they were now...it thrilled her to the point where she had to close her eyes and hold the bliss she felt, hold it tight up against her heart. All the gods, she had not known anything could be better than music.

Four pages to practice, first running through them without stopping, regardless of the mistakes, then repeating note by note, measure by measure, only moving on when to her own ear it sounded perfect.

Aunt Lani's call broke her concentration. The sun told her it was mid to late afternoon. She'd been practicing too long. She rubbed her left wrist for a minute, easing the ache, then put the practice violin away.

Jorie was huddled at the table, looking like a jellyfish caught out on the sand for two days. Aunt Lani was dishing up an early supper — she was going to a luau that night, celebrating the anniversary of the artists' collective she'd belonged to for many years.

Bree pressed her lips together, trying not to laugh. She eyed the squid and pasta with chopped tomato. The pungent seafood and garlic aroma made Bree's mouth water. The dish was one of Jorie's favorites.

"Not fair, mom." Jorie was swallowing rapidly.

"But it's your favorite." Aunt Lani proffered a plate with a too-innocent smile.

"I can't eat it."

"Oh, I didn't realize." Aunt Lani sat down at her place and scooped up a large forkful. Curled tentacles dangled as she looked squarely at Bree. "Would you like to tell me the truth about last night?"

Her blush was hot and immediate. Did Aunt Lani know? What had given her away? She sputtered a word or two and could only stare at Jorie, who had her hands on her temples.

"Start with the phone call," Aunt Lani said.

With a pang of pure relief, Bree remembered she hadn't mentioned Jorie was drunk when she'd called from the rink. She tried to stay ahead of Aunt Lani's reasoning. "Well, when — "

"Bree hauled me out of the party, Mom. It was a bad scene. I was already drunk." Jorie could not seem to look away from the pieces of squid dangling from Aunt Lani's fork. "She didn't say because I asked her not to. I didn't want her to feel like she had to decide if she was going to rat me out. You'd know anyway."

Bree closed her mouth and wisely scooped up her food. It was a good lie. It could work. She abruptly wondered if she wanted to get good at lying to Aunt Lani. She'd never had a reason to do so before.

It didn't seem right.

"Jorie's just protecting me," Bree admitted. "I didn't want her to get into trouble."

"So you lied by omission," Aunt Lani summed up. She sighed and popped the squid into her mouth.

Jorie's swallow was audible.

Bree just nodded, not planning on defending herself. Aunt Lani trusted her to tell her the truth. But then she realized she had a reason that Aunt Lani would understand. "You guys have been sniping at each other constantly, and I don't like it. I was trying to help."

Aunt Lani's expression immediately softened. "Okay, I deserved that, I think. But peace between Jorie and me is up to us."

Bree nodded, feeling better. She *could* talk to Aunt Lani about anything, including what Aunt Lani did that hurt her, like fighting with Jorie. And including the fact that she was in love with Jorie and always would be. She wanted to say it, right then. She even opened her mouth, but Jorie spoke first.

"Yeah, just stay out of it." Jorie dropped her head onto her arms, tears abruptly wetting the table. "I think I'm gonna die, Mom."

Aunt Lani did not tell Jorie it served her right, though Bree could see it in her eyes. Instead she made Jorie some salty chicken soup from the can and brought over the whole box of saltines. She didn't dangle any more squid, either. When she left for her party Jorie said she was going to have a bath. She looked almost human again.

Bree stood awkwardly in the doorway to their room after a towel-wrapped Jorie emerged from the bathroom.

"An early night?" Bree tried to sound nonchalant. Jorie wasn't undressed for her benefit. It was just like it always was.

"Yeah. My head is pounding. I don't ever want to get that drunk again."

"Probably a good idea."

Jorie turned with her pajamas in her hand. There were words forming on her lips, but they never made it out of her mouth. She just stood there, staring at Bree.

Bree was helpless to do anything but look the truth at Jorie. She wanted her, would give anything to hold her again.

Finally, as if from within a mist, Jorie said, "It wasn't a dream, was it?"

Bree shook her head.

"Do you — do you want to? Still?"

Bree could only nod.

"Why?" Jorie clutched the pajamas across her breasts suddenly. "Are you...?"

For the first time Bree wished she could talk like music, could make words flow like Brahms, crash like Mahler, seduce like Chopin. What was there to say? What more could there be than the three words she chose? "I love you."

"It's not right," Jorie said quickly. "We're...you're my — "

"No, I'm not. Never in all these years have you made me feel like I was, either."

"Mom won't, I mean, we can't."

Bree's head was pounding with pain and fear. She wanted to get down on her knees and beg Jorie to love her back. She loved Jorie and it wasn't wrong. "I do."

"Because you're...you're like that."

"No," Bree said firmly. That she'd kissed another girl once was meaningless. "That's not why I love you. I don't want any girl but you."

"Why?" Jorie seemed about to cry.

Bree left her nervous position in the doorway. Her knees were shaking but she kept moving toward Jorie. Her gaze swept over Jorie's body. She could tell Jorie was breathing hard, trembling. There was gooseflesh on her arms.

She thought she would stop when they were close, would wait to see what Jorie would do. Instead she took the pajamas out of Jorie's hands and then pulled Jorie's naked body into her arms.

She was as deliriously soft as she had been the night before. Bree tipped her head and kissed the parted lips.

"Bree," Jorie breathed when their mouths parted, "Why?"

"Because you're beautiful." Bree tried to find words, but it was so hard. She thought of Jorie's Rachmaninoff. The music shivered through her, mingling with the feeling of Jorie against her hips and stomach, her small, hard nipples pressing through Bree's shirt. "You are music for my heart."

Jorie shuddered as Bree kissed her throat. Bree didn't know where she found the courage to speak, let alone hold Jorie like this, bending her back so she could kiss her shoulders.

Jorie moaned, a rising note that had meaning. Bree took it for desire, for longing. A similar note was building in her.

She gently propelled Jorie to a sitting position on the edge of her bed, then quickly knelt on the floor so she could take Jorie back into her arms. She wanted to prove to Jorie that she loved her. Jorie's breathless noises were encouragement as Bree kissed her stomach, then moved slowly but deliberately to the nipples that beckoned to her mouth.

Jorie had one hand on Bree's cheek and the quiet "oh" was lost in the sound of Bree's lips closing around one pointed tip. Her tongue knew what it wanted as it slid over the roughened flesh. Nothing seemed as sweet as it had last night, but maybe because Bree knew she wanted more than sweet and quiet and soft.

She put one hand on Jorie's thigh. She wanted to be inside Jorie again and feel Jorie explode with her. She wanted to put her mouth there. Did that make her a carpetmuncher, a muff-diver? No — she just wanted to show Jorie she loved her enough to do that. It would feel so good. Her own hips moved. It would feel so good to both of them.

Her hand urged Jorie's thighs open and Jorie fell back on the bed, one arm over her eyes. The light made it so real, so unavoidable. She was between Jorie's legs. She could see everything. Jorie was wet there and all the gods, head to toe, Bree wanted to taste it.

She kissed her way up each of Jorie's thighs, giving Jorie a chance to say no, that she didn't want it. Jorie's hips were moving in time with the choked gasps of her breathing.

She kissed the soft mound then, and her head filled with the intoxicating scent. She reached out with her tongue because nothing would stop her now and Jorie's hand was on the back of her head. Jorie wanted this as much as she did.

It was not like she had thought it would be. The taste was like her own, the slick, shuddering flesh, the walls that seemed to quiver with welcome for her tongue — she had imagined all that. She was starved and thirsty for this one thing and she feasted on it, listening to the music that flowed from Jorie's gasps. Present always was more beauty than she could have ever conceived — it was Jorie she was loving this way.

It was Jorie.

Jorie's legs were around her. Jorie's unrestrained cry filled her ears. Jorie was rising off the bed to kiss Bree's wet mouth and cheeks, kissing away the triumphant smile even as her hands went to Bree's T-shirt.

After that there was nothing to hold back, no reason not to shed her clothes, her secret, no reason not to let Jorie know how much she had wanted her. "I've always loved you," she murmured, though she did not think Jorie could hear her. They were on the floor and Jorie was on top of her, kissing her even as her hand finally touched the proof of everything that Bree told her. Her thick, black hair surrounded Bree, enclosing her in a private world that held only the two of them.

Again, that it was nothing like she expected surprised Bree, but this time it took her breath away. She thought she was saying, "Please," but later was never sure she had managed to speak. Jorie was stroking her to an incoherent scream. She wanted Jorie inside but this was enough to make her legs circle Jorie. The only words she knew were orgasm and come and neither described the needle-hot contractions inside her that left her in tears and frantically kissing Jorie's mouth over and over.

When she could hear herself, she was saying, "I love you, I love you."

Jorie was smiling, a little, then she kissed Bree hard and pulled her up on the bed.

More of the same, doing it all again, loving it again. The summer sun set in the distant sea and a breeze swept through their room, cooling their bodies until they came to a rest, at last, arms around each other.

For years Bree would wonder what might have been, what might have lasted, if she had not been so foolishly in love, so trusting that the love she felt was enough.

That was the big lie, that love could fix anything.

She should have let Jorie fall asleep. She should have just left it alone for a while. Maybe if she'd given Jorie time to get used to the idea of being in love it might have happened.

Instead, she had whispered, "Let's tell Lani in the morning, okay?" She felt guilty about the lie of omission she'd been caught in. Saying nothing when they were so happy together was the same thing.

Jorie's body had been curled in relaxation, spooned in front of Bree on the narrow bed. Her breathing was slow and steady though Bree knew she wasn't asleep. At Bree's words she stiffened and the spoons separated. "No."

"Why?"

"I — Bree, my head is splitting again. Can't we just leave it?"

"I don't think she'll get mad," Bree said, meaning to soothe.

"I don't care what she thinks," Jorie snapped. She rolled over in bed, taking the last of Bree's sense of peace. "I don't tell her every time I have sex, okay? It's none of her business."

Bree wondered if the dark hid her confusion. "But...but she'll want to know how we feel about each other."

"How do we feel about each other, huh?" Jorie sounded angry, now. "You don't know anything about life or being in love. You just think you are. I'm the only person you ever talk to who isn't part of music. You only want me because I'm here and I'm...willing." She choked to a stop. Bree thought Jorie was going to kiss her. "You don't love me. You can't."

"But I do. Don't you — don't you love me?" As she asked the question she knew it was a mistake. This was a kind of death she was facing, like the swan. She felt it come upon her very quickly and there was no music that could stop it. From last night came Jorie's hurtful words, *I hate that thing!*

Jorie got out of bed to turn on the light. "Bree, I — "

"You don't, do you?" Bree got to her knees, for the first time in a long time not feeling weak at the sight of Jorie. "You let me — you let me do that to you but it was just...just like with some boy." The thought stabbed at her.

"No boy ever did that to me."

"You'd let me do it again, huh? Wouldn't you? Just because you want to get laid." Boys' words, hurtful words were welling up in her. As far as Jorie was concerned she was just like some boy wanting to feel her up. Wanting to...to...fuck.

Jorie came back to the bed. She looked so much older than Bree felt at that moment. Bree wanted to trust that Jorie would take away all the pain swirling inside her.

"It wasn't like that. You're not just — you're not like that." She sat down. "I care so much about you, Bree, I always will..."

70

Bree didn't know much about love or life or anything, but she knew a *coda*, an ending, when she heard one. "But you don't love me."

"Not the way you love me."

"But you still let me suck you."

"Don't."

"You want me to do it again?" Bree shoved her hand between Jorie's thighs and wanted to cry at the wet that seemed endless.

"Stop it!"

"You didn't say that a half hour ago!"

"I wish I had!"

They struggled, straining, then Bree let go of Jorie, pushing her away. "I'll never touch you again, not even if you beg."

Jorie clutched her head. "Fuck you, okay! Why can't you just shut up?"

Bree felt a hot pain between her shoulders and knew she should shut up. *I hate that thing!* Voices welled up inside her, warning her that she was destroying something she could never have back, something that could only be mended, but wouldn't be the same as never broken. "I'm not going to shut up. I'm going to tell everyone you liked it."

Jorie went pale. "You can't — "

"I'm Sabrina Starling," she said, finally gaining her feet. Jorie hated her. Hated her violin. Hated her. "I'm going to be a fucking star, and nobody cares what famous people do. But someone like you, yeah, they'll care that you like it with girls."

"Stop it, Bree! For god's sake!"

The pain inside her was immense, so powerful that the voices became very faint. "You think Cici will still be your friend? She'll drop you so fast — "

"Shut up!"

"And your job, what about that? You could get kicked out of that sorority you wanted to join this fall, you could — oh!"

Jorie's slap ended Bree's tirade and she staggered back a step. Jorie was scrambling into her clothes while Bree cupped her cheek. The voices were loud again and they all called her a fool.

"I'm sorry — I didn't mean it."

71

"You did so!"

"I'm sorry — I won't tell anyone. I won't," she promised Jorie's departing back.

Even though she was naked, Bree ran after her, following her out onto the porch. Jorie was a rigid silhouette.

"Leave me alone, Bree. I'm not like you, I could never be like you. Just leave me alone!"

Jorie was gone into the night, a flash of long hair and legs, running down the driveway toward the road. Running forever out of Bree's life. Until the next time they were alone, the next time they were vulnerable. But all the next times turned out like their first time. *I hate that thing!*

The figure on the porch moved to the stairs as Bree parked. She was shaking and didn't like it that Jorie would know, but there was no escaping it.

She got out of the car slowly, even though she knew that seconds wouldn't make a difference to her vulnerability.

The shadow moved. "Aunt Bree!"

The relief was so strong she felt weak, then she hurried forward to the welcome and tearful hug, painfully aware that Penny looked just like her mother had at seventeen.

"Mom had to go get some chairs. She'll be back in a bit. We were starting to worry."

"I had to drive for a while," Bree admitted. It had always been easy to talk to Penny, even when Penny had been, good lord, fourteen. Three years since they'd snuck off at night to gossip over ice cream. A steady stream of e-mails — hard to write this last year — had kept Bree from feeling like a stranger.

"I know," Penny said. "If I had a car I'd go driving myself. The house is so empty."

There was no speaking around the lump in her throat. They gathered up Bree's suitcases and Bree let Penny lead her to the new addition to the house which included a bedroom for Penny and a second bathroom.

"I'll let you have the bed. Mom says that there's no way you'll want to sleep on the floor."

"Your mom is right." No matter what Jorie's reasoning had been, she'd come to the right conclusion. She pushed away disappointment — what had she thought? That Jorie would countenance them sharing a room again? Every time they did they had sex. It was still their little secret, still their reason to fight and try to hate each other. "I can sleep in the workroom, though."

"It's stuffed, Aunt Bree. Aunt Lani had slowed down a lot this past year."

"Okay. If you don't mind."

"I've got an air mattress. It's no problem."

As far as Bree knew Jorie had never told anyone but Aunt Lani about their trysts. Not Penny's father — wherever the hell he was by now, hopefully in hell, Bree added, as she usually did. Jorie hadn't told any of the men who had come in and out of her life, most likely. Certainly not Penny.

With a shiver, she could hear Jorie's voice from one of their pasts. "Nobody does it the way you do, Bree. I can't believe I ever said no." And soon after, it was, "I'm not like you, Bree, and I never will be."

Morning always came. The fight always started. *I hate that thing!* And if Jorie started up with her this time...no, it wouldn't work. This time Bree would say no. She should have said no the last time she visited. She should have said no when Jorie had surprised her in Los Angeles.

Her heart twisted and she felt tightening between her legs...Jorie had wanted her so much. If Jorie didn't want her then Bree might have been able to let her go.

Aunt Lani was dead. Her funeral was tomorrow. She couldn't be thinking about sex right now. She didn't want to be wondering if Jorie would want it and how cheap that would make her feel later. She was tired of the fatal pas de deux. She was the one who died the next morning, but, all the gods...

She sank down on the bed and let Penny hold her while she cried.

73

She wished she'd told Aunt Lani about Jorie herself. Maybe if she had, maybe...she would have never needed Diana. She missed Aunt Lani with a profound ache that touched her more deeply than the reality of the unending pain in her wrist.

She'd already thought she'd lost more than she could bear. And then she'd lost what really mattered.

She realized that Penny was crying, too, and she shifted so she could wrap one arm around the girl. Not a girl, she reminded herself. As much a woman as Bree had been when she'd left this place — her only real home — for Vancouver and the music conservatory. It had been hard to be some place so cold and so far away. She'd lived for packages from Aunt Lani and letters from Jorie, even though the latter were always full of friends she'd made at school and which man in her life might be likely to pop the question.

She wondered what Penny's hopes and dreams were but right then didn't have the strength to ask.

"*Milimili keiki*," she murmured. She held Jorie's daughter in her arms and soothed away the tears, finding a way to ease her own in the process. There was a tickling in her shoulder blades and she realized that this was still her *'ohana*, still the people she loved best in the world. Jorie and she were not meant to be lovers, but they were still family.

CHAPTER FIVE

"Hey, Scooter." Bree didn't remember why the nickname had stuck. Penny snuffled into Bree's shoulder. "Yeah?"

"I'm starved. Want to go grab a burger? Is Falco's still open?"

"Sure. I mean the bar will be and they'll toss something on the grill if we ask nice. Buy me a beer?"

"Not a chance. We're just going for food."

Penny grabbed her purse and led the way. As Bree passed her old bedroom door she couldn't help but look in. The room had been changed since her last visit. Gone were the separated, cramped twins and the mismatched dressers and tiny desks. A double bed centered the room now, with matching dresser and nightstands made of a light-colored teak. Above the headboard was one of Aunt Lani's tapestry arts, in the vibrant reds, oranges and greens that Jorie had always liked.

It was the room of an adult woman. And no way could Bree share that bed with Jorie and not repeat all the same mistakes.

Falco's was a local dive the owners left unpainted and unkempt to keep out tourists. Bree would have liked to have a drink, but it didn't seem fair to say no to Penny over a technicality of three years and indulge herself. Instead she got them Coke floats and a couple of burgers and sides of mac salad. One whiff of island sweet onions sizzling on the grill made her weak in the knees.

"How is your mom holding up?"

Penny shrugged. "What would be considered okay at a time like this? I mean...how can she not cry sometimes? I do. Just because she's older doesn't mean she's supposed to hold it all in. Gramma would have said let it out now and get on with life."

Bree studied Penny's grave expression, remembering how serious she could be. It was startling, still, because Bree knew she had never been that wise at Penny's age. She hadn't been wise at any age, at least not without a violin in her hand.

Stop, she thought. She massaged her wrist under the table.

"How about you? How are you doing?"

"Floats up!" The cook's call gave Bree time to think about her answer. She'd made light of her situation when she wrote to Penny, not sure what a teenager could understand about such a loss. She realized Penny could probably understand a great deal. She reached for the two glasses, one for each hand, before she remembered. Stupid Pain jabbed at her like a hungry viper, needling into the bones of her wrist. She picked up one in her right hand and found Penny at her side, reaching for the other.

They were seated again when Penny said, "I'm sorry, I forgot about your wrist. When will it be better?"

Even steeled for questions like that, Bree had to take a deep breath. "It won't get better. The damage is permanent. The scar tissue from the second surgery was worse than the first. There are all these carpal bones at the base of your hand, and they connect to the two big bones in your forearm here." She gingerly flexed her left hand to demonstrate the connection point. "I broke seven of them and there's a little tiny screw right there." She pressed hard, making it hurt to distract her mind from crying. "It's made out of a strong ultra-lightweight polymer that NASA invented, but even then it just isn't flexible enough. The scar tissue is the real problem though — "

"Aunt Bree, I'm so sorry." Penny put her hand on Bree's wrist. Bree had never let anyone but a doctor touch it. "I didn't know. I don't think mom knows, either."

"I've only accepted it myself recently." Accepted it? She was a long, long way from that. "There's been almost no improvement in over a year." Her shrug was a lie.

"Did Gramma know? She was so mad at herself not being able to get on a plane. She tried but just couldn't do it."

"I know. I didn't want to put her through that. There wasn't anything she could do." Bree sipped at her float. She fought back regret. It was her decision not to come home since it happened. She'd been afraid she'd find herself telling Aunt Lani about Diana. She couldn't have borne it if Aunt Lani had looked at her with reproach and disdain for what she'd done. She had lost so much. She couldn't afford the loss of Aunt Lani's respect, too.

Penny nodded, her eyes scanning Bree's face. "You must miss your music."

"You could say that." She took an extra long pull on the straw and tried to lose herself in the creaminess of it. Ice cream and Coke was one thing she'd never outgrown. Even when she'd been playing sophisticated games she'd kept this one taste of childhood. She'd introduced Lila to them. She'd introduced Lila to a lot of things. She'd shared them with Diana, but she didn't want to remember that. Not now, not ever.

"Burgers up!"

Penny went to get the tray and Bree was lost again in how much Penny looked and moved like her mother. Lila had walked that way, too, as if all the muscles in her body were one unified, sinuous curve. It was one of the first things she'd noticed about Lila, when she finally allowed herself to think of Lila as a woman and not just a fellow musician.

She hadn't thought about Lila in a long time. A rueful smile touched her lips. She had thought she'd never get over Lila. But hurting about Lila had gotten lost in a magical time when she began to believe she could be a professional musician. This memory she could handle so she let it come to her like fresh air.

"What'd you do this time?" Lila reached for the biscuit on Bree's tray and Bree speared the tomatoes from Lila's salad. Their mealtime custom was to always get everything in the cafeteria line, then swap whatever suited them.

"Nothing new." Bree bolted the tomatoes into her mouth and ground every ounce of juice out of them with her molars. Canned. Disgusting. But it was better than the cookies she could have had. If she skipped the gravy on the meatloaf and the cookies she could afford the soft-serve ice cream in diet Coke she'd have later. "I am ignoring the basics."

Lila rolled her expressive brown eyes. "You did the basics ten years ago. What is it with him, anyway?"

Bree shrugged. She and Professor Tolan had objected to each other from the moment they had met. He declared her advanced repertoire unfit for her immature hands. She objected to his lack of a musical soul. He appreciated music, but he did not experience it like a musician. He only heard notes, she thought with pity.

"Feed up." Derek dropped onto the chair next to Bree, his tray laden with the same choices she had made. Lila quickly swapped him half her fries for half his cobbler. "You know we're not going to get any brie and pate tonight."

Musicians were invisible at gigs. Bree acknowledged that fact. Her scholarship covered her tuition and her trust fund covered her expenses. She supposed if she'd asked she could live in her own apartment and have brie and pate every night. But she'd agreed with Professor Stockwell and Aunt Lani that it was time not to be so isolated. The dorm was good for her.

She had joined the trio of Derek, Paul and Lila for the practice and to have money she did not have to account to anyone for. She'd also helped them make The Island Breeze a little more authentic. It was ironic that most people took Lila's New Jersey born and bred complexion for Hawaiian ancestry, while not making the same assumption about Bree. Being neither nor both bothered her, still.

"I don't care about food," Bree admitted. "It would be nice if someone listened. And we didn't have to do 'Tiny Bubbles.' "

Paul ambled up with his tray. Bree offered half her fries for more tomatoes. "Hey, we did take the 'Hawaiian War Chant' out of the repertoire," he reminded her. "That's something."

"Are we going to try out 'Ahe Honi'? I think we're ready." Bree watched Lila demolish her meatloaf in four bites. Aunt Lani would have approved of Lila's appetite. It wasn't fair she stayed so slim with no exercise, though. At least she didn't think Lila exercised. Bree had found since leaving Aunt Lani's cooking that her hips wanted to expand.

Bree felt as if she would kill for fresh pineapple. "If you guys think so. I really appreciate you giving me the chance to compose something."

"It's perfect." Lila speared three fries and hummed a bar from the song before popping them into her mouth. "Would you let me do it as part of my recital?"

"Sure," Bree shrugged.

Paul swatted Derek's fork away with his own. "I'm eating all my cobbler. I missed breakfast."

"What's her name?" Derek smirked at Paul, who had an odd little smile.

"That would be ungentlemanly," was all he would say.

Bree had to dash to her theories of composition class, followed by her time in practice studio. She wrapped what was left of the meatloaf between two slices of bread. "See you guys at six-thirty."

Vancouver in the dead of winter was frostbitten. It had been sleeting earlier in the day, but the sun had improbably broken through the clouds, adding a hint of watery yellow to otherwise gray skies and buildings. The University of British Columbia's Conservatory of Music sat on the edge of a spacious campus, surrounded by botanical gardens and large tracts of wetlands. When everyone had complained of the so-called heat last September she had scoffed. Now they were scoffing at her. The natives thought the weather was mild, but she was shivering under her sheepskin jacket.

She gobbled her sandwich as she hurried from her dorm toward Arts & Humanities. She was glad of the gig because otherwise Lila had been insisting the two of them ought to go to one of the gay dance clubs not far from campus. Lila had heard that the music and dancing was better there than anywhere. Bree wasn't sure she wanted to go. She didn't want anyone at school to find out she was gay and she didn't want to pretend she wasn't, either. She was a musician at school. Besides, Bree didn't want Lila to think she was after her. Not that Lila wasn't attractive. She just wasn't Jorie.

The whole matter would have occupied her more if Professor Tolan hadn't been the one teaching theory of composition. He took a fascinating subject and turned it into three-day-old poi.

It didn't help that he was her instrument advisor, the instructor who was responsible for guiding her training with the violin. Professor Stockwell had liked his credentials and he'd had several students who had turned out impressively. Their discussion before lunch had been the same as always. He wanted her to spend more time on the basics, unlearning what he called bad habits with fingering technique. Her hands weren't mature, he kept saying. Bree had reached a stage of nodding and agreeing and only following his instructions when he was actually in the room. If she survived to the end of the term, she could request a new advisor.

She felt better after practice. She always felt like a lumpy mattress when she went in, but was sleek and smooth when she came out. Today was no different. She hurried back to the dorms to change. The frequent dash across campus helped with her hips.

She waited with Lila for the guys to pick them up. The gig was at a private party in one of the Horseshoe Bay estates on the golf course. It was a short drive and the party planner had her act together. They often arrived at gigs to discover that chairs, electricity and other general arrangements outlined in the contract had been overlooked until they arrived. They were often expected to string extension cords and move furniture themselves.

The contract called for three seventy-five-minute sets with no repeating music. Paul tuned his Hawaiian guitar, then plugged into the low-level amplifier. Derek set up his drums while Lila turned on the mixer. Derek would fuss with that later. Bree saw to her own tuning and right on schedule sat down next to Paul to open with the light and breezy "Crazy K Highway."

The party was in full swing within thirty minutes, but Bree's heart sank when she saw that Professor Tolan was somehow one of the guests. She ignored him and hoped he didn't notice her. He would, though. There was nothing wrong with her fingering technique, and she worked well within the quartet, but she could already hear the lecture.

Lila finished a charming version of "Island Home" at the end of their first set and they retired to the kitchen — it was too cold to go outdoors for fresh air — where Bree managed to swipe a spear of reasonably fresh mango. The kitchen was crowded with waiters filling champagne glasses to circulate the main rooms again and a radio was tuned to an endless disco station. Bree didn't mind disco as much as Derek did, but some of it did make her teeth ache.

They were arranging themselves for the second set when Lila gave an odd little gasp. She sounded half strangled.

"What's wrong?" Bree signaled Derek not to begin.

Lila turned a stunned face toward them. "Don't stare." She rolled her eyes meaningfully to her left and barely moved her lips. "Over there."

Bree could see nothing noteworthy in that direction, but Lila was standing. Bree coughed, rose to smooth her dress and looked again.

It was sheer habit that kept her from dropping her violin. Numb shock gave way to terror.

Paul likewise casually rose to his feet, then sank back to his seat with a choked swallow.

Derek, behind them, would have had to crane in an obvious way to see what they all saw. "What? What is it?"

Paul whispered the name, but Bree could hardly take it in. They were about to play their simple pseudo-island music for a personage so lofty as to be a god to them. The sleek gray hair, the prominent hooked nose — there was no doubt about it.

Derek gave them a few beats, then led them into a quiet, moody piece about fire and love. Playing helped Bree regain her composure, but she doubted everything she had ever learned. She was sure she was out of tune. Her bow arm suddenly seemed to weigh a ton. She was sweating.

She caught sight of Professor Tolan glaring at her and felt herself falter. To make any kind of mistake in front of the Personage was unthinkable. She could never meet his standards. Who was she kidding?

Her shoulder blades went hot.

Then, under the music she could hear the hum of *wiwo'ole*. Courage, she told herself. This is what your life is all about, this moment.

She calmed her heart and let the music flow through her again and as she steadied so did the others. They were making their brand of music, and Bree felt a sparkle in her fingertips.

When the Personage came into their sight he even nodded in their direction, a professional courtesy. When they finished the piece he nodded again, and quietly clapped fingertips against palm for a few beats.

Don't start shaking, Bree told herself fiercely. Derek moved them into one of Bree's adaptations of an island tune that blended with the prominent folk melody in Dvořák's Symphony from the New World. There was a lovely vocal stretch for Lila, a solo for both violin and guitar, and Derek got to show off his smooth-as-glass percussion that held the piece together.

It was her own work and Bree was very proud of it. She ignored Professor Tolan's continuing scowls and let her fingers do what they knew to make her contribution shine without leaving the others behind. They were a quartet. It wasn't a solo concert. This was background music at a party, she reminded herself.

When she realized that the Personage had broken off his conversation to give undivided attention to the music her stomach turned over. His stillness was attracting attention and other guests turned as well to discern what he was studying so closely.

One hand, tucked under his opposite arm, moved slightly to their tempo. The room had gone still. Bree had never seen anything like it at any of the parties they'd played at. Usually when people liked the music they started to dance. Nobody actually *listened* to background music.

It wasn't just in the background anymore. The music was all there was. The Personage smiled slightly. A lazy gesture of his vastly expressive left hand indicated they should increase their volume.

Bree was halfway through her solo. She heard Paul respond to the gentle command and knew she had no choice. The Personage would never remember her, but many musicians would go their whole life without being heard by a virtual god of music. She would at least be able to tell herself later that she had played her best.

She gave the violin its voice and let Dvorák fill the room. The music spoke to her of new shores and ancient mysteries, then lapsed into the bittersweet lament of going home. Her solo concluded, she eased to Paul and smiled her pleasure at the way he slid his steel bar across the chords, giving a true Hawaiian edge to the music she'd written.

There was actually applause when they finished. Terror of terrors, the Personage approached them. Bree realized she was going to have to find her own voice or look like an utter idiot.

"Well done," he said simply. "Is that an original arrangement?"

They all nodded. The lined face eased into a smile, as if he knew the effect he had on four lowly students. "It was very evocative and well-constructed."

Bree felt her face flame. He noticed. With another lazy but expressive gesture he indicated her violin. "You have an unusual fingering technique, but it's very effective. Where did you learn it?"

She found her voice. "I've had mostly self-guided lessons under the direction of Professor Stockwell at the University of Hawaii. I'm having my first formal and regular instruction now," she added.

"Don't let them change you too much. You've made a good start. Do you know any of the Brahms Paganini Transcriptions?"

She nodded.

"Choose one, and let me hear about twenty bars."

He was serious.

She couldn't move.

Her shoulder blades felt as if they were on fire. Only when Paul coughed and nudged her did she take up her violin.

She chose number one because it was the first one she thought of. Not exactly an inspired decision, but at least she wasn't standing there like a mute rock.

The Personage wasn't looking for timidity. He had played and heard and conducted so much music in his life that the last thing he needed was an amateur. *Wiwoʻole.*

She struck into the piece boldly, feathering the rising scale with the fingering that suited her, that she'd refined in Aunt Lani's workroom with countless hours of mindless practice. The conclusion of bar twenty-three was a logical break and she drew her bow the last time with a flare, punctuating Brahms's musical intention with a closing note that would keep the unfinished piece from echoing in her head for the rest of the night.

He had not moved nor altered his facial expression while she played. When she was done he nodded and fished in his pocket. "You are all fine musicians and you have fulfilling careers ahead of you. Never forget that earning your living through the thing that gives you the greatest joy is a blessing." He handed Bree two business cards and spoke directly to her. "For you. When you call, tell Markham you have the other card as well. The very best of luck to you. Perhaps our paths will cross again."

He turned and rejoined the host, who had been hovering anxiously. Bree put the cards in her pocket and found her companions were all grinning at her. Derek tapped a beat and they went on with their second set as if nothing had happened. She still felt numb when they played her "Ahe Honi" and the Personage turned for a moment and nodded to himself.

Bree could feel the business cards like they were on fire. When the set ended and they hurried to the kitchen again she took them out.

One said, "Markham Powell, Musical Agent" and gave a single phone number. The other was blank except for the Personage's name.

Derek and Paul embraced her heartily. Bree felt the same way she had the day Aunt Lani had taken her to the concert at the *heiau*. Another giant had just blessed her.

She had no idea what she'd done to deserve the blessing. But later she would look back and realize that was the moment when she'd begun to truly believe she would be a success.

When Lila had suggested they go dancing after the gig, she'd numbly agreed.

"Aunt Bree?"

Penny's voice startled Bree back to the present. The throb in her wrist returned and the quartet's music faded away. The simplicity of Island Breeze's music was as inaccessible to her as the Goldbergs. "Sorry."

Penny set down the tray of food and immediately scooped up a ring of grilled onion. "You looked happy about something."

"I was just remembering how I found my agent. Not that there's any reason to have one now." Markham wanted her to continue her lectures. He'd even suggested that she promote her compositions. But she wasn't a composer. Everything she'd ever written had been through the voice of her violin.

"Is it really that way?" Penny was blinking back tears. "I never got to hear you *really* play."

Bree tried to sound philosophical as she reached for her burger. She didn't feel so hungry now, but she had to eat. "Believe me, I wish it weren't so, but we don't always get what we wish for."

We don't always get what we wish for, Aunt Lani said from the past.

Sometimes we get what we wish for, Lila whispered in her ear, from a long way away.

She didn't want to feel good right now. She didn't want to remember that night. The world had been, to quote a young Penny, her toaster. She would never have that back.

85

She didn't know exactly when it was that Penny's focus on her wavered. She studied the change in Penny's face, wondering what caused the sidelong glance at something over Bree's shoulder.

A tall, broad shadow fell over the table a few moments later. Penny feigned surprise. "Riki! What are you doing out and about?"

Though the boy had made the effort to stand next to their table, he looked across the room. "Nothing." Then his handsome face cracked into a smile and he looked right at Penny. "Until now."

Even Bree wasn't immune to the charm, but the effect it had on Penny wasn't what Bree expected.

"Go use that line on your girlfriends, Riki."

Bree would not have said she had any maternal instincts, but she learned in a split second that she did. Riki was handsome, charming and not so deeply tanned as to indicate unemployment. He was, therefore, dangerous.

"I'm Penny's aunt," she said firmly, holding out her hand.

Riki dealt her a smile so likeable that Bree nearly responded with a grin of her own. "I know," he said. "I think I've grown a little since you last saw me."

"Bree! Bree Starling, it is you!"

Stunned, Bree recognized Momi hurrying toward her. She did a double-take at Riki. No way was he Momi's son — not the gangling, tongue-tied, pimply-faced Richard the computer geek. He'd grown up into a god. She remembered then that he had always been Penny's shadow, and Penny had always been very aware of her limitless power over him.

Given Penny's abrupt agitation, tables had turned, perhaps. Penny was probably wishing now she'd been a bit kinder and not quite so dictatorial.

Bree rose to embrace Momi and blinked back tears. Of all Jorie's friends, Momi was the one who had been the friendliest to her, through all the years. She vividly recalled when Momi's sweet, light voice had been the only music in her life. Momi had sent flowers after that disastrous San Francisco concert. She barely remembered them now. Diana had swept all other memories away.

She was momentarily overcome with the picture of what her life had never been — a certain destiny. Momi had always known what she wanted from life, a strong *'ohana*, and she'd achieved it. No one could take that away. It seemed the much better choice, devoting oneself to home and family, rather than the vagaries of a performing career.

She wanted to stop feeling like this, like she'd never known happiness in her past when she knew that she had. She'd known since conservatory that she would be a performing musician and quite possibly a star. But it was so illusory. How could a stack of CDs, a case of awards and boxes of playbills possibly compare to Momi's riches? There was a gnawing certainty in her that what she had known of joy was all there would ever be. Her ancestors had stopped speaking to her. The violin was lost forever. Music was all static.

Momi returned her hug with all the warmth of long friendship, but even that didn't seem to touch Bree. Had there ever been anyone besides Aunt Lani she had cared for? She'd never loved Jorie enough to fight for her, or to set both of them free from their destructive pattern. She hadn't loved Lila, not any of the others.

She hadn't loved Diana. Not even Diana.

CHAPTER SIX

"It's such a loss," Momi was saying as she gently separated herself from Bree's intense hug. She had the solid, unbreakable feel to her that Aunt Lani had always had. "I miss *lehua* Lani a dozen times a day."

"I know," Bree managed to reply. "I can't believe she was there one moment and gone the next."

"God wanted her. It was over in seconds, the doctor said."

Bree was momentarily speechless with rage. What evil-minded, selfish god could Momi mean, that would take goodness out of the world? How could any deity worth believing in need someone like Lani more than the suffering world? No god she would ever believe in.

The flash passed and she knew it was just how Momi comforted herself. She glanced at Riki, who was listening to them gravely. "I didn't recognize your eldest, here."

"Yeah, he popped straight up one day. Grew an inch a day for three months, it seemed like." She smiled proudly while her gaze flickered to Penny speculatively.

Bree now recognized kindred maternal instincts. "I hadn't eaten and Penny is taking pity on me by joining me."

Momi nodded. "I stopped in to borrow the large soaking pan. For the party."

"We'll make sure the ancestors hear her coming," Riki added. His gaze never left Penny.

Bree quirked an eyebrow at Momi, glad of any distraction from the pain that her entire body seemed steeped in. Momi rolled her eyes slightly and glanced meaningfully at her son. "We'll have to get together for...a long chat," Momi said, far too nonchalantly.

Bree sought for something that would carry her concern but not be translatable by the younger people. "Age?"

"Right." Momi nodded firmly. "Although..."

"Oh. Right." Bree recalled that Momi had married Riki's father at nineteen. As far as she knew, they were still married. Oh, that was awkward — how to ask? "Still. Safety."

Momi looked around. "Come see the new drink mixer."

It wasn't the most subtle ploy, but Bree could tell that Riki and Penny bought it. She scuttled across the room with Momi and gazed raptly at the appliance.

Momi said, through a forced smile, "I can't get Jorie to realize it's serious. She says Penny's too young and she's agreed to abstinence. But look at them!"

Bree did turn and look. All the gods, had her feelings for Jorie been that easy to read? "That particular tide is going to come to shore," she observed dryly.

Momi laughed. "You sound just like *lehua* Lani. Will you talk to Penny about it — I mean, maybe sort of mention safe sex and your feelings about it? I'm not thinking they'll get something from each other, though gods. I know he's a good boy, but he's a *boy*. Remember Cici?"

"Of course."

"She can't have kids. First guy she was ever with gave her PID and now she's infertile. I love Penny and I think Jorie is being foolhardy. She just insists Penny's too young to know what she really wants. Therefore nothing will happen."

"Christ," Bree said without thinking. "I was having sex by her age." She might have blushed if Momi hadn't been nodding.

"Exactly! So was I. So was everybody, including Jorie, so this is like some sort of blind spot for her. I want our kids to be happy. I don't know if this is the long haul for them, but if it isn't neither of them should pay for the rest of their life, you know? And I don't think Jorie is ready to be a grandmother."

It was a shock to even contemplate. "I'll see what I can work into the conversation." Bree pointed at the machine. "I've seen all I want to see."

Momi laughed and hoisted the needed pan from the bar. Riki, in possession of one of Penny's onion rings, promptly took the heavy pan out of his mother's arms and fell into step with her on the way out the door.

"He seems to have turned out to be something rather nice."

"Yeah." Penny picked at her fries.

"I remember when he was your shadow."

"Yeah."

"He seems to get along with his mother."

Penny shot her a suspicious look. "Don't you start, either. We're not...that way."

Bree forked up some macaroni salad. It wasn't as good as Aunt Lani's, but it was the best thing she had tasted in years. "Why not?"

Penny gaped. "Aunt Bree!"

"Just a simple question."

"I've known him forever."

"I see."

The suspicious look intensified, then Penny's eyes filled with tears. "Aunt Lani said the same thing. I don't — I'm too young."

"For what?"

"For...sex and forever."

90

"They go together?"

The tears melted into the glimmer of a smile. "They're supposed to. Or so I've been told repeatedly."

Bree swallowed a large bite of her burger. "Tell you a secret. I've had sex and so far no forevers." She choked and hoped Penny thought she'd swallowed wrong. Hmm, given that Penny knew she was a lesbian, it was hard to bring up condoms. Before AIDS, the thought of safe sex had never crossed her mind, either. She had no real business preaching safety after some of the things she'd done in the past. "A little love along the way. I tried hard to be safe. Heart and body."

"You're not very much like Mom, are you?" Penny sank her teeth into her burger with a sigh.

Though it cost her a pang, Bree agreed with apparent equanimity. "I've led a different life."

"I'll bet. Did you always know you were gay?"

Puzzled by the change in topic, Bree nodded.

Penny subsided into a thoughtful silence for the rest of the meal. Feeling as if a vast emptiness had been filled with delicious, comforting *'ai*, Bree studied the young face across from her. So like her mother at that age, but so much more open. She could tell nearly every thought that crossed Penny's mind. She had never been able to read Jorie. For that matter, she'd never been able to read anyone she'd slept with.

Her mind was back to Lila, she realized, as she shepherded Penny out of the door. Lila, like so many others, had been a mistake. It just hadn't seemed so at the time.

* * * * *

"I can't believe he gave you his card!" Lila hadn't stopped dancing around Bree the entire time they packed their equipment into Derek's van. "We need to celebrate!"

Bree wanted to play it cool, but a smile kept flashing out. "Maybe..."

"What maybe? Let's go out!"

Glancing at the guys, she asked, "What do you think?"

"I have an early exam." Derek patted his pockets for his keys again.

"Let's go to that club, you know. In West Van — the gay one."

"Count me out for sure," Derek said. "I don't need some sissy Mary trying to jump me."

Paul stumbled slightly. "I have an early exam, too," he said.

"You guys are no fun!" Lila stamped her foot. "Bree and I would dance with you. No one would think you were gay."

"Like that matters to those people," Derek said.

"Don't be a boor," Lila scolded. "What about you, Bree? Come on, it'll be fun."

"I don't know..."

"I'm sure you'll have fun." Paul opened the passenger door. "The music is good."

Derek stared at Paul, who shrugged. "You're...you're..."

"You're not my type, man." Paul's shoulders were rigid.

"I mean — how come you never said?"

"Why would I? It's not like I want to date you. Can we go? It's cold."

Bree could feel eddies of hostility like a frigid tide around her ankles. "Yes, let's go."

Derek wasn't so easily distracted. "What about your family?"

"They don't know yet."

"I mean, can't you give girls a try?"

Lila snorted as Bree said, "Derek, geez!"

"I'm not looking to get cured, Derek. I like it this way, okay?"

"But it's sick!"

Bree couldn't take it. "Shut up, Derek. What difference does it make to the music? For that matter, I'm gay, okay?" The words were out before she considered what she was doing.

Derek's reaction wasn't what she expected. Instead of more disgust, his expression cleared. "That's different."

"Why?"

"You're a girl. Girls can't... I mean they can try, but not really."

"You are *so* ignorant." Lila opened her door. "I swear if I didn't like guys it would be so much easier to live with a girl. The seat would be down and someone would actually help clean up."

Bree got in beside Lila, relieved that Lila wasn't freaking. "It doesn't matter to the music."

"No," Lila said slowly, "I don't think it does. But I'm serious. Let's go dancing. Paulie come with us, please. You can be our protector knight."

Paul was hunched deep in his jacket as he settled into his seat. "It's not like you're in danger. None of the guys are interested in you."

"True," Lila allowed. "Derek, you can swing by there, can't you? Save us a cab ride?"

"But we're wearing gig clothes," Bree protested. "I look like a carnival escapee." The bright orange *kihei* knotted over one shoulder was hardly club attire.

"You look great. Just take off the fake lei." Lila tossed hers in the back of the van with the equipment. "Turn left."

Derek hardly spoke to them as they got out. At the last moment Paul joined them in the bitter night air. "I'll get my stuff tomorrow," he told Derek.

Derek took off without another word.

"Well," Paul said. "You guys might need another guitarist. I'm not putting up with that."

"And a violinist," Bree said.

Lila tossed her hair. "Derek'll be the one looking for a new group. It bugs me that Bree's okay and you're not, Paulie. I didn't realize he was such an idiot."

"Guys? I'm freezing." Her sheepskin jacket couldn't compensate for the thin cotton of her Hawaiian stage dress.

"Wimp." Paul led them across the street to the club entrance. Bree could feel the throb of dance music through her feet, reminding her of a waterfall. The bouncer looked her and Lila up and down, then gave Paul a "you must be joking" look.

"They're cool," Paul said.

Bree proffered two twenties for the cover charge, enough for all three of them plus some extra.

Over the pounding grind of the music, the bouncer said, "It's not fag hag night!"

"One is and one isn't," Paul shouted back.

Lila laughed and opened her long coat. "You can't tell me some of the guys won't want to ask me where I got my dress!"

Feeling suddenly lighthearted, Bree likewise flashed her *kihei* and the bouncer laughed. He took Bree's money and said, "If anyone asks, I'm not the one who let you in."

Inside the club the wall of sound was so intense that Bree winced. At the coat check Paul stripped off his Hawaiian shirt and put his leather jacket back on. She and Lila checked their coats and bags and they all pressed their way to the dance area. The high-pitched vocals were unintelligible at this level.

"Don't make that face," Lila shouted. "We're not here to listen!" She seized Bree by the hand and wormed her way out to the dance floor. "We're here to move!"

They danced apart for a while. Bree felt very self-conscious but slowly realized she could have been invisible for all the notice the men around her took. Men dancing together had no reason to be restrained or gentle, either. They swung, kicked, spun and collided with all of their strength. Their exuberance infected her. She thought of the business cards tucked in her bag and was suffused with joy at proof that her dreams could all come true.

She could even like disco music if she didn't think of it as music. It did have a language. It said dance with all you've got. Move, feel the rhythm and don't stop. Thank god it's Friday because it's the last dance on the midnight express. Don't be misunderstood, move, shake your booty and move, give in to the Saturday night fever, move because there ain't no cure for the rhythm. You should be dancing, so move.

A new song began and men were yelling, "Time Warp!" Bree ducked flying arms and legs and looked wildly about for Lila. She felt hands on her hips and managed to turn. Lila threw her arms around her and they held on for what felt like dear life.

It was so crowded that Bree could have lifted her feet and not fallen. Once or twice she and Lila got caught in the crossfire, colliding with shoulders.

It made a lot of sense to hold Lila very close even after the floor cleared a little. Their combined mass took up more space and the men granted them more room.

"All these guys," Lila said in her ear. "Water, water everywhere and not a drop to drink for little ol' me."

"There's not exactly a drop to drink for me either." As far as she could tell, they were the only women in the place.

Lila's laugh had a sultry edge. One hand slid down Bree's backside. "Don't be so sure, Bree."

Startled, Bree found herself shifting her hips so that Lila's were flat against hers. They moved together in an increasingly compatible rhythm. Lila cupped her ass and Bree felt warm lips at her throat. It felt way too good. She hadn't been with anyone but Jorie, and it wasn't like she was saving herself for that to happen again. Jorie wasn't interested. "I thought you were...you know."

"I am. I think I might like girls, too. You sure do feel good to me."

"Have you?"

"No. But I've thought about it, a lot."

"Uh..."

"Oh, don't be a prude. This place is all about sex and freedom to just enjoy it. Let's enjoy, honey."

What about tomorrow, Bree wanted to ask. What about dating and love and what about Jorie? What about the fact that Lila liked guys...Lila kissed her, then.

Through the thin material of their dresses she could feel Lila's small breasts hardening against hers. It was hot from the number and closeness of other bodies, and Lila's dress clung to every curve. Bree managed to work one hand up to caress first ribs, then the soft, inviting side.

Lila shuddered. "God that feels different when you do it."

The kiss that followed left Bree dizzy with want. Any confusion she felt about right and wrong, safety and danger, gay or not became rapidly irrelevant. Lila didn't want her heart. Lila didn't want anything except sensation and the moment. It was obvious she wanted Bree to touch her. What was wrong with that?

Their dance became a slow grind, with Bree's hand on Lila's breast, her thumb teasing the nipple that felt like a rock through the skimpy fabric. Bree knew how to undo the knot at Lila's shoulder and that underneath there was only pantyhose. Her mouth was watering. Lila

95

moved like liquid. She would find what she craved between Lila's legs. She wanted it bad. She hardly cared that it was Lila — her mouth was so hungry for the taste of a woman again.

Her tongue danced in Lila's mouth. It was a prelude, warm-up, practice. Lila's hips were moving in a continuous pulse of openness that bumped Bree in the right places. She pulled Lila toward the edge of the dance floor, into the hallway that led to the bathrooms, up against the wall. Lila let out a little cry as Bree's hand went under the dress, sliding over the thighs damp with perspiration.

The music made it hard to think. Bree could only feel. More kisses, more heat, more dizziness. It was Lila who pulled her into the women's restroom. She hardly noticed the two men they interrupted. Neither took any notice of them fumbling their way into a stall. Lila was right — it was about sex and the freedom to enjoy it.

Lila braced herself against the wall as Bree went to her knees. She pushed up the dress and buried her face in the crotch of Lila's pantyhose, smelling what she wanted and delirious with wanting to taste it.

Lila's hand was suddenly between Bree's mouth and the fabric. With a shudder that was close to climax she watched Lila's long red nails tear it open. No barriers now.

She forgot to breathe while she swam, reveled, tasted, pushing Lila's legs farther and farther apart. Her heart pounded to the throb in the floor below her and her ears rang with Lila's short, desperate gasps.

"There, there, do me there!"

The sensation of Lila's wet trickling down her chin left Bree gasping. She clambered to her feet, pushing her fingers into Lila, kissing her on her shoulders, her mouth, her eyes. Lila's hips thrust down on her hand and Bree wanted to feel the rush of Lila coming on her palm as she pressed Lila into the wall. Lila shrieked once, then again, as she wrapped one leg around Bree's thighs.

"Yeah, baby!"

The light seemed to flicker and sparkle. It all felt so good. Bree felt like a god. Only when Lila was gasping gratitude into her shoulder did she think of Jorie and wish...and wish that it could have been her. The thought wasn't fair to Lila, so she shook it away.

After a minute of breathing hard, Lila murmured, "My roommate is at her boyfriend's tonight. Come back with me."

Why not say yes? Why not? Yes was easy with Lila. Lila was hungry for everything Bree wanted to give her.

On the bed, Lila said what she wanted. "I can't believe the way you make me feel."

Bree explored Lila's body, tasting everything, touching everywhere. She surged between Lila's legs, feeling strong and sure and knowing exactly what would make Lila respond.

"Inside me, be inside me," Lila pleaded and Bree gave her that, too. She felt as if she was falling into Lila's desire and fulfilling passions that only she could touch.

She left Lila exhausted, which pleased her. Lila's tentative touches had been enough, and Bree trusted that time would give Lila more boldness to take Bree to the same places Bree carried Lila to. They had a lot of time.

What to call the pain of inexperience and foolishness? For a precious week Bree walked a tightrope of happiness. She dreamed again of having a woman in her life, *'ohana* of her own. She found the courage, two days after her affair with Lila began, to call Markham Powell. Mentioning that she'd been given the other card as well opened doors like magic.

The gray skies gave way to a bleary sunshine on the day that Markham Powell was flying in to hear her play. Bree had received guardedly hopeful permission from Professor Tolan to use the recital hall for an audience of one.

She dressed carefully for her appointment with Mr. Powell, choosing a plain skirted black suit common to orchestra musicians. Full of high spirits, she skipped across campus to Lila's dorm, swinging her violin case as she walked and feeling like singing something from *The Sound of Music*. She bolted up to Lila's door with the idea of asking her to come with her. She'd felt funny about it — Lila was a musician, too. A talented singer. But an opportunity to audition for the most exclusive musical agent in North America wasn't coming to Lila. She didn't want to make Lila feel...inadequate.

Maybe Lila wouldn't feel bad. After all, Bree knew perfectly well that Itzhak Perlman existed, and she'd never be as good as he was. That reality didn't make her feel less assured about the gifts she did have, though.

Her knock on the door brought a muted response. When Lila opened the door she gaped at Bree. "I wasn't expecting you."

Bree burst past Lila, hardly noticing she was in her robe in the middle of the day. Setting her violin case down, she said, "I was thinking. Do you want to — "

She didn't know if it was good or bad that she didn't know the man huddled in Lila's bed. She stared at him for a stunned second, then reeled around to face a flushing Lila.

"I never said — "

"No, you never did," Bree snapped. "I shouldn't have assumed." She'd been with Lila last night. Lila had liked everything. Just last night.

"You're right."

"You said...you..." Bree was at a complete loss. "What do you need me for?"

"Oh Bree." Lila laughed. All the gods, she laughed like Cici, like Jorie, like everyone did when Bree didn't understand the rules because she was a stupid outsider. Well, damn it, she didn't understand the rules to this game. Was this not supposed to hurt?

"I get it. I get it. I was kicks. You got off. Not that you ever wanted to do much in return."

"I'm not — "

"You're not what?" Bree advanced on Lila, feeling like she just wanted to smack her. "Not queer? You're not queer because you never screwed me?" Pathetic, Bree thought. You wanted a woman so much you had one that didn't want you back.

"Don't be a prude, Bree."

All the while the guy watched their exchange without a word, the sheets crumpled over his crotch. Bree gave him a look of contempt. She didn't hate guys, she just had no use for them in bed. "Yeah. This was a mistake. Well, you got something out of it." A lot of somethings. Screaming, shaking somethings. Somethings that Bree would have liked to have by more than her own effort.

Okay, fine. You're not here to have sex, she told herself angrily. You're not even here to be happy. You're here to become the best goddamned violinist in the history of the world. And that's exactly what you're going to do.

"I was just curious, that's all," Lila said to Bree's back. "It's not like you could really fuck me."

Dimly, Bree heard the guy say, "She doesn't have to go."

A scherzo of rage boiled inside her, but words failed her. She didn't know the rules. She wasn't a prude. But she wasn't going to wait around to get hurt even more.

She was halfway down the hallway to the stairs when Lila yelled, "You forgot this!"

Bree turned to see Lila holding out the violin case. She had no choice but to go back for it.

"I guess it's a compliment," Lila said. "That you could forget about it for once."

I hate that thing!

"Why are you treating me this way?"

"I thought you didn't care. Because you're...you know. Lesbian. Sex doesn't mean anything." Lila shrugged. "I'm sorry you're hurt, but I'm not going to give up men for you."

"I don't think I asked you to." Bree knew, though, that she thought that was what Lila had done. That she hadn't — she struck out in hurt. "I just thought you might stay out of bed with someone else long enough to change the sheets."

"So now I'm a slut?"

Bree shrugged and reached for the violin case.

Lila let it drop to the floor with a thud. "Fuck you, Bree."

"It's not as if you ever did." She snatched up the case and then stood erect with the pittance of dignity she could muster. She never wanted to feel this way again. At least Jorie had seemed to like touching her, tasting her. At least Jorie had wanted Bree to feel good. From here on out she would make damn sure someone wanted her before she got involved.

She hurried down the stairs to the street and out into the cold afternoon. Was she not supposed to have cared about Lila? Were lesbians just supposed to take being treated like they didn't matter? Did lesbians sleep with any woman and then move on to the next? Were those the rules?

Her shoulder blades itched and burned as she raged at trees, benches and cars. She was glad of the walk to the recital hall.

Her anger carefully banked, she was surprised to find Professor Tolan and two of her other instructors waiting for her. Lila faded to a bad dream as the necessity of the performance took over. It was more meaningful than Lila could have ever been.

"Game face, that's good," said Professor Tolan. "I would tell you that this is the most important moment of your life, but I think your life is going to be one important moment after another."

Professor McConnell, who taught theory and early music, added seriously, "But there's no such thing as guaranteed destiny, Sabrina. Statistically, there must be thousands of brilliant musicians throughout history whose names we don't know because their timing was off. You have to control your fate by rising to the challenge of every day."

Was she brilliant? Her shoulder blades itched again, and she heard the murmur of *wiwo'ole*.

Professor Tate, who was too young to be frightening, simply said, "Have fun out there."

"What are you going to play?" Professor Tolan turned toward the door. "It's too cold out here for your hands."

"I thought the first Brahms Paganini transcription."

"The fourth," Professor Tate said quickly. The others nodded.

Inside the hall it was cold, so they all insisted she keep her coat on until she walked out on stage. Was this what it was like to be a performer? Other people fussing about your well-being?

"One other thing, Starling." Professor Tolan sounded as gruff and unfriendly as ever.

Warily, Bree asked, "Yes, sir?"

"Forget everything I've tried to teach you."

Bree's anxiety melted away. "Not everything, sir."

He made a humph of disapproval that she was arguing with him, but said nothing more. In a flash of unaccustomed wisdom, she realized his attempt to change her in some way was a desire to play some part in her future.

The rear doors opened and the three professors converged on the lone man who strolled through. He was tall and elegant, though dressed in slacks and a thick Shetland sweater. He glanced past the greeting committee to where Bree stood, still clutching her violin case.

She did some deep, rhythmic breathing while her teachers introduced themselves, and then, with the air of admitting the agent into a hallowed presence, escorted him along the aisle to meet Bree, calling her by her full name.

They shook hands.

"You need warmers," he observed. His glance at the others seemed to be full of wonder that someone had failed to provide something so critical to her success.

"Yes, sir."

"Our mutual friend gave me to understand you have some talent."

Bree swallowed. "I think I do, sir."

"Please don't call me sir. Markham will do."

"Yes, si — Markham."

He laughed and glanced at the professors. "They're only this age once, right?"

They all chuckled, then Professor Tolan said seriously, "Miss Starling is far older than she seems."

"Let's hear her real age, then."

Professor Tate was the one who took her around the wings to the stage stairs. "You're going to be fine, Bree. Let it be fun."

The stage was dark, but as she found the center, a single spot came on. She nodded thanks, kissed her violin between the tuning pegs and snapped out her left arm. She couldn't see where anyone was sitting, but said loud enough to be heard, "I need to do a little warmup."

"Sure," came the answer.

Scales, quiet and musing, then with increasing precision. She paused to adjust her tuning, then ran the full strings. She wished she'd arranged for a pianist. She wouldn't feel so alone. *Wiwo'ole*, sang the voices. It was no time for fear. No time to think about Lila.

Brahms had always spoken to her of light. Sunshine dappled on a garden, shifting patterns of stars on a clear night. Like all music, Brahms was mathematics, a dazzling geometry building bridges from simple to profound. She let her fingers slip over the strings like sunrise, coaxing thoughts from the violin, giving it full voice.

Markham would work with her later about how much she moved while she played, reminding her it was a concert and not a dance. But as the critics took notice and the response to her name on a symphony's schedule grew, he acknowledged that part of the charm of seeing her live was the way she responded to the music she played. Symphonies eventually vied for her contract, wanting to open seasons with her on-stage, many offering to undertake any piece she chose.

Bree slipped out of the past, remembering that the maestro in San Francisco hadn't made that offer, but had been gentlemanly about negotiating the piece. San Francisco...

Abruptly she was aware of Penny's chattering and the sway of the car around a corner. They were almost home and she didn't want to think about San Francisco. It was too new. It hurt too much. It led to Diana and she couldn't handle that right now. She didn't think she'd ever handle it.

"...don't you think?"

"I'm sorry," Bree said automatically. "I didn't hear that last part."

"You haven't really been listening," Penny accused. "But it's okay. I — I'm not used to going home yet and not finding Gramma there."

"I know what you mean." She struggled to find words. Feeling clumsy, she added, "Life can be hard."

"Yeah."

"Look, it's none of my business, but I would be really concerned for you if I thought you weren't being safe."

Penny snapped, "I'm not doing anything."

"I know what it's like, Penny." Bree felt as if she was pleading for Penny's life. At least for her future. "I know that it's so easy to get overwhelmed. It's easy to forget the rules. It's so easy to forget that sometimes things that feel good aren't good for you. You can't act like other people don't have feelings. You think you won't get hurt, but you do — "

"It's okay, Aunt Bree. It's okay."

She realized that Penny was trying to comfort her. So much for maternal instincts. None of that had been about Penny. Jorie, Lila, Diana. There were others. The list was longer than she liked to think. Teena. Christ, she didn't need to think about Teena right now. That was a completely different kind of guilt.

"I'm sorry, honey. Everybody makes mistakes. You'll make them — it's called life. But you shouldn't pay for them forever, you know?"

"I know."

She turned instinctively into Aunt Lani's driveway in a condition she might have called numb if she could have thought about it at all.

"Mom's home."

Her whirling mind finally translated "mom" to mean Jorie. Jorie was there.

As before she saw a figure in the window. It moved toward the door as she parked.

Penny was out of the car first. "I'm back," she called. "Aunt Bree's here."

Bree found herself propelled into the moment. She couldn't think, she couldn't avoid, she couldn't do anything but get out of the car, walk on robot legs toward the slender figure waiting in the semi-dark of the porch.

A flash of a tremulous smile, then a wave of grief.

"Bree." It sounded like pain. "Oh, Bree."

Jorie's tears were scalding, a flood of anguish. "I know." Bree's tears were threatening again, but this was her time to be strong.

"I still can't believe it."

"I know." There was nothing else to say as she patted Jorie's back,

103

trying to forget for the sake of her sanity and Jorie's comfort how Jorie could move when she was aroused.

It was too hard to separate, and for a dizzying moment Bree straddled past and present.

Jorie was hot against her. She wanted no more of the past and she tried to put it away. Her shoulders itched fiercely — what could her ancestors want with her? She had nothing to give them, nothing to give anyone anymore. Her wrist was screaming at her as she struggled to hold Jorie close — she couldn't even do that well. In the past, she had...Jorie had...

Jorie moved, one hand wrapping around Bree's waist as she cried. All the gods, Bree thought, I can't do this. She didn't have any *wiwo'ole* left. The past hadn't left her any.

CHAPTER SEVEN

Their hug went on. The tears didn't stop. There was a tickle of rosemary and sage from the garden's night air. Christmas. Jorie's arms around her. The smell of goose and papaya and the lilt of Aunt Lani's voice. Jorie's arms around her.

"Conservatory agrees with you." Jorie pushed her hands into the back pockets of her jeans.

She had no right to look so nonchalant. She disturbed Bree's sleep, invaded fantasies when Bree was tired. Bree put down her suitcase and slung the useless sheepskin jacket over the chair. "It does. I like it a lot."

"Me, too."

"Gonna marry anyone yet?" Bree meant that to sound nicer than it did. Since Lila she thought about sex all the time, wondering if she'd ever meet any woman who actually wanted her back. What was the point of Markham telling her she was gorgeous when she couldn't, well, she couldn't get laid, she thought. Sometimes it seemed as if that was all she lacked to be happy. A little sex. The violin was the only thing that made her longing for Jorie stop.

Not that she had a lot of time to fantasize about her dream woman or even an array of slightly-less-than-perfect women. She barely had time for sleep now that Markham had her on a limited schedule of performances, all of which had been agreed to by her professors.

Jorie was frowning. "No. I think I'm going to put it off for a while. Work on school."

"Sounds like a good plan."

"Mom approves."

Bree smiled at that. "Well, that's something."

Jorie shrugged. Her shirt was pulled tight over breasts Bree remembered hardening against her mouth. Stop it, she warned herself. Stop or she'll know. "When do you go back to Oahu?"

"A bunch of friends are planning a hiking trip on Kahoolawe. Some of them have been doing environmental measurements for school to see if there's been changes in the soil because of the treatment. A missile target range takes a while to heal. So I need to be back by the twenty-seventh to go with them. When do you head for Vancouver?"

"I'm part of a New Year's broadcast, and there are rehearsals continuing. I have to be back on the twenty-eighth."

She could feel Jorie's sigh of relief. Only four days to get through. One was Christmas, the others surely taken up with seeing friends. "Mom has a show at the big gallery. She sold a lot over the holidays. There are tourists everywhere it seems like. The Japanese really like her stuff."

"That's good." Bree edged toward the door. "I know I smell angel volcano cake."

Jorie's mouth split into an easy grin. "Yeah. I think it's the fatted calf for both of us."

Dinner consisted of so many favorite dishes that Bree hardly felt she could do justice to any of them. After wolfing down an enormous piece of cake, Jorie did indeed head off to see friends. Though Bree had expected it, she felt hurt. But she did have the pleasure of telling Aunt Lani all about Lila and being soothed and comforted.

"No one should be treated that way. If you were an experiment she might have said so sooner." Aunt Lani slowly stirred the pot full of sugar and cocoa. The aroma of chocolate permeated the kitchen.

"It was only a week. I don't think she knew what she wanted. Except it sure wasn't me. Except, you know, when she wanted, well, you know."

"Wipe away the pain, Bree. Your life is too full to carry it around." Aunt Lani peered into the pot and adjusted the flame underneath it. "I talked to a friend about Markham Powell. I am glad that someone of that status is interested in your career, but I wanted to be certain he wasn't after money today and not caring about your tomorrows."

Bree could smile at that. Markham set aside time every week to talk to her by phone, going over potential performances he might be able to sign for her. But he always asked about her finals or practice schedule first. He was more likely than she was to rule something out as being too much interference in her studies for the value — money, exposure or experience — she would get for it. "And?"

"His reputation is sound. He has clients who have been with him for twenty years. His agency is highly regarded. Does he handle you personally?"

"Always. Occasionally an assistant might call about something, but he's the only one who talks to me about what I could be doing." There were only a few other students at the conservatory who had agents and Bree knew how lucky she was to have Markham nurturing her career.

"I know I had objections about you becoming a working professional." Apparently happy with the fudge, Aunt Lani poured it carefully into a shallow pan to cool. "But this seems to be very good for you."

"Better for me than Lila. I'm really thankful that he thinks I'm worth his time." Bree tried to edge a finger into the fudge, but Aunt Lani whacked the back of her hand.

"You'll burn yourself. He's the one who should be thankful, Bree."

Feeling seven again, and willing to believe she could always feel this carefree, Bree watched Aunt Lani's favorite television program with her and went to bed.

She wasn't quite asleep when Jorie came home. She listened to the furtive sounds of undressing and her earlier happiness fled. Now she could remember all the rest of the days of summer, when Jorie flitted away like a bird every time Bree came within two feet of her.

Was that her shirt falling to the floor? Her bra? Were her hips bare? Surely she was naked by now. Why wasn't she getting into bed? She couldn't be looking Bree's way. Bree imagined Jorie crossing the room, whispering her name.

I'm yours, I'm yours. I want you. Let me touch you. Let me inside your heart. I am music for a lifetime.

At last she heard the rustle of bedclothes and hoped it covered the sound of her shifting to wipe her eyes.

Christmas Day came with a blaze of sunshine and hot windward breezes. Bree finally felt warm again. She'd found a lovely weaving shop in Vancouver and so gave Aunt Lani an array of Persian and Egyptian silks. For Jorie she had bought a wildly expensive monogrammed pen and scented paper, remembering she was fussy about what she wrote with. Aunt Lani's gift to her was twelve squares of brilliantly hued tapes tries hand-woven by a friend. She could arrange them on the background fabric any way she liked, changing them every day if she wanted. Jorie gave her a small certificate that said she was now a member of the Fruit-of-the-Month Club.

"You sounded so hungry for fresh fruit in your letters."

The name sounded so silly, but Bree was deeply touched. Jorie had read her letters enough to think of it. "I think that's the hardest part. Everything is canned."

After phone calls to relatives on other parts of the island and other islands, Aunt Lani fussed with the goose and dressing as the house began to fill with artist friends who brought a wonderful variety of foods with them. When everyone was too stuffed to consume another bite, cars were crammed and everyone headed north for a drive of about an hour to Spencer Beach.

Sun and waves, like childhood, Bree thought. She had missed it. This beach was her favorite, with its long, gentle swells and shaded sand. She held hands with wading *keikis*, remembering when she had been amazed to go so far from shore and yet only have water up to her calves. When a lone giant *honu* swam by, Bree shooed away the kids — all of whom wanted to touch the scarred shell — and swam alongside for a while. Grace and elegance, she thought. It took far more effort than she had thought it might, but finally, she could recall the song her mother had sung about graceful *honu*, grandmother of the sea.

She had of course put her practice violin in the car, and when asked was happy to play carols. No one seemed to notice that she had stumbled over the Hawaiian words to the "Twelve Days of Christmas." She danced her way through "Kana Kaloka" and reveled in the feel of sand between her toes.

But at no point was she not aware that Jorie was laughing with other people, putting a casual arm around anyone but her.

"I've missed the sound of you practicing," Aunt Lani admitted when Bree emerged from the back room.

"I'd forgotten how good it sounds in there. No bounce at all. I can hear every fuzzy note and sloppy bow movement."

Aunt Lani put her arms around her. "I miss you, too, you know."

"Yeah." She hugged the older woman back with all her strength. "It's good to be home."

"Will you come back for Easter?"

"I don't know — I'm sorry. Markham is trying to sign me into a TV thing. It'll be good timing in terms of school. But there's ski week in March. Can I come home then?"

"Of course." Aunt Lani chuckled in her ear. "You never have to ask."

"I'll remember." But she knew as she said it that she didn't want to be home if Jorie was here. It hurt too much. Maybe, given time. But not right now.

Jorie was quiet through a dinner of leftovers. When they were just about to begin clearing up, she said, "I've decided to go on the hike to Kahoolawe. It'll be something I could write a paper on."

Bree saw how stricken Aunt Lani was. It reflected how she felt. So. Jorie was leaving tomorrow.

On the surface, the evening seemed easy. They laughed through gossip and listened as Aunt Lani read them a piece of a novel she'd found amusing. At the point when they might have gone to bed they decided to make mango shortbread, working in the kitchen with easy familiarity. For a little while, everything seemed like it had been before she and Jorie had been together.

It was nearly midnight when they were able to sample the delicious cookies. They all agreed enthusiastically that fresh-squeezed pineapple and orange juice over ice was the perfect accompaniment. Jorie's imitation of one of her professors trying to swat an irritating mosquito made Bree laugh so hard she nearly wet her pants.

Like children, safe and happy, with none of the stress of love and sex, or success and failure, Jorie finally put a hand on Bree's forearm as she talked.

It felt too good and Bree jerked her arm away.

Jorie gave her a long, hurt look that was too intense for Bree to maintain. The house suddenly seemed so small.

"Play us something," Aunt Lani said. "Something you like."

Jorie nodded and Bree wondered if she imagined that Jorie was steeling herself to listen. I hate that thing!

For this special time she didn't turn to the practice violin. Instead, she spent a minute showing them both the new violin that Markham had recently arranged for her to purchase. The long-distant trustees had released the funds for it and the insurance. "I'm not really supposed to take it out of the safety deposit box, but I wanted to show it to you. It was made in the seventeen-hundreds by an Italian

110

named Guarneri. It's very like the one I borrowed for that competition in Los Angeles. The real magic of it seems to be in this curve of the sounding box." She ran her hand over the nearly imperceptible swell of the violin's belly.

Aunt Lani ran her sensitive fingertips over the strings. "This is a lovely piece of work."

"Playable art," Bree said with a smile. "Okay, how about this?"

She played "Ahe Honi," aware more than ever that she longed for even the lightest of kisses from Jorie, to be wrapped by her affection like a gentle island breeze. It wasn't Jorie's fault they couldn't have simple affection, she realized. It was her and her desire that was the problem. How could she ever conquer it? So far, it had ruined everything.

The melody rose like a pleasant memory and Bree gave herself to the music then, using it to banish all the chill she felt in cold, dank Vancouver. When she was done she saw a glimmer of tears in Jorie's eyes and for just that instant she felt complete.

"That was just lovely." Aunt Lani sighed. "It makes me want to get my hands into some silks and clay."

"Sunrise at Haleakala." Jorie swallowed the last of her juice. "The light shooting over the clouds."

"Thank you. I was very homesick when I wrote it."

"You *wrote* that?" Jorie seemed stunned.

"Yeah." Bree almost felt sheepish. "I write lots of stuff, but that is probably the best I've done so far."

"That piece you did for one of Jorie's birthdays," Aunt Lani added. "I liked that a great deal. You spent hours on it."

"Which?" Jorie's glance at the violin made Bree set it on her shoulder again.

Jorie's face split into a gigantic grin at the opening strains of "Stairway to Heaven." "You didn't write that."

"Not that part," Bree said. "I wrote the bridges though, and arranged the segments of the Fantasia so they echo the structure of 'Stairway.' "

"Oh. I thought — I thought you learned it from sheet music. Like the Rachmaninoff."

"That's how I learned the Fantasia." Bree let the melody float into

111

the air as they talked. She swayed to the peace and whimsy of it. "I had to learn the Fantasia first to be able to adapt it the way I wanted."

"Wow. I always liked that, too. I hope you write lots of music, then."

"Thanks." Bree felt an ease in her heart. Perhaps Jorie didn't hate her or her music after all. And she told herself she could be happy knowing just that.

Aunt Lani went to bed, but Jorie lingered, having another cookie and making them mango tea. It was very late, Bree realized, but what was a holiday without a late night or two?

"Let's walk up to the top of the hill," Bree suggested. "I miss the warm nights so much. You wouldn't believe how cold it is in Canada. The wind is never anything but biting."

"Making for hardier people, perhaps?" Jorie followed Bree onto the porch and Bree felt a pang at the memory of Jorie running away in the dark.

"Hardier but maybe not quite as fun. It doesn't seem like anyone laughs, but that could just be school."

"Is it hard?" Jorie passed Bree on the footpath, leading the way to the fallen tree that had served as bench and stage for all of them as children.

"Sometimes. I — " She didn't know how to express her fears and excitement so Jorie would understand.

Jorie sidled onto the tree, leaving lots of room for Bree. In the warm moonlight she seemed to swim in silver and gold, her dark hair shining like the glassiest of 'a'a. "What?"

Bree sat down, aware that her thigh was only an inch from Jorie's. "I think I'm going to be famous."

Jorie laughed, but it wasn't the cruel cutting laugh of earlier years. She seemed genuinely amused. "Oh Bree, was there ever any doubt?"

Bree didn't know where she found the courage to ask, and her voice warbled. "Do you mind?"

Jorie's laughter faded. "No — I don't feel like the big sister who doesn't measure up any longer, if that's what you mean."

"No, not exactly." Big sister, all the gods, Bree thought. "You've always been there to help me, and give me advice. But I never thought

112

of you as my big sister. You're my friend, one I could trust to tell me truths."

Jorie was very still. Bree thought she could hear the rhythm of Jorie's heartbeat, rapid and uneven. "Maybe living away from home makes it easier to look back and realize I could have been different. I was pretty shitty to you — "

"No, you never asked for me to live with you."

"It's not about that," Jorie snapped. "That was just the way it was. A kid resents sharing her stuff and her space. I didn't mean that. I'm not a kid!"

Mystified, Bree tried to interpret the flare of anger in Jorie's eyes. "Then what?"

"It's about...Jesus Christ. About this, you idiot."

The kiss took her by surprise. For a split second Bree felt frozen, then heat swept over her, a fire of pent-up anguish and need. She fiercely kissed Jorie back, desperate to take all she could, as fast as she could, and tuck the moment somewhere inside of her where she could always have it, unmarred by any pain that might follow.

All that mattered was the sound of Jorie's ragged breathing and the warm *aniani* that swirled around their bodies. Bree's shoulders were hot with the sensation she began to realize was her ancestors. Notice this. Remember this. *This is Important.*

Jorie gasped against her mouth and Bree stiffened in pleasure as fingertips found her breasts, gently stroking.

"I was scared," Jorie said when Bree let her breathe. "I was so scared."

"I still am," Bree answered. "I love you. I've loved you for years."

Jorie seemed to quiver. "I just can't believe it. Why?"

Her lips against Jorie's throat, Bree murmured, "I could play it for you, but words...are hard for me to find."

Bree wasn't sure which of them pulled her shirt off, but it was Jorie who turned Bree on the bench so she could unhook Bree's bra. Bree had a flash of terror that they'd be seen, but that faded with the insistent teasing of Jorie's fingertips. With the heat of Jorie at her back, Bree thought they could have been any two island girls from any time, joined in the act — natural and easy — of loving each other.

113

Jorie's hands slid down Bree's stomach to the buttons of Bree's shorts. Her fingers eased them slowly open and all the wide-ranging music in Bree's mind centered to an urgent, single pulse. "Touch me, please."

Jorie moaned. Her fingertips pushed aside Bree's panties and the little gasp she made told Bree she was pleased at what she found. "This is okay?"

Bree arched back against her. "God, yes." Her legs spread wide, inviting Jorie to feel everything. Lila had barely touched her. No, fool, she told herself, this isn't about Lila. It's Jorie, all the gods, this is Jorie and she wants you.

Jorie held Bree while she lifted her hips toward the pleasure of Jorie's fingers. An aching knot made Bree want to cry out. She needed...she needed Jorie to...then Jorie was inside of her and the knot was unbound, sending shock waves up Bree's spine.

"Hold me — "

"Yes, Bree — "

"I love you — "

Bree only knew the sky from the land because of the stars. She seemed to be reaching for their brilliance, a strand of energy meant to fuse with white and yellow glory. Jorie made her feel that way.

Jorie...

Jorie was beautiful, naked in the moonlight. Her smile was tremulous and quickly faded when Bree touched her. "How can you?"

"How can *you*?" Bree pushed eager fingers into Jorie. "I love to touch you this way."

Jorie's weight was resting on her hands behind her and her hips responded like a swollen, rolling ocean to Bree's stroking. "I can't ever stop remembering that you — that you..."

"What?" Bree leaned forward, her voice husky. She'd learned a few things from Lila, and to use them to make it better for Jorie suddenly seemed the whole point of having been with her. "That I did this?"

Bree filled her mouth with the tender, wet flesh just above where her fingers were easing slowly into Jorie again, proud to hear Jorie's cry of pleasure. It was heady, to feel Jorie moving for her like that, pushed beyond control to make sounds that could only mean she loved what was happening.

Stars fell from the sky around Bree, sparkling on her skin. All that mattered was here, loving Jorie, sharing the most intimate pleasures with joy and abandon because their hearts were already joined.

Jorie was sobbing for breath when Bree finally raised her head. Profoundly happy, she wrapped her arms around Jorie's shoulders.

In those short minutes while Jorie panted and Bree held her tight, Bree dreamed a lifetime. A mansion built of music with all windows facing the sea, filled to the top with *'ohana*, surrounded by flowers and orchards of fruit — she dreamed it for her and Jorie so they would never be apart again.

"How can you do that to me?" Jorie stirred, one hand stroking Bree's hair.

"Same way you get to Carnegie Hall." Bree grinned into Jorie's bemused stare. "Practice, practice, practice."

She expected Jorie to laugh.

She expected Jorie to take her to bed.

She expected — for the last time in her life — for her dreams about Jorie to come true.

"Practice? With who?"

Blithely, not even seeing the ending that was coming, Bree answered, "Nobody important."

"Another girl?"

Finally, Bree took in Jorie's odd expression and sensed rising anger. "Yes, of course."

"You said you loved me this summer."

"You ran away — told me to get lost."

"You say you still love me."

"I do!" Bree scrambled to her feet, peering down at Jorie in the dark.

"Is that how you're always going to show it? Practicing on someone else? Someone who doesn't ever matter?"

"Of course not. I thought — I thought we'd never be together again." Damn Lila. Damn. What was she supposed to have done? "Was I supposed to pine away to nothing for you? Would it be better if she'd mattered?"

Jorie began scrambling into her clothes. "No."

"Then why are you mad? Don't tell me you weren't in bed with any of the guys you wrote me about."

"I wasn't. I didn't. I was trying to figure out how I felt. About what we'd done." She jerked her top over her head. "I don't want to be a queer if this is the way it is."

"What the hell does that mean?"

"Sleeping around."

"One girl. I was with one girl — and she hardly touched me back. She went back to guys. Just like you did."

"And what if I did! So what if she did — does that make it okay that we're just practice to you?"

"What the hell is your problem? You rejected me. I wanted us to — "

"I'll never have a piece of you that's mine." Jorie threw her hair over her shoulder. "I thought...I thought at least I was the only one. That it was about me and not just that I'm a girl you can have. I thought — oh, what does it matter! I'm not like you and I never will be!"

She was running away again, leaving Bree abruptly aware of the cooling breeze on her bare body.

She stayed under the stars for at least an hour, wiping away tears, but hoping if she left Jorie alone that she'd calm down so they could talk. Stupid hope. Stupid pain. All the same thing.

The sight of Jorie's packed duffel in the hallway was a shock, as was that of Jorie sitting at the kitchen table eating what looked like a sandwich of leftover goose. It was nearly four a.m.

"Where are you going?"

"I'm catching the first ferry to Kahoolawe. No point in waiting."

"You can't — "

"I can do whatever I want." Jorie had never sounded so cold before.

"What about Lani?"

"I left her a note. One more reason for her to snipe at me. You tell her whatever you want."

"I won't." Bree choked on the promise she'd made in the summer. "I won't tell anyone."

There was a long silence, then Jorie asked, "Where were you?"

116

Where does she think? On Mars? Her mansion was broken to pieces and her ancestors had gone silent. "Out screwing the first woman I could find. How many guys are you planning to do in the next year?"

Jorie wrapped up the remains of the sandwich and tucked it in her backpack. Through tight lips, she said, "Hundreds."

"Great. Then for sure you won't be like me."

Bree wanted to wither at the blast of contempt she felt lancing into her from Jorie's eyes, but she stood her ground. She wasn't going to be the one who walked away.

"You don't get anything, do you?" With that, Jorie turned on her heel, grabbed her duffel and disappeared into the night.

Through ears ringing with a thousand bells of tin, Bree heard the sound of a car and a slamming door.

Jorie's tears soaked through Bree's shirt and she let go of the memory of the fight, of Jorie's jealousy. All these years later, Bree could still feel angry about how unreasonable Jorie had been. They might have had something, but Jorie had turned it to dust by running away. For months the only things she'd had of Jorie were shipments of pineapple and grapefruit, sweet yet bitter.

She was intensely aware of how Jorie's body had changed over the years. Yet she still knew that body and the soul it contained, and she had looked for the dreams of a life with Jorie in every woman she'd met since. Especially Diana. All the gods, she could not do that, think about Diana with Jorie in her arms.

Her past had created a long list of women, enough to justify any jealous impulse Jorie could still have. Not that Jorie cared. Lila and Jorie weren't lesbians, and Bree wasn't going to make that mistake again. She wasn't going to make any mistakes again. There was no point to trying. If she didn't try she couldn't fuck it up anymore. Dr. Sheridan had said giving up wouldn't fix anything, but Bree couldn't see any other path.

"I miss her so," Jorie gasped in her ear. "Everyone tries, but only you would understand. I'm so sorry for all the petty things I did to test her love for me. I had to do everything she told me not to do. God, I did some stupid shit." Her grip tightened. "I said a lot of stupid things."

"You struggled because you loved each other."

"I could have made it all so much easier. She was so wise. Oh — " Jorie's hand swept over Bree's neck. "You've cut your hair!"

Bree didn't want to explain how difficult long hair was to keep clean or remotely tidy with one good hand. She wasn't about to say that she'd chopped it off herself. Right after that Dr. Sheridan had coaxed her into signing an agreement about hurting herself, as if it had any meaning.

"Let's go inside," Bree murmured. Jorie's arms were around her waist. She strengthened her resolve to ignore the way that made her feel only to have it crumble when Jorie's cheek inadvertently brushed against her own. A kiss...

It wasn't her imagination. For a moment, Jorie pressed her mouth to Bree's, then stepped away with a startled gasp.

Bree wanted to clarify — for the record — that it wasn't her fault. Just like the time in Los Angeles, she had not made the first move. Penny hadn't seen it, though, so she said nothing.

Jorie had her hand over her mouth, her red-rimmed eyes gleaming in the dim light. She shook her head once, vehemently, but Bree couldn't tell which of them the gesture was meant for.

She couldn't do this again. She couldn't fall into bed with Jorie only to have Jorie hate her for it all over again. No, she wouldn't. How much more pain do you need? No Jorie, no straight women, no married women, no groupies, no women at all!

She would have cried if she'd had any tears left. There was so much pain, from the scream in her wrist to the red blaze behind her eyes. You can't fight nature, she told herself bitterly. Nature made you love her and her not love you back. Your paths were never meant to run side by side, *'ohana* or not.

She felt numb again and it took two prods from Penny to get her moving into the house. She followed Jorie to the kitchen, badly needing a drink of water and just to close her eyes.

She blinked twice, but the slender Caucasian woman slicing oranges at the counter didn't go away. She could remember herself, all those years ago, learning to slice oranges with that very knife, standing in that very spot.

Jorie said something but Bree didn't take it in.

"I'm sorry. Too much crying. My ears are ringing." This time she concentrated on what Jorie said.

"I was making introductions. Bree, this is Mea, my partner. Mea, this is Sabrina."

Ma'e'ele
(Benumbed)

CHAPTER EIGHT

Mea made them tea.

All the while Bree knew she must look as if she was listening and speaking, as if she was actually there.

She wasn't there. Whatever was happening in the little kitchen was happening to someone else. She was drowning in a lake of pain, full of ice and razors.

Everything she thought she knew...everything she thought she was, none of it was right.

She had felt this way reading clippings about her interrupted career, about the failed surgeries and the lists of her final performances and recordings. It was all happening to someone else.

Jorie was living with a woman.

Was there a smile on her face? Jorie and Mea acted as if nothing was amiss, so perhaps she looked as if she was there. Was that her own voice asking how long they'd been together and why it had been such a secret?

"Mea moved in about six months ago. I didn't know how to tell you," Jorie admitted. "I felt, well, at the very least rather foolish for taking so long to figure out that while I got along with men..." She briefly linked her fingers with Mea. "Mea came into my life at just the right time."

Had Jorie told Mea about their five nights? No, it wasn't her asking what Mea did for a living and discussing the specifics of teaching morphology and physiology. Mea asked after her wrist, and winced when Bree told her the names of the broken bones and torn nerves.

The freezing lake was closing around her. She was drowning in it. Her arms wouldn't move now. She'd always loved Jorie, but at least she'd been able to tell herself the fact that they weren't together was because one gay and one straight didn't add up to forever. But that wasn't why at all. Jorie didn't love *her*. Not just a lack of attraction to all women, but a lack of attraction to *her*.

She'd fallen out of the conversation. Mea asked her something, but she was drowning in oceans of cold salt.

She drank the sugary tea Mea pressed on her and then let Penny put her to bed. She tried to explain that she'd been up for over thirty hours now, unable to sleep until she was home again, but she wasn't sure her mouth was working. If she'd had a violin, she could have played it so they understood.

She fell into the bed, shivering.

It had to be a dream, she thought. Memory never played true. Memory was flawed. Memory told her Jorie was straight, but that was wrong. Dreams then, of applause and awards. Dreams of the years after she'd given up on her heart and concentrated instead on music.

Not that she'd lived without sex. Every symphony had its groupies, though they wore evening gowns or tuxedos. It was easy to love for a night, to share breakfast and goodbye. What was her name? Marsha? The one who liked limousines and nightclubs? She'd learned a lot from Marsha.

She was glad her ancestors had left her, and her mother's voice had long fallen silent. She didn't want them to see all the things she'd done. Bree would have been ashamed, but it was only a dream, wasn't it? She had never slipped out of the nightclub into the limo with Marsha, had sex, then gone dancing again. She turned down the drugs, but not the hard-bodied woman who had also caught Marsha's eye. In the limo again a gasping arrangement of whispers and sobs spilled over her ears. Whose hands were on her head? Who was inside her? It was only a dream. It was only sex. A present for her twenty-sixth birthday, Marsha said. Even geniuses came down off the mountain for sex.

She played MacDowell, Scriabin, Wagner, Moussorgsky, Schumann, her own compositions. She immersed herself in the very old and the very new and everything in between. She bowed and she danced while she played. She came into her trust fund and played for the joy of it. There was money for condominiums in Los Angeles, Toronto, London and Sydney. Every symphony had its groupies. She closed her eyes and pretended they were all Jorie. Jorie's ghost was always there to turn her back on the music Bree played.

Music could lift her to ethereal heights, to the point of understanding the ticking of the universal mind, and when a performance had been that good there was always someone to help her come down. Lovers either wanted to elevate her with tenderness or bring her down to earth with need. In music, in bed, in the moments of life made up of neither, she traveled extremes with a variety of tutors.

It was all so easy, life in these dreams. Had it really been like that? Did she float through days and nights with the ease of the *honu*, always moving toward her goal — more music, more performances — with single-minded purpose? Had school become a joyful but secondary pursuit? Had she played in Vienna, Beijing, Auckland and Moscow and all points in between? Was her artistry graced with the insights of other musicians whose names were so lofty she was always stunned to see her name paired with theirs on a marquee?

Her female professors had warned her that being a woman would count against her, but so far she hadn't noticed. Neither had being a lesbian. Was she that good? She still felt an irreconcilable pang when *haoles* called her exotic and other Hawaiians called her a mainlander. As Aunt Lani had said, being both and neither wasn't always comfortable. Mr. Proctor's advice to always be a musician on stage — letting all other roles play out in other facets of her life — had begun to make sense as she matured artistically and personally. When she played the violin, all conflict and contradictions blended to reason. Her music and her voice made it all so easy.

And if she said yes to a woman who made her feel more real than Sabrina Starling ever seemed to be, was there harm in nights filled with free give-and-take?

Home was always there, but Jorie and she always seemed to just miss each other. Aunt Lani knew only what Jorie had told her, but Bree kept her promise about never saying a word, though she longed to. Aunt Lani was her closest confidante and the thing that hurt her most was the one thing she couldn't talk to her about. Jorie and she would be together for an evening, never a night, and never alone.

Were these dreams? Or memories? Whose arms were around her? Whose lips were on hers? Whose thighs spread in eagerness, whose body was on hers, undulating like the *alania* ocean? Diana? No. Diana would not and could not be in her memories. Diana had never happened.

She wanted to believe that with all her heart. Diana had never been in her life. If there was no Diana then there would be no Pam. The dreams of Diana's mouth, her kisses, her tears were all fevered imaginings. She couldn't remember what had never happened, could she?

She only accepted that what was coursing through her mind were memories when she slipped into dreaming — she knew the nightmares for what they were. Her wrist pinned in a vise, turned by an unseen tormentor, ever tighter. A violin of stone crashing down on her hand and everything shattered on impact. Instead of applause, audiences jeered and jagged rocks broke her skin. A pack of wolves slavered, always behind her. Teeth sank into her arm. Her wrist was everything, the source of pain and genius. Violins still spoke to her, but she couldn't give them voice. She heard their yearning for music, but she was wrung dry. Her wrist...

"Bree..."

Before the pain had been that night in L.A., when Jorie had sought her out for the first time. When Jorie had wanted it so badly she had begged... She couldn't hear Jorie's voice over the pounding drum wired to her wrist.

"Wake up, Bree."

Something soared past her face and she reached out with her good hand, catching the hard shell. Pulled firmly through the darkness of her nightmares, she seemed at last to rise toward the light. The wise, gentle eyes turned toward her briefly, then the great *honumaoli* faded away as Bree surfaced out of the dream.

Her swollen eyes wouldn't focus on the still unfamiliar face. It took longer than it should have to recognize Mea gazing at her in concern.

"Penny and Jorie went out for the flowers, but it sounded like you were having a nightmare."

"I guess," Bree mumbled. She shoved her hair out of her face, aware that the T-shirt she was wearing was probably Penny's and as such a bit snug. Light and fresh air streamed through the open window.

"Do you have pain meds I can get for you?"

"Yes. I mean, yes, but I'll get them. I forgot last night."

Mea just nodded and left the room, leaving Bree to struggle with her throbbing head. She managed sufficient sips of water to get down one pain pill. She'd need to eat before she could take the second one.

Sometimes she thought there was no point to the pills. The pain always came back. So why bother sending it away?

"I made you some eggs," Mea said. "Jorie told me you used to like them scrambled. I hope you still do."

Bree managed a low, "Thank you," and blinked back tears. She made herself eat for the sake of another useless pill.

Mea's hand on her shoulder caught her by surprise. She wanted to

125

put her cheek on it and cry. Such an act would be far too weak. She didn't want to like Mea. She ought to hate her. Who was she, anyway?

But the contact was genuinely warm, and it was with obvious concern that Mea watched Bree struggle to swallow the second pill. But she didn't ask about surgeries or prognoses. Instead she gently propelled Bree into the rhythm of the day. Time to shower, time to plan what she would wear. Time to let Aunt Lani go.

She needed Aunt Lani so much, but she was gone forever.

She went into Aunt Lani's room and selected a bright, beaded *muumuu* Aunt Lani had worn often. She turned with it in her arms to find Jorie in the doorway. "I thought — she hated black."

"I had the same idea," Jorie said. "I can't wear black. Anyone who really knew her won't be in black."

Bree could only shake her head. The pain pills were working, a little, and when she moved she felt a little off balance.

"She wanted a party, not a funeral. Besides, no *pule* addicts for her."

Someone laughed and Bree realized after a moment that it was her. "Then let's do this right."

Penny thought it a good idea and Jorie also selected one for Mea. Bree tried not to let that hurt. Was Mea *'ohana*? Bree didn't want her to be, but it wasn't for her to say, was it? If Mea was Jorie's husband she'd at least give him a chance. She didn't want to give Mea a chance. She wanted to hate her.

She'd tried to hate Pam, too. That hadn't worked either.

There had been performances so anticipated, so practiced and stressful that Bree had had to actively fight letting them become a blur. When she went on autopilot she didn't perform as well. She had learned how to keep control of herself, and saved automatic behavior for social settings.

How many people would ask what was wrong with her wrist? How many times would she have to pretend it didn't really matter?

Aunt Lani had parted with tradition in wanting an immediate cremation and disposition of her ashes. Her soul had been set free

126

two days ago. This party was for those who grieved for her and wanted to let her go.

Aunt Lani's lifelong friend, Hamu, opened the service with his usual, gentle style. "'*Ua koʻokoʻou i ke anu na mauna.*' The chilling storm is on the mountains. We feel the cold, the empty because she who was warm, Laniakilani, has gone to the gods."

She let the memorial become a blur, lying to herself that she could have resisted the strange detachment if she'd wanted to. She tried to use happier memories for comfort. They were there, somewhere in her mind. Countless images of Aunt Lani's unconditional love and support. From Christmas fudge to always listening to Bree's thoughts and worries, Aunt Lani had been the best mother Bree could imagine. She wished she'd told her.

I understand, even when you have no words, Aunt Lani said from the past.

Her shoulder blades rippled with the harsh silence of her ancestors. The memories she sought wouldn't come. There was only a parade of images she didn't want to look at and couldn't handle. Sex, she thought. Think about sex, you could always escape into sex. She made herself think about that encounter in Marsha's limo, even that night when Stacy had taken her to bed after the poker game. It trod perilously close to thinking about Diana because Diana had been there and had watched Stacy seduce Bree. She'd gone with Stacy because she couldn't consider Diana. Diana was with Pam and had been for eighteen years.

She veered her mind from Stacy then and instead found herself in the front seat of a car. Who was she with? She couldn't see the other woman, not yet. The kisses said the woman was coming upstairs to Bree's condo. London? Who was it?

The other woman bit Bree's lower lip. "Let's get it on."

That voice — London, after the recital where she'd first played with Itzhak Perlman. She'd been so high on adrenaline that night. All the gods, that was Teena she was making out with.

Teena had made it clear she was ready for anything and she backed up her flirtation throughout the post-concert reception with breasts or hips bumping into Bree. She was a track competitor, Teena said, but she really preferred to do her exercising at night.

Teena wasn't averse to cars and pulled Bree's hand under her short dress. Muscled thighs parted and Bree enjoyed the sensation of kissing that receptive mouth while her hand stroked between Teena's legs. Teena's moan was her favorite kind of personal music.

"Do you want to start this here?" Bree kissed Teena's throat as she realized that Teena was wearing garters with her stockings and nothing else.

"Yeah, you're making me very hot."

Her fingers slipped into Teena's ready fire. "Like this?"

"Yes, don't stop!"

Bree shifted her position slightly, trying to get the parking brake out of her hip. She bumped the switch for the overhead lights and sprang back with a laugh. "Sorry!"

Teena giggled and Bree flipped the switch back off. But just before the light went she saw Teena clearly for what felt like the first time.

Teena grabbed Bree's wet hand, putting it back where it had been. "Finish me and then I promise when we get inside that you'll like what I can do."

Bree could feel Teena's excitement. Teena was lovely and seductive. That Teena liked what Bree was doing was unmistakable.

She didn't have to stop. Teena wanted it.

"There, right there, please do it!"

Bree pulled her hand away and turned the light back on.

Teena blinked in the glare.

All the gods, Bree thought. *What am I doing? How could I not have noticed?* Her shoulder blades tingled, but Bree ignored it. She didn't need any help to know what she had to do.

"What's wrong? Do you want to do it inside? Whatever you want is okay with me."

"How old are you?"

"Eighteen."

Bree just looked at her, feeling like Aunt Lani waiting out a lie.

"It doesn't matter. Inside I feel way older than I am. I know what I want."

"I'm twenty-five. How old are you?"

Sullenly, Teena muttered, "I'll be sixteen in a couple of months."

Bree wanted to scrub off her hand. She felt incredibly dirty. She started the car. "Tell me where you live."

The evening ended with Teena flouncing out of the car after informing Bree that she *hated* her. Even a scalding shower didn't make Bree feel clean.

Had sex become her drug of choice? How could she not have realized Teena was so young? Never mind that she had known at Teena's age what she wanted. Let Teena find a girl her own age to experiment with. How could Teena's parents let her wander around dressed like a twenty-something woman who left parties with strangers?

Aunt Lani, she thought then, thank you for caring what I did and who I was with. Thank you. *I wish I'd told you what you meant to me, but you knew, didn't you?*

Bree's ancestors tingled along her shoulder blades as she fought down the grief. How could she be thinking about Teena at Aunt Lani's funeral? All the gods, it was horrible enough that her ancestors might see her past, but could Aunt Lani see it, too? She was ashamed, ashamed of so many things. She didn't want Aunt Lani to know.

There were tables laden with lotus flowers, over a hundred of them. Each person picked up one as they left the service. Jorie held hands with Mea. Riki kept one protective arm around Penny's shoulders. The walk to the shore was solemn and Bree did not want to go. She didn't want Aunt Lani to be gone forever. Let other people set their lotus flowers in the water. She thought nothing of the one she held and it drifted away with none of Bree's grief in tow.

Jorie was crying, but she had Mea's arm around her. Penny had Riki to hold her up. Bree had nothing left.

"Miss Starling?" Bree turned to Hamu. "Would you be able to play for us today? It doesn't have to be *'uhane* — something joyful instead, something Lani would have liked."

Bree called what she felt the Thoughtless Pain. It came out of nowhere, and layered on top of all other kinds of pain. How could

Hamu not know? When she answered it was as if someone else was moving her mouth. "That's no longer possible." She lifted her wrist.

His gentle face creased with concern. "I'm so sorry — I didn't know. Perhaps you could sing for us. Lani said you and she would sing while you cooked."

She wanted to refuse. Singing was music. Music was pain. She didn't sing very well, but part of conservatory rigor was vocal training. She'd not really kept it up. Everyone would expect her to sing like she played the violin.

"Please, Bree." Jorie took her hand. "She loved 'What a Wonderful World.' I know the words too."

There was a murmur of agreement and she had to go along. Jorie's hand felt so right in her own. Remember Pam, she told herself, and she let go of Jorie. She found a pitch she could live with and began, sounding as gravel-voiced as Louis Armstrong. "I see skies of blue..."

Jorie took up the words, her voice sweet and soft. Momi joined in and Bree took comfort in her sure, steady tones. Then voices rose along with the sea breeze, and the music spread out over the waves.

Bree felt as if her spirit was out over the water, too, trying to get the lotus back, but the flowers were almost out of sight.

Food seemed to spread for miles. There wasn't any part of the kitchen that wasn't covered with a dish or platter. It was a good thing, because hundreds of people seemed to fill the small house, spilling out into the garden and on up the hill to the fallen tree. Bree wished she were hungry. She hadn't had so many of these dishes in so long. But the aroma of roasted macadamia nuts, coconut and bananas made her feel ill.

She drifted from conversation to conversation, saying much the same to everyone. She explained about her wrist with unfeigned nonchalance. She didn't feel anything at all now and it was better that way.

She was passing the bathroom when she heard someone crying. She peeked in and saw Jorie blowing her nose on a tissue.

"Mea says it'll get easier now that the memorial is over. It just all has to come out. Penny's worried about me — could you close the door?"

If Jorie was surprised that Bree chose to be on the inside of the closed door it didn't show. Bree didn't really recall making a conscious choice to stay with Jorie.

Jorie had Mea.

She needed to remember that.

"I never thought she would go this way, so fast. She always used to say to live each day as if it was your last. She did that, but I didn't understand what she meant. I didn't even get to say goodbye."

"Neither did I." Bree reached for a tissue herself. Why was she crying? She felt nothing at all, not even the persistent tingle that always rose in her when she was alone with Jorie.

"I know, but you and she had something special. You didn't have to work at it. It was so hard sometimes. She was so *good*." Jorie dabbed at her eyes. "It was so hard to measure up. To her. To you."

"Me?"

"You were good, too."

Bree's laugh had no humor in it. "Not getting into trouble is not the same as being good. I just didn't get caught..."

"You didn't envy anyone anything because of...you were always so finished. Even when you were little. You didn't need anything."

Only a violin, Bree thought. A violin for so long, and then I needed you. Her right hand went automatically to her wrist, which began to pulse.

"Does it hurt?"

Bree could only nod.

"Is it really hopeless?"

Not this, Bree thought. I can't bear to see pity in her eyes. She'll say that I'll move on to other things when there are no other things. She won't understand because she's never understood what it meant to me. "Yes."

"I'm so sorry, Bree." Jorie moved awkwardly, putting her arms around Bree's shoulders. "It must be just terrible for you."

What was she supposed to do? Jorie's body left her feeling seared.

The bathroom was so small. There was no place to run. Her arms wouldn't let go now. She felt so empty and it would be easy to fill herself with Jorie.

She'd tried that with Diana.

Jorie's arms slipped down, moving to Bree's waist. "I'm sorry about everything else. The older I get the more I see how I was — I was foolish and young. And I should have told you everything when I had the chance. Who knows — "

"Don't," Bree whispered. "I can't handle talking about the past right now."

Jorie stiffened, then relaxed again. Did she really not feel the danger? Her hand came to Bree's face. "I understand. We made some mistakes."

Did any of them matter as much as the one they were making now? Didn't Jorie remember that if they touched they lost control? Even when they knew it was a bad idea they couldn't stop. Every night together had proven that.

All the gods, was Jorie cupping her waist or was that memory? Were they back in Los Angeles? Her head spun with that same, heady dizziness, reeling with the knowledge that Jorie wanted her.

Was Jorie whispering "I've always wanted you" or was that another dream to be shattered? Bree no longer knew where she was. She could only hold Jorie close and live memories she wished were only dreams.

Bree shrugged back her wet hair and peered through the security glass before dazedly opening the door.

"Surprise." The bright smile was at odds with the whisper. What on earth was Jorie doing in Los Angeles?

Bree recovered herself and waved a hand. "Come in, please, of course."

"You actually live here?" Jorie gazed around the spacious main room.

"It's a good investment." The high-rise condominium was one of her favorite places to spend time since it was high enough to glimpse the ocean. An early spring mist hid it from view today, but she knew it was there.

"I didn't know what to expect," Jorie said. "It's more austere than I imagined it would be."

Austere? Bree looked at the room with new eyes. She supposed it was cold, perhaps. She hadn't moved a thing the decorator had done. She liked the location and what she could see out the windows, but otherwise it was just another place to stay in between trips. "Sometimes," she said slowly, "it seems like someone else lives here. Sabrina Starling does, and she's more grown up than I am."

She realized Jorie was studying her, and Bree was aware of the silk bathrobe clinging to the parts of her that were still wet. "I got you out of the shower."

"No, I was done. I have a charity cocktail thing to go to later." She had a date with the general manager of the Los Angeles Philharmonic. Sort of a date. They'd gotten together after the performance three nights ago and tonight's arrangement, Bree conceded, had been made to make them feel like their night together hadn't just been about sex.

"I should have called. Mom gave me your address since I was here."

"It's okay. You're really lucky I was here. I'm leaving tomorrow for Seattle," Bree said. Just looking at Jorie was like food for her soul. Every line and curve, the hint of her smile, the way her eyes rested on Bree's body — all of it made her remember that night on the hill.

She realized in a heart-pounding flash that none of the women she'd tried to fill the empty place inside her touched what she felt for Jorie. She'd been sleepwalking. Since Teena she'd been far less interested in casual sex. The general manager had been the first in quite a while.

She still loved Jorie.

Jorie swallowed hard and Bree was abruptly aware that the wet robe had chilled her breasts. Was Jorie noticing?

For a large room it got very warm, very fast. Bree could almost believe that no time had passed since their last night together.

Fool, she told her body. Jorie looked unbelievably attractive in slacks and a denim jacket over a form-fitting shirt. "What brought you to L.A.? Can I get you a drink? Have you had dinner?"

"I'm looking into other schools for teaching. It was time to see the world. I...I wasn't sure this was a good idea."

Bree stood there, her hand on the liquor cabinet. She wanted a drink right then because Jorie was looking at her with an obvious mix of trepidation and desire. Bree realized that she'd been drinking more since cutting back on sex. Why did she want the liquid courage now? To say yes or to say no?

"Bree." Jorie's mouth trembled. "I came because...I was stupid, before. After we...you know."

Bree couldn't help her bitterness. "It took you seven years to figure that out?"

"There were reasons. None of them good. I was afraid of a lot of things. I'm not like you, Bree — "

"And you never will be." Bree decided she needed Scotch.

"That's right. I'll never have your courage or talent, your money or confidence. I'll never look like you." She spread her hands to take in the condo. "I'm just now realizing I don't know you."

After a long swallow, Bree turned to face Jorie. She was aware of her robe loosening and wondered if she imagined Jorie's jaw going slack for just a moment. "You do know me, Jorie. Better than anybody."

"I never felt that way."

Bree walked toward Jorie, not sure if she was a willing gazelle or a prowling tigress. She felt both. She stopped when she was inches from Jorie, who hadn't moved. "You know what I like."

Jorie's breath caught. "I, I didn't come here for that."

"Yes, you did." Bree wasn't going to touch Jorie, not now. "You don't care that there have been others anymore?"

Jorie shook her head. "I shouldn't have been...it's not like you promised me anything or I gave you reason to think I expected you to do anything because of me. I misunderstood..."

"There have been lots of others," Bree murmured. "None of them made me forget you."

"Bree, please...this is still not a good idea. I just wanted — "

"Wanted what?"

"I wanted...wanted...oh fuck." Jorie's rapid breaths caused her breasts to rise and fall as Bree stared at them.

"Tell me what you want."

Jorie's voice broke. "You. I want you."

"But it's not a good idea."

"No...but..."

"But what? If you want something, ask."

It took Jorie two tries to hook her finger in the tie of Bree's robe. "I didn't come here for this, but I want to go to bed with you."

"Are you sure?"

Jorie's nod was timed with a pull on the tie. Bree's breasts were almost completely exposed.

"What if I say no," Bree murmured.

"Please don't." Jorie licked her lips quickly, then gazed helplessly into Bree's eyes. "Please say yes."

Bree said nothing while Jorie swayed slightly.

Finally, Jorie gave the tie another tug, making a noise of desire that nearly broke Bree's control. She wanted to sweep Jorie into her arms, spread her out on the bed, taste her, devour her. She wanted Jorie inside her head, inside her body, a part of everything. Every day had some pain in it because Jorie wasn't there.

The robe fell open and with a half sob, Jorie went to her knees. "I want this."

The feel of Jorie's lips on Bree's thighs left her feeling utterly exposed. She couldn't hide how she felt as she groped for the chair behind her, falling back and opening herself completely to Jorie.

It felt so good. Remember, she tried to tell herself. This is just electricity. This isn't about feelings. This is about the sex. She wants you now. She won't tomorrow. Remember and it'll be okay.

Jorie pulled Bree's legs over her shoulders. "I can't believe how much I want you. You're so beautiful."

You're the one who is beautiful, Bree wanted to say. The shock of Jorie's tongue finding her drew a choked cry in response and they surged against each other. This was nothing like the first time, when every gesture had been so sensual. This *was* about sex and desire, hard, fast and unstinting. Jorie's mouth was ravenous and Bree responded until Jorie raised her head.

"You want this, too, don't you?"

"God, yes, Jorie. Can't you tell?"

"I want you on a bed," Jorie said hoarsely. "I want to feel all of you."

Trembling, Bree led Jorie to the bedroom. Every nerve seemed to respond as Jorie pushed the robe off Bree's shoulders and seized her naked body for a hard kiss. She had dreamed so often of being with Jorie again, but had never imagined Jorie could be in this kind of forthright and needy mood.

She was aching for Jorie now. Jorie had only removed her shirt and bra when she slid on top of Bree, and the difference between the silky warmth of Jorie's breasts and the rough texture of her slacks made Bree feel even more wanton. She had to have Jorie now, like this.

The only way to make it real, not to treat Jorie like all the other women she'd been with, was to do what she had never done with anyone but Jorie — she surrendered. She gave up all her distance, all the self-protection she had built over the years without Jorie. She said it again though Jorie never believed her. "I've always loved you."

She felt fingers teasing her. Jorie's mouth was at her breasts. "I want to do this to you," Jorie gasped.

Bree didn't recognize her own voice, husky with desire. "Then do it."

It was different. Every time with Jorie was different.

Her body was more lean, and Bree didn't know the hard muscles in Jorie's forearms. Her breasts seemed impossibly more full and responsive to Bree's touch. She had never before felt the way Jorie's hips moved to add force to the fingers that seemed to reach every place that Bree had kept hidden from all other lovers.

Would Jorie realize that Bree had changed as well? She'd always found it easy to orgasm, but she knew now that waiting would make it better. She tried to hold it back, to give Jorie as long as she wanted to enjoy the way Bree felt under her.

Another minute and she had no choice. She gave it up and sobbed out her love, even knowing that underneath she was angry that it was always Jorie's decision whether this would happen. She knew there would be pain because she trusted no other outcome.

Save yourself, she thought, with the feeling of Jorie deep inside her. Stop this now.

She forgot about the party and her date.

She forgot about the call she'd promised her agent.

She forgot where she was and the past, even the future. There was just the present and Jorie's hands and mouth.

When she was exhausted and thought she couldn't move, Jorie persuaded her that she could. The gray sky deepened to black and they continued to roll over the bed.

"I can't." Bree must have said it a dozen times.

"But you want to."

"Yes." Honesty, at last. "Just tell me you want me and I will."

"I want you, baby." Jorie's teeth rasped over one nipple, drawing a responsive shudder.

Bree felt like a ship, broken on the rocks, her inner secrets spread out in the light of Jorie's eyes.

Some time later, shaking and dizzy, Bree kissed her way down Jorie's body. It seemed like it had been hours and she had yet to taste her, though the slacks had been pulled off finally.

Jorie's voice was hoarse. "Do you want me now?"

"Yes. I've never stopped wanting this."

Jorie ran one sensitive fingertip down Bree's spine, then repeated the gesture only this time running up Bree's abdomen, between her breasts to brush over her lips.

She wanted Jorie in her mouth but Jorie's fingers were teasing her. How could she be wet again? Was this how Jorie wanted her, helpless to resist?

Jorie held her so tightly Bree could hardly move against her fingers, so instead Bree let words spill out of her, adoration and passion. She was crying when she came that last time. Bree had given Jorie everything and Jorie seemed to want it all.

It can't last, she told herself.

She hardly knew which way was up, but she still fumbled her way between Jorie's legs. Jorie was shaking under her as Bree regained some measure of control of herself and this moment. She wasn't helpless. Jorie needed something from her, too.

* * * * *

She didn't remember falling asleep, but her first thought in the morning was that she was alone, the second that parts of her ached. She winced as her thigh muscles protested any movement. It came back in a wave of hot recollection, the way she had wrapped her legs around Jorie, over and over.

She heard the shower then and was relieved when in a few minutes Jorie emerged from the bathroom wrapped in a towel.

Bree smiled shyly. It was the morning after and they were alone. That was a first. "Did you sleep okay?"

Jorie nodded. Was that a blush? "I was pretty tired. You?"

"Tired."

Bree started to get out from under the covers when she realized they were no longer anchored to the bed. She gathered a sheet around her and escaped to the bathroom.

A hot shower made her feel more alert, and she was no longer able to ignore the questions that bubbled in her head. Why had Jorie finally given in to her desires? Was it at all possible that Jorie wanted to talk about a future?

There it was, she realized. No matter how guarded, hope was hope. She wasn't going to get hurt this time, she promised. Now that they both had the sex out of their system, they could talk about the future like adults. They'd never really been adults together. She could save herself. If Jorie gave her any reason to think this wasn't about a future, she would save herself.

She realized that Jorie was on the other side of the shower door, watching her.

With a grin, Bree grumbled, "What're you lookin' at?"

"The woman I'm going to fuck."

Bree dropped the washcloth.

This couldn't be happening. Her traitor body was eager and willing to be taken to bed again, wet hair spread across the sheets to cool them as the temperature rose. Jorie remembered everything, it seemed, and Bree fell into helpless response as Jorie excited her, pleased her and lifted her to a climax that eclipsed all of the previous night.

They staggered laughing to the kitchen and foraged for something more substantial than olives, cheese with unexpected blue streaks and pickles. A can of soup proved the best bet and they shared it between them.

Bree held her spoon aloft, a noodle dangling. "Do you remember when you were so hung over and Lani tried to make you throw up?"

Instead of sheepish, Jorie gave her a wicked look. "Of course I do — it was the day after our first night together."

Bree wondered if her smile was as nostalgic as Jorie's. "What took you so long?"

Jorie's answer was immediate. "I had to make lots of mistakes first."

"You didn't write much, I thought you were, well, having your life the way I was going on with mine."

"I was trying, anyway." Jorie was pensive, now.

"I've missed you. Not just, you know. But the girl I grew up with. I didn't have many friends. I still don't."

"I know. I missed you, too."

Bree could feel the cautious pulse in her throat. It was hope and she was scared. Don't trust happiness, she thought. "Why now?"

"I couldn't see my future any more." Jorie looked away. "I had to make some decisions. Every time I thought about the next stage of my life I would think of you and feel unsettled."

"I think we took care of some unfinished business last night and this morning." Bree almost added that it was the single most memorable night of her life, but she'd learned from experience. No comparisons. No references to practice.

"I want...I have to tell you some things."

A deep bell of warning rang in Bree's mind. Listen, she told herself. At least she's talking and not running.

"It's just that I'm not sure you'll understand that a person can do something foolish, believe they feel something when they don't because believing it makes life easier."

Was Jorie talking about them? Was she trying to say she wasn't going to storm off, but she was still going?

Jorie sighed. "I can't go on pretending about it — "

"About what? About me? How foolish being with me is?" Happiness, she decided then, was a big fat lie. She had been an utter fool thinking this time was different. She was not going to be destroyed again.

"No, that's not what I meant at all."

"It sounded like it to me." Bree felt cold in spite of the soup. "You believed something last night, even this morning. But now you don't believe it anymore. Just like every time."

"No, you're not listening to me. Bree, please!"

"I can't do this again." Bree got to her feet. She felt very calm. She knew this pain and could handle it. "You don't know how much you hurt me — "

"Christ, Bree, this isn't about you. It's about me. There's some shit I need to fix, that I need to decide about." Jorie was flushed now and also on her feet.

"Well, then, let me help you, if I can. We can fix it together."

"What if I don't want it fixed? Or if I do I don't need your help to do it?"

"Okay," Bree said shakily. "I'm not saying you can't handle your own problems.

"I don't need to be rescued." Viciously, she added, "Not by Mom, not by you. Not by anybody."

"Okay. I only want to help."

"You haven't a clue how to go about it, do you?"

"What's that supposed to mean?"

"What was my major, Bree? What exactly do I teach?"

Flabbergasted, Bree struggled for words. She realized then that she wasn't sure of the answers. "Archeology? You always wanted to go on digs."

"Cultural anthropology, specializing in Polynesian cultures. I'll be a lowly part-time college professor next year. You have no idea what

140

I want to do with my life. And I look around this place and I don't see anything of the you I thought I knew. We're strangers. I felt it last night and now it's so clear."

"Was that what last night was about for you? Sex with a stranger?"

"No — "

"We're only strangers because you keep running away!"

"China bowls and crystal milk glasses." Jorie gestured at the table. "Where's the Oreos and potato chips? The paper plates and Ritz crackers?"

"I barely live here — "

"That's not the point. You've changed."

"Is that so terrible?" It was too much, to be rejected because she'd changed. Jorie had taken seven years to knock on her door.

"No — "

"Look!" Bree jerked open the deep drawer at the end of the counter where she looked over statements from Markham. Going to her knees she pulled out a handful of papers and spilled them across the floor. "Programs from performances. Here. Reviews. Photos. Publicity packets." Another handful. "More of the same. There's me and the Mayor. Me and the Governor's wife, more programs — that's a review Markham sent from the *New York Times*."

Jorie knelt to pick up a photograph. "I get it, Bree. I can't even begin to comprehend the life you lead."

"You never tried."

"I'm not the only one guilty of that, am I?"

"All this has changed me, yes, but it's so intense, so focused that there are parts of me it doesn't ever touch..." Bree realized Jorie was staring at one of the photos.

"Who's this?"

"The conductor of the Women's Symphony of Southern California."

"Do you — is she special?"

"Do you mean did I do her?"

Jorie winced. "I'm sorry, it's none of my — "

"I fucked her." Bree flushed. Jealousy? Hardly any contact in seven years and now she was getting jealousy? She dove into the drawer,

141

dumping the contents on the floor. She sifted through the stack. "Here, I fucked her, too."

Pictures from parties and press meetings. "Fucked her. And her." She tossed them at Jorie's feet. "And this one. Fucked her twice. Fucked this one — here, who knew, a supermodel that likes classical music. Fucked her. And I've got a drawer just like this in Toronto. In London. The one in Sydney is twice this size because Australian women are hot for it. Fucked her, and her, and her — "

"Bree, stop it!"

"No!" Her shoulder blades burned with a warning, but she ignored it. "You want to judge me, go right ahead!"

"You could never see past that damned violin!"

I hate that thing!

Bree choked on tears. Had she been that self-centered? Yes, of course. But Jorie's letters had been so sketchy. Her anger abruptly fizzled. Bree knew she had asked questions about school. She didn't know Jorie at all. How could she love someone she didn't know? "Why are we fighting?"

"Because you're not hearing me." Jorie nudged the pile of pictures with her toe. "I don't care about this."

"You don't care about my life's work — "

"I don't care about the women."

"Then what? Just tell me, because I can't stand waiting for the pain. Just tell me and get it over with!"

"I'm married!"

After a stunned silence, Bree managed barely a whisper. "What?"

"I'm married. I got married almost four months ago."

"How could..." She felt numb, then another eruption of hot anger burst out of her. "How could you do this to me? How could you!"

"I'm trying to tell you — "

"That you needed your fix? I'm not going to be here next time you have to have it." Her vision went to a flat, murky gray. She could hardly see Jorie for the anger and agony. Married. All the gods, married.

"You never could listen to me. Everything is about Sabrina Starling and her music. Sabrina Starling and her Guarneri, her Stradivarius. Sometimes things are about me!"

"I don't even know you anymore. How does my being a self-centered bitch justify you cheating on hubby to get a lesbian fuck on the side?"

"That's not what it was about, and you know it."

"I don't know anything. I don't know you. I can't believe I thought I loved you all these years, and I had no idea you could be so — so cruel. So low!"

"You never loved me," Jorie snapped back. "You just said it because you wanted to get it on with me."

"Who knocked on whose door last night? You can't put last night on me. You wanted it."

"Things are always different in the light of day with you. Always." Jorie rubbed her hands over her eyes, her shoulders, her belly. "Okay. This was stupid. I thought I could..."

"Could what? Have it both ways? Well, it's not going to be me doing the lesbian bit for you. I have some standards and I'm not going to bed with a cheat. I feel dirty enough as it is. Next time you need it with a woman I'll give you the name of a couple of clubs where you might get lucky."

"I assume you know them well, then."

The barb found its mark and a jolt of pain surged across Bree's shoulder blades. They were playing with knives and neither of them would survive if they didn't stop. "You should go."

"I want you to remember this, Bree. I tried. I didn't run away. I promised myself I wouldn't. I run when I'm hurt, but I'm trying to do better."

"I've only ever wanted to love you."

"On your terms. Always on your terms."

Jorie stalked to the bedroom and emerged an impossibly short time later rumpled but dressed. "I won't be begging at your door again."

"There's no reason for you to. I was in love with someone who didn't exist."

Jorie had her hand on the knob. "Bree..."

"Give my regards to hubby."

Jorie's face twisted and a moment later she was gone.

Bree dropped to her knees where she stood, too spent to cry. Part of her wanted to wail, to cut her hair as if a close friend had died, to give in to grief in the ancient Hawaiian way. It would be faster, she thought, but she couldn't find tears.

CHAPTER NINE

Was Jorie in her arms again? For a disorienting minute Bree had no idea where she was. All she knew was that she was kissing Jorie and that her wrist hurt. So, it was after then. After the incident.

"We can't do this," Jorie whispered when the breathless kiss ended.

"I know. It's just a...relapse. I'm sorry."

"We're not ourselves right now."

Bree studied Jorie's bloodshot eyes. Swirling grief was foremost but underneath something familiar. No, she thought. Don't look. Don't fall. Don't believe in it. When you stopped believing in it the years were all good. All safe. "We agreed..."

"Yes." Jorie's hand cupped the back of Bree's neck. "We did. So we need to stop."

The next kiss was intoxicating. Bree had never stopped craving Jorie. Even though their horrible fight in L.A. had ushered in what critics termed her "mature" work, it had been empty of Jorie, of any meaningful love or commitment. Even sex had failed to distract her. She'd worked, and worked hard. Her travel agent told her she'd logged enough air miles to circle the world over a hundred times. She'd sunk her toes in sands on every continent and told herself she was happy. She was living a dream. She had her violin, her music and being able to concentrate exclusively on that made her a better musician.

She was as happy as she possibly could be, craving this kiss, this woman.

And then she remembered Mea.

With a gasp, she pushed Jorie away. She wouldn't hurt Mea like this. Even if she thought Mea was the greatest bitch on the face of the planet, she wouldn't do this. Not after Pam.

Jorie gripped the sink with her eyes closed. "I'm so sorry. I didn't mean for that to happen. Please, believe me, Mea and I are — "

"It's okay. It just happened. Like I said, a relapse. Does she...know?"

Jorie shook her head. "What's to explain?"

"Indeed." Bree had no idea a single word could hold such bitterness.

"I'd better get back. There wasn't enough mac salad, I'm sure."

"When is there ever enough mac salad?"

Jorie attempted a laugh as she slipped by Bree and out the door, startling Penny, who looked back and forth between them.

Afraid that Penny was far too perceptive, Bree quickly said, "It's hard to find a place for a quiet word right now, isn't it?"

Penny nodded. "I need to use the bathroom, though."

"Sure." Bree followed Jorie into the living room, but turned away from the kitchen. The gardens would be better.

The sandalwood tree had been planted when Bree was ten or so, and it was now glorious with summer leaves. Bree passed by the people gathered in its shade, pausing only to gently caress the soft *limu* that grew on the shady side.

Aunt Lani's garden was thick with herbs and flowers. Her nose was tickled by the minty *pakaha*. The bank of heart-shaped anthuriums were so vivid with red that her eyes watered. She kept walking, moving faster and faster until she was nearly running. She went out the side gate to the driveway, then down to the road choked with cars. She needed to think.

Reliving that night in L.A. left her drowning in what if — what might have been? She'd been the fool then, hurting before she was hurt, thinking she was somehow saving herself. She'd been wrong, so wrong.

She stumbled on gravel and caught herself on a car with her left hand. Contact pain shot up her arm and she clutched her wrist to her, trying to cradle away the agony. She had thought, mistakenly, that carpal tunnel was unbearable. Another thing she'd been wrong about. Carpal tunnel had sidelined her ten years ago and led to the last time she and Jorie had forgotten it wasn't a good idea to touch each other.

"Two months? You've got to be kidding!"

The sports medicine specialist gave Bree a sober look. "If you want to play again free of pain, you need to rest your wrist. I will give you a regimen of escalating exercise and anti-inflammatories."

"You have no idea what you're asking me to do."

"Miss Starling, I've heard you play. I know what an enforced rest will do to the muscle tone in your left arm. However, muscle memory in practiced musicians is vast. Once the constrictions in your wrist have eased, tone and expertise will come right back. But the choice is very clear. Rest now for two months or possibly rest forever."

"Can't I wait until October to take the two months rest?"

"Your decision. You're playing Russian roulette with your wrist. The pain will intensify and the possibility of irreversible nerve damage goes up. Then we may be looking at surgery. At your age, eight months to a full recovery — by that I mean recovery to the extent that *you* would require, which is a dexterity far beyond the everyday uses of the wrist. When was the last time you had a vacation, anyway?"

"I don't remember," she muttered.

He made a quick note on her chart. "It must be an amazing thing to have a career that seems like a vacation."

She glowered at the doctor. Two months. The pain wasn't *that* bad. Damn Markham for insisting she get it checked out. Two months of work to cancel. And without the practice time this summer, she'd have to cancel the season opener with the New York Philhamonic. Now *that* hurt. Happy thirtieth birthday, Bree.

She called Markham from her car phone and he accepted the news with his usual aplomb. Calls would be made. He would instead make sure she began the following year's season with the NYP. She was to consider her only job to be healing. She could do anything she liked, as long as she followed every edict from the specialist to the letter.

Her next call was to Aunt Lani, whose instant sympathy carried across satellites and into Bree's heart. "That's just terrible, *keiki*. But it will get better?"

"Yes, they promise me it will. I just have to be good."

"Why don't you come home for a while and just relax?"

"I promise I will for part of it." She wanted to go home and soak up Aunt Lani's love and macaroni salad and fish stew and that unbeatable Hawaiian sunshine and slow pace of life, but how pathetic was that? A little injury and she ran home? Pathetic at her age.

"Good." Aunt Lani sounded especially satisfied at the idea. "The house isn't the same without you. Shall I expect you when I see you walk in the door?"

"Yeah," Bree agreed. "I'm going to practice not having a schedule. No — you moron!"

"What?'

"Sorry, this idiot just pulled out in front of me."

"Concentrate on your driving, then, and take very good care of yourself."

Bree said goodbye and resigned herself to learning to get by on her own.

After a week of inactivity in L.A., Bree couldn't stand it. Summer in Toronto was always lovely, but there was no more for her to do there than in L.A. Without the whirlwind of performing, practice and travel she came to the realization that she lacked something most people took for granted: friends.

It was a sobering thought.

It wasn't as if she could call any of the women she'd been with. After a year it would be awkward, she figured. What would she say? "Hi, I can't play the violin right now, so I'd like to ease my boredom by playing with you." No, that wouldn't work.

Okay, what were her other options? Money wasn't really an object. Why not travel for non-business reasons for once? To places where music wasn't the reason. Live without it for a while? If she couldn't play it, it seemed a lot easier to just do without.

She'd always wanted to see Alaska, she told herself, so she let her travel agent arrange a three-week trip up the Inland Passage and through Denali preserve. Chilled to the bone by the end of it — though she felt it was one of the most beautiful places she'd ever experienced — she could think of only one thing: Kona and Aunt Lani.

She'd managed a month on her own, so it didn't feel like she was licking her wounds and crawling home when she got off the plane. She shopped her way through the growing number of specialty boutiques and arrived at Aunt Lani's carrying only a small suitcase of toiletries and undergarments and two bags of summer-weight clothes. Her Alaskan gear had gone on to Markham. One of the assistants would get it back to her place eventually. Times like that Markham wanted her to have a personal assistant, but she'd tried it and been miserable. She'd rather pay Markham a little more for the use of his assistants and travel light. She knew how to tell someone backstage when she needed water and hand warmers.

"Bree!" Aunt Lani's embrace was full of all the things Bree could want. She felt immensely better just from that one hug. She'd hardly said two words the entire time she was in Alaska, but now she was chattering a mile a minute about the details of carpal tunnel syndrome — no, not from typing, from the rapid finger movements required for playing — and how much longer she had to wear the brace. Yes, the specialist thought her fingering technique made it worse, but at this stage in her life she couldn't change it. No, that didn't mean she would ever think Professor Tolan might have been right.

She didn't need the violin to express herself, she thought with relief. She just needed Aunt Lani.

"You look wonderful otherwise," Aunt Lani said. "I'm so glad to have you here. No, not that room."

Bree paused outside her old room, puzzled.

"Sorry, Jorie's using it." Aunt Lani looked very pleased with herself.

Stunned, Bree said, "I thought she was on Oahu, teaching." She hadn't heard from Jorie except at Christmas time the last three years, and that was a formal card.

"She was, but when they opened the U of H extension campus in Kona she relocated."

Suspicion dawned. "And you didn't tell me this when I called?"

"I'm staying out of it." Aunt Lani was far too smug.

Okay, so hubby and Jorie lived here now? It was upsetting, thinking of Jorie sharing her room with someone else. And evidently Jorie had asked Aunt Lani not to tell Bree, thinking Bree wouldn't visit while the arrangement lasted. Well, she wasn't going to give Aunt Lani the satisfaction of asking questions. "I can camp in the fabric room, no problem."

Aunt Lani was cheerfully resigned. "I'll just clear off the bed and we'll get some fresh sheets."

Somehow, while they tended to mundane matters of moving stacks of fabric and finding sheets and towels, Bree found it in her to ask calmly, "So, is Jorie's husband nice?"

Aunt Lani's response was completely unexpected. The air of having managed a coup of some sort fled. She regarded Bree with complete seriousness. "This is just ridiculous. You two have no idea how this feels to me, and you never have."

"What?"

There was the sound of a car in the driveway and Aunt Lani shrugged. The smug smile came back. A door thudded shut, then another, followed by light footsteps on the front porch. Bree's heart began to pound and she wasn't sure she could face a married Jorie.

Jorie looked twenty, like always. Bree's heart began to pound as she

150

recalled those firm legs around her. "I don't know whose car that is, sweetie. We'll just have to find out." She stumbled to a stop at the sight of Bree.

Aunt Lani spread her hands and said, "Now you'll have the conversation you should have had."

Bree's gaze dropped to the little girl at Jorie's knees. She was just like Jorie's baby pictures, all eyes and tummy. How old was she? Three? Two? Bree had no way of gauging. A baby. Maybe it was none of her business where Jorie lived and with whom, but why hadn't anyone told her about something so...so *crucial* as a baby? That was a matter of *'ohana*.

"I'll take Keneka in for her snack while you two talk."

"Go with *tutu*, Penny."

Penny? And where was the husband?

Jorie took her out to the garden but before Bree could burst out with all her questions, she silenced her with, "I tried to tell you. I tried."

"Tell me what?"

Jorie took a deep breath. "That I'd gotten married and it was a mistake. That my future wasn't going to ever be anything unless I knew for sure how you felt. I tried, but when you said you didn't know me I realized that I didn't know you. I knew you liked SpaghettiOs™ and wearing orange, but nothing about the inside you."

Bree didn't know what to say. "So you're divorced?"

"Not exactly. Some process server somewhere is trying to find him, but it costs an arm and a leg. He left after ten weeks of wedded bliss."

Bree just stood there with her mouth open.

"I'm not a cheat, Bree." Jorie paused to swallow. "It really hurt that you could think so."

"I'm sorry, but you never said he was out of the picture."

"You didn't let me. You jumped on the first opportunity to fight and then I realized why I was there."

Some of the shock was wearing off. Now Bree just felt sad and stupid. "Why?"

"To be rescued. If you loved me, you'd save me — "

"I'd have given you *anything*, done *anything* to help you!"

151

"I know. But it was my mess."

Her mind whirling with dates and time, Bree asked, "How old is Penny?"

"You don't need to find a calendar. I was nearly two months pregnant when I saw you."

Bree felt as if Jorie had punched her in the stomach. Little things she'd have never noticed made sense, like how Jorie had kept her slacks on for a long time. Had she been afraid she was showing? She groped for the garden bench and sat down heavily. "I'm having a hard time taking it in."

"I was ashamed of what a fool I'd been. He took everything, Bree. It was all a sham. He took all my savings, my credit cards which he then maxed out, everything. And left me my shining Penny." There were tears in her eyes, but she blinked them away. "He said he was obsessed with me, addicted to me, that I was intoxicating — it all sounded so dangerous and alluring. I thought it would fix all my uncertainties about who and what I was."

"I'm so sorry, Jorie."

She held up a hand. "It's okay. I can't begin to describe how healing it was to hold Penny in my arms the first time. It was like I got to start over learning how to love."

"I — I'm just stunned, that's all. I wish you'd told me."

"He was probably a bigamist, but no one knows for sure. Hence the divorce papers. Or seven years, whichever comes first. So I needed a heap of rescuing. And I realized, after being with you, that you were a virtual stranger. That's when I knew I had to keep the baby. The baby was all I had."

She dropped her voice and said quietly, "You must never tell her I even thought about it. That's why I was in L.A. That was the appointment I didn't go to. Instead I went to see you. Whatever else, Bree, whatever this *thing* is between us — Penny is in my life because you were home that night."

Bree wiped away tears. "You could have sent me an announcement. I'm still *'ohana*."

"I — I know. I kept telling Mom that when you came home on

152

your own schedule I would tell you. I didn't think it would be so long. And part of me was afraid you'd come — "

"Mommy, mommy!" A bolt of energy flew across the garden to seize her mother by the knees. "Mommy! *Tutu* says this is my star lady!"

"I know, sweetie. This is Sabrina Starling."

Penny clambered up onto the bench to sit next to Bree. Rapidly thinking back over the elapsed years, Bree realized she had to be approaching four. "I'm Sabrina, too!"

"You are?" Bree gave Jorie a puzzled look, but Jorie only smiled.

"Yes I am. My name is Keneka Sabrina Pukui. I'm going to be four. Everyone calls me Penny." She pointed at Jorie. "That's my mom. *Tutu* says you like fudge."

Deeply touched, but not wanting to frighten the child with more tears, Bree nodded. "I do like fudge."

Penny leaned toward her with the air of a conspirator. "If we ask *tutu* very quietly she might make some."

"Then let's ask her later."

"Aunt Bree and Mommy aren't done talking, honey. Can you go finish your snack with *tutu*?"

The imp skipped back into the house without a backward glance, leaving Bree with a mind spinning with information overload. What had they been talking about? She absent-mindedly rubbed her sore wrist. "I wish you'd told me. I'd have helped even if...you know."

"I know. But I made it on my own. With Mom's help when Penny was born, of course. She knew he was no good." Jorie kicked at a rock. "I hate it when she's right. She told me I should have told you sooner, but I didn't want you to know I was in such a mess."

"She was right. Everybody makes mistakes."

"Not you." It was said with a smile that took out all of the sting.

"I don't have the free time to make mistakes. Considering how bored I've been on this hiatus so far, it's probably just as well I don't have much." She'd drunk far too much every night in Alaska, at first to keep the cold away, then just to pass the time. She wasn't happy when she was idle and yet there was nothing in her life she cared about except her music. If she wasn't actively playing she found it hard to listen to music. She could read about it for only so many hours a day.

Jorie sat down next to her and lightly touched her wrist. "This is going to be okay?"

"So they say. I am following orders to the letter."

"Good. I know it means a lot to you. I mean, we knew each other as kids and we've drifted as adults. But I'd like to get to know you again. We don't have to be enemies, do we? Just because..."

"Because what?" Bree felt abruptly overwhelmed and her eyes again stung with tears. "Because we have this *thing*?"

"Because we've hurt each other."

She wanted to snap back that Jorie was flattering herself. Four nights in what, thirteen years? That didn't even qualify for a *thing*. But part of her knew it wasn't true. There was something they couldn't ignore, even now. Women who were intelligent, attractive, witty and accomplished had all been held up to the Jorie standard, and none of them came close to making Bree feel the way Jorie did. Second dates were rare, third dates even rarer.

She felt the raw electricity even if Jorie didn't. But Jorie seemed to want to get beyond it. Okay, Bree would try. It hadn't brought her much in the way of happiness. "The times we...it was never a good idea, was it?"

Jorie shook her head. "I don't regret it. But it's never going to work..."

Bree looked at Jorie for a long, sad moment. She hadn't ever envisioned this, a time when they both agreed that what had never really begun was definitely over. Jorie needed to move on. She was a parent, now. "So, let's go back to being friends. I was the one who changed that."

"Don't be sorry."

"I'm not." How could she be? Were there more than a dozen total hours when she had believed in forever, had happily dreamed that she and Jorie would spend their lives together? They had been the only hours when she'd known real happiness without a violin in her hand.

Jorie stared into the distance. "Mom has been really hurt by the way we've been. It would be good if we could work something out."

Bree felt optimistic when she agreed. Jorie had mellowed. Hell, they both had. So there was this little flare between them, still. They made better friends. It was time to let Jorie the Woman of Her Dreams go. She had never truly existed. Time to let someone else into her life. At least she could try.

Being friends was easy to do, on the surface. Penny's presence in both their old bedroom and their lives kept things between them simple and light. Aunt Lani was so happy to have them speaking again and it looked as if their *'ohana* was finally intact. Thirteen years, Bree mused. A foolish waste of family love over a little thing like sexual obsession.

She could even believe that was all it had ever been.

Feeling happy was dangerous — it could go away so quickly — but it was another risk she was willing to take. Jorie's summer teaching stint wasn't for several more weeks, and there was plenty of time to lie in the sun, swim and build sandcastles. There were four giant *honumaoli* at Pu'uhonua o Honanau when they all took Penny to visit the monument. She held Penny as carefully as her Stradivarius so she could watch the massive turtles glide silently between the rocks and through the clear water toward the sea. It was all so innocent.

After a week of warmth and gentle fun, Bree was only slightly shaken to learn that Jorie was going on her first date since Penny was born. When she looked for one of Penny's toys in Jorie's handbag she tried not to let the condom packet upset her. She didn't want Jorie that way any more. It was so much better to be friends now. Everyone was happier.

She couldn't sleep that night and prowled the garden, wondering where Jorie had gone with blond and blue-eyed whatever-his-name was. Why wasn't she back yet? They were probably at his place. She kept thinking about the night when she'd pulled Jorie out of that party. *She's a grown woman*, Bree reminded herself. *She doesn't need you rescuing her. She's proven that.*

Could he possibly make Jorie feel the way Bree had? Did he care that she liked to be held tight and close when she was coming, and kissed gently afterward?

When she heard the car well after two a.m. she thought about scuttling into her room, but instead stayed on the back porch, illuminated by the small reading lamp. If Jorie wanted to talk, she would join her. If not, that was okay, too.

When Jorie's shadow fell over her, Bree was deeply pleased.

"Couldn't sleep?"

"No. Thinking about my schedule," Bree lied. "How was your date?"

"Okay. We drove up to Waimea for dinner."

"Nice." It was a long drive. That alone could account for the lateness of the hour.

"Yeah, it was nice not to have to cut anything but my own food." Jorie sat down next to her. "I'm out of practice for dating, though."

"It's no fun, most of the time."

Jorie loosened the waistband of her simple black skirt. "God, that's better. I hate holding in my stomach."

Bree wanted in the worst way to know if she'd had sex. She just wanted to know, but she couldn't just ask. "He was nice?"

"He's quite good looking. A year younger than me but that doesn't matter, I guess."

"No, not if you get...you know."

Jorie regarded her suspiciously. "Are you trying to ask me if I had a *good* time?"

"Sorry. I saw the condom in your bag."

"It's still there. I mean — it's been a long time, you know. Since...you. And I thought I was ready to get back on the bicycle. He was my type."

Well, that said it all, starting with the pronoun, Bree told herself. "So why didn't you?"

"He got a little grabby a little too early. And it turned me off. I had no idea my libido was so fragile."

Bree wanted to laugh, then sobered as she realized she was thinking she was in competition with this guy. Jorie liked guys. Sometimes she liked it with Bree, true. Maybe she was bisexual — didn't researchers say almost everyone had the capacity for it? "You were the one who warned me about grabby guys, you know."

156

"Was I?"

"You gave me all my dating advice. It turned out to be mostly useless, but I do know how to wither a guy with a glance. Since they're not my type."

"You've never?"

"Not interested." Bree shrugged. "I'm a lesbian. Women do it for me. The same way you know guys do it for you."

Jorie seemed to search for words. She cleared her throat. "Is there anyone special?"

"Well, there's a problem — either I find someone interesting with her own life and our schedules never jibe. Or there's someone who wants to move in the next day, start putting her clothes in my closet, you know?"

Jorie laughed. "I remember your place. The closet was already full."

Bree humphed. "I suppose that's a decent metaphor for the situation." *I'd have emptied the closet for you*, she wanted to say, but with unaccustomed insight she asked herself if that was true. Would she have slowed her performing schedule? Or would she have expected Jorie to live her life? Well, throwing those pictures at Jorie had ensured she'd never had to make that choice, hadn't it? "Maybe I'm just not cut out for permanence."

"I'm not having much luck with permanence myself. Not like Momi. She found her guy. She had her first about the same time I had Penny — took them a long time to conceive. Lucky me. I think I got pregnant the last time I was with the lying rat bastard."

Bree patted Jorie's hand. "If you need to vent sometimes I don't mind listening. Look, I was thinking, let me pay for the process servers and get it over with. I have more money than I know what to do with, really. You're *'ohana* and not only should I offer my help, you should accept it. Aunt Lani let me pay for the roof and the new septic tank. She doesn't have the money for big expenses like that." She left her hand where it was because right then she couldn't move it.

"That's — that's very sweet. I mean...okay. If you can."

"I can." She could offer so much more, but she would let this be a beginning. She had four places to live all by herself. She could easily find Jorie and Penny their own house in this neighborhood, or they could add more rooms to this house. Penny needn't ever worry about college expenses. She could give them both so much, and she wanted to.

"Okay, then." Jorie was breathing hard. Bree felt a tingle in her hand, running up her arm.

She would remember, later, Jorie trying to explain in L.A. that sometimes a person can do something foolish, believing they feel something when they didn't because believing it makes life easier. But right then she forgot about that, and told herself she believed she was mature enough to handle all new rules for her relationship with Jorie. They'd grown. Neither of them was committed to anyone else. They had needs...why not take care of them together?

It would be the mature thing to do, wouldn't it? Why couldn't a friend help another friend? Just let it happen, feel good and move on?

Jorie slowly eased her hand out from under Bree's. "It's been a really long time and, well, okay. I'll admit that you probably shouldn't touch me right now. I really wanted to tonight and...well..."

"It's okay," Bree said softly. "There's nothing wrong with how you feel."

"We agreed...we said it would be a bad idea."

"Maybe we were wrong."

Jorie swallowed hard. "What are you trying to say?"

"Why not..." She ran one finger down Jorie's bare arm. "It's just a *thing*, right? Why are we saying no to it when it might just feel good and let us get on with our lives? It's not about tomorrow, it's just about tonight. It's — it's been a while for me, too."

Jorie watched Bree's fingertip travel over her arm. Hesitantly, she said, "So it wouldn't mean anything."

"It would mean something. I care so much about you, Jorie." Bree believed if she didn't say she loved the Jorie she had gotten to know this past week, all grown up and full of fire and wit, wise and gentle with her daughter, then everything would be okay. "But I'd give you a massage if you needed it. Isn't this the same kind of physical comfort?"

It sounded so rational put that way. Jorie was silent for a long while.

"I can't..." Jorie took a deep breath. "I do want to. It's not that I don't. I remember L.A."

"So do I. In Technicolor."

Jorie's smile was pleased. "It seems too easy. Damn, really, what is it about you?"

"I have no idea," Bree answered with a grin. At least Jorie admitted there was something. "It seems easy to me, too. Maybe that's why people who aren't lucky enough to have friends who care about them think it's wrong. *Pule* addicts."

Jorie laughed. "Spoken like someone raised in this house."

Bree took Jorie's hand again, and pulled her to her feet. "I know where we can be a little more private and...decide."

There was no decision left to be made. Jorie's hand was soft and warm and Bree had no trouble believing her version of what was happening.

It was just friendship.

For friendship she led Jorie to Aunt Lani's workshop, where she'd spent so many hours practicing away from the house. They were out of the cooling breeze of very early morning, and the night seemed soft and welcoming.

For friendship she ran her hands under Jorie's skirt, nearly delirious with wanting to strip off the pantyhose. She pushed Jorie up onto the workbench. She wanted to kiss her hard, make her mouth open in gasping response, but instead she kept her kisses almost completely free of the passion that was boiling inside her.

It was all for friendship.

Jorie said nothing while Bree gently kissed her cheeks, her eyes, her lips. Her shoulders arched as Bree slowly unbuttoned the turquoise blouse.

"Is this okay?"

"Yes." Jorie pulled Bree down for another kiss, this time on the lips. With a soft moan her mouth opened and it felt to Bree like that first kiss, full of sensation and surprise.

She pushed the blouse off Jorie's shoulders and unhooked her bra. A back massage wasn't the worst idea, Bree realized, and she set aside the pulsing drive that wanted to push Jorie back and spread her legs. Not this time, she thought. It won't be that way this time.

She held Jorie against her with one arm and used her good hand to stroke and smooth her back. Her head filled with the fragrance of Jorie's light perfume. Jorie felt like the whisper of a cello, the hint of sublime counterpoint. Bree could hold her forever.

Jorie's bra slipped downward as she finally leaned away from Bree. She cupped Bree's cheek and drew her head far enough down so that Bree knew that Jorie wanted Bree's mouth on her breasts. The feeling of Jorie's nipple hardening in her mouth took her breath away. Bree's hips started to move, not able to stay still in the slow tempo she had chosen.

"I like that," Jorie murmured. "Please don't stop."

Bree stopped only long enough to say, "Whatever you want." Her hands went to the zipper Jorie had already loosened, and she pulled it down, eager to get Jorie's skirt out of the way. Jorie's hips were moving now, in time with Bree's.

Jorie's belly was more plush than it had been. Bree found it alluring as she kissed her way across it. A life had been here, that beautiful child. It seemed sacred, but that feeling fled as she inhaled and recognized the scent that her memory knew was Jorie's alone.

One finger touched Jorie's open center and the effect on Jorie was electric. She arched back on her hands. "Please, Bree, I can't take being teased any more!"

Dizzied by her own fires, Bree said lowly, "I think you like it."

Jorie gasped, her hips lifting off the workbench as Bree's finger went away. "Please."

Did a friend, giving mere physical comfort, tease another into a frenzy? Bree heard the familiar murmur of her ancestors, then, warning her that she was lying to herself. Her tongue flickered over Jorie's copious wet, making Jorie cry out.

She kept every contact light, frustrating, never more than a hint of what she could and would do. She'd have kept it up longer but Jorie's hand was suddenly in her hair, pulling her down hard and fast. Bree groaned and stayed where Jorie wanted her, stayed there for a long while.

160

Jorie's fingers were still wound in her hair when Bree finally rose and Jorie used them to pull Bree to her for a long, hard kiss.

Bree fell into the kiss. How could a kiss like this be about mere friendship? She felt Jorie's hands on her breasts, then, and moaned into Jorie's mouth.

"I remember that you like that," Jorie whispered against Bree's lips.

Bree felt drunk on that kiss, and wished her pulse wasn't so frantic. But Jorie's fingers were so precise in their teasing.

Jorie released her finally. "Take your shirt off."

She had stripped for other women, confident in her allure, aware of being watched. She couldn't find that same assurance with Jorie. She fumbled instead, her arms trembling.

Jorie slipped a finger under each bra strap, slowly lifting them off Bree's shoulders. With tantalizing slowness, she pushed the soft fabric down until her fingertips could close around Bree's excited nipples.

A shudder of pleasure ran through Bree that was so intense she could almost believe that what she felt was all about sex, about the sheer pleasure of being touched by someone who knew how to please her. But there was more because behind the pleasure was memory, and memory reminded her that pleasure could lead to joy or to disappointment.

Not this time, she told herself. Not this time.

Jorie took her with sweetness, with a murmur of delight. Part of Bree wanted it to be like it had been in L.A., full of harsh and needy words, and Jorie taking complete control of her. But what Jorie was doing reached past the ache in Bree that needed release. It spilled like the tide into Bree's heart, filling her emotions with the beauty of Jorie's touch.

It wasn't about friendship. The lie was washed away. "Please," she pleaded. She was asking Jorie for forever, now. "Please."

Jorie's tongue became more persistent. "Let it feel good."

Bree wanted Jorie's answer but she didn't remember the question. Music was so easy but this...this was so hard to follow, to make sense of. Her climax was unbearably close. What words could even matter? But she needed more than Jorie's touch. "Please tell me you love me!"

Jorie ceased all movement and Bree could only hear her pounding heart, like timpani in her ears. "Don't — don't stop!"

Jorie's fingers surged into her, deep and hard. Bree cried out as orgasm raced over her like a waterfall, churning her heart and body from passion to vibrant, searing ecstasy.

It was several minutes before Bree recalled where she was, and that the friendly passion they'd agreed to share wasn't supposed to include a profession of love.

Jorie's arms were around her, soothing, patting, as she murmured, "I know, I know," into Bree's ear.

"Thank you," Bree finally managed. She tried to make it sound light.

"I do love you, Bree. I always will, you know that."

Jorie had heard her. Bree had known she was exposed, vulnerable, but even so the knife of that inadequate response was completely unexpected. Jorie might as well have said, "But not that way."

Not what way? With Bree's scent on her mouth, Bree's wet on her hand, what way didn't Jorie love her? What was wrong with Bree that Jorie couldn't admit this wasn't a *thing*?

Don't ruin it, she told herself. Don't break everything apart now. Her ancestors were warning her of *pilikia*, of trouble she could never mend if she made a mistake now. She felt closer to Jorie than she had since that first night, and she'd broken that feeling to pieces. It felt healed now, but fragile.

She wanted more from Jorie than Jorie would ever give her. Accept that, she told herself. Accept that and live with it or go away forever.

"Thank you for saying that," Bree said. "I made mistakes, and sometimes I think you must hate me."

"Never that."

They rocked together. Bree wanted to cry because she had lost something she would never get back. What she had instead didn't fill the void. Live with it, she told herself. Your only other choice is to live completely without her.

"I have a confession to make," Jorie said. She gently pushed Bree away and began dressing. "As you know, I have a complete collection of Sabrina Starling CDs."

"I know." She fumbled for her clothes. "So does Aunt Lani. I mean, if your *'ohana* doesn't have your music, who should? That's why I send them." She thought she sounded light-hearted.

"Well, I listen to them."

The idea took Bree's breath away. "Really?"

"A lot. I think I like her stuff. A lot."

"You've never — you've never said that before."

Jorie's fingertips brushed her cheeks. "I wanted to, but sometimes I'm stubborn. I didn't want to sound like just another fan."

"You'll never be that." Bree fought back tears. "Thank you. That's the nicest thing I think anyone has ever said."

They walked hand in hand to the house and parted with a quiet kiss at the back door.

Don't cry, Bree told herself. If you do she'll know.

So she held back all the tears, even those that had risen when she'd left for L.A. to get the specialist's permission to return to practice. She held back the tears for years, planning visits with seeming ease, never letting anyone see how much she cared when Jorie moved in with Brian — he was decent enough — for a couple of years. She and Brian had drifted apart and when Aunt Lani had hurt her hip, Jorie and Penny had returned home. Bree had been happy to pay for the new rooms on the house to make the arrangements easier on everyone. She'd grown used to Penny's noise, like joyful timpani sprinkled into a beautiful day.

For nearly two years, Jorie had taken a series of teaching jobs that allowed her to follow the Polynesian journey, from New Zealand to Tahiti, Fiji and Somoa. She'd come home again with a complete dissertation, though Bree swore she'd never call Jorie a doctor. Bree stayed longer with Aunt Lani while Jorie was away. It was easier to relax and recuperate, though the house seemed so quiet with just the two of them.

Those visits, sandwiched between concerts and a growing number of lectures, had been free of any nuance from Jorie that she remembered the way they had been together. That is, until the very last visit. Bree had become so good at pretending she didn't love Jorie that when Jorie had reached for her one night she'd actually been shocked.

Late at night again, sitting in the garden, giddy from too much hard cider and finished at last wrapping Penny's gifts from Santa, Jorie had eased her head onto Bree's shoulder. "It's hard to believe she's nearly as old as we were when...you know."

Bree had been startled. Jorie never brought it up. After all this time it seemed like it had happened to someone else. "She's almost as old as I was. Well, in a year or two."

"We did some stupid shit when we were younger, huh?"

"Yep." Bree had almost reached the point of believing she didn't feel what had never gone away.

"I think a lot, especially since Brian, about the last night. About friendship and what..." Her hand slowly circled Bree's waist.

Into the silence Bree heard the rising sound of her heartbeat. "What are you trying to say, Jorie?"

"That...we said we were friends. And..."

"I can't," Bree whispered. She didn't want to say why. But if Jorie touched her again something inside would snap. She was only okay if Jorie didn't touch her. She hadn't expected this — she wasn't ready to be strong. She wanted to pull Jorie into her arms and never let go. Desperately, she sought refuge in a lie. "There's someone."

"Oh." Jorie sat up. "I didn't know — you didn't say. I didn't mean anything, just, okay. It doesn't matter."

"Okay, it's okay."

"Is she nice?" Jorie's voice sounded very tight.

"Yes. Sort of special. It's early days yet..."

"I understand."

"I don't have to perform as much to stay in form, and I'm spending more time in Boston at Berklee."

"So someone nice in Boston. That's wonderful. You deserve it, Bree. Someone who loves you." Jorie's voice broke. "I'm really happy for you."

"Thanks."

"And she's good for you? She knows...?"

Bree realized Jorie was staring at her breasts. "Don't do that," Bree snapped, unable to help herself. All the gods, she wanted to give herself to Jorie, completely, and take everything Jorie could give. It had never gone away. Jorie couldn't look at her like that.

"I'm sorry." Jorie's smile seemed false as she fanned herself. "It must be hormones, that's all. Look, I'm just beat and Penny will be up at dawn."

"She doesn't believe in Santa anymore, you know. She's fourteen."

"I know. But she *thinks* that I think she still does. We enjoy the lie."

Good for you, Bree wanted to say. Nice that someone can enjoy a lie now and then. She certainly wasn't getting any joy out of hers.

It had made her angry, again, that it was always up to Jorie. If they kissed, if they had sex, even if they were friends. She'd trailed around like a lapdog all her life, it seemed, and never once had she had any real say in what happened.

Jorie had driven her to the airport when it was time to leave that visit, and anger had finally cracked Bree's restraint.

They'd been saying goodbye as the first class passengers were called, when Bree added, "It may be a while before I come back."

"Oh? Why?"

A flash of intense irritation shook Bree. She'd seized Jorie then, kissed her hard, with all the need she'd bottled up for those lying years. There was no friendship in it. And when Jorie's mouth had softened, had seemed to welcome Bree's fierceness, Bree had pushed her away. "Because it's not always up to you."

With a shock, Bree surfaced out of the past, realizing the streaks on her face were rain mingled with tears. Rain danced on the cars around her. The sound might have been the beginning of the piece she'd composed for Moscow. She shoved that memory away, then regretted it. It would hurt less to remember music than all the broken pasts with Jorie.

Dr. Sheridan would be pleased that anything seemed more painful to her than music.

She was quickly soaked to the skin, and she lifted her face to the refreshing water. She closed her eyes and pictured Jorie today, walking hand in hand with Mea.

Jorie had found a woman she loved, finally. Bree was certain it was all very rational. Something in Jorie's life had changed, and she was finally open to an ongoing relationship with a woman instead of wanting to fuck Bree every five years or so. Bree didn't want to hear about it. She didn't want to act like a friend. She wanted to hate Mea, but couldn't.

She wished she felt anything but pain.

She'd had absolute control of her career until San Francisco, and no control at all over Jorie or her heart.

She told her ancestors she really had loved Diana. There was nothing but silence in response. Her ancestors had tried to save her from the worst mistake of her life, but she'd ignored them.

A clap of thunder filled Bree with memories of Diana, her kind eyes, the easy laugh and the shimmering happiness that surrounded her. She wanted to strike out at it, slice Diana out of her mind. Instead she scrubbed her face with the rain, wishing it was purifying, but knowing there was nothing that could wash her clean.

CHAPTER TEN

"Are you sure you won't come with us?" Penny paused in the bedroom door. "It's supposed to be a good movie."

"I have reading to do." Bree hoped the presence of her little-needed reading glasses helped with the lie. "You guys enjoy yourselves."

The house was full of empty noises when they were gone. In the two days since the memorial Bree had found it almost impossible to move. She feared the pain medication now, having used it so long that it was wearing off. The doctors had indeed warned her it was moderately addictive, but that she would find the relief necessary for good sleep. Sleep and rest were the only hope there was to a recovery.

Not that she had any hope.

Dr. Sheridan said from the past, *And how does that make you feel?*

Like I want to stuff that fucking question down your stupid throat, Bree thought. The flash of violent anger left her limp.

She left the book about Bernstein's theories of musical language based on the work of Noam Chomsky on the table. There had been a time that just considering his commentaries had left her breathless. There had been a time when she almost understood what he meant.

What was the point to trying now?

She watched the sun slipping toward the horizon and ate the last of the muffins Mea had made. Mea was good with Penny, Bree conceded that. Mea seemed to love Jorie, too. Bree thought as long as she lived, she'd never understand Jorie, but she'd grown into a wonderful mother. She deserved some peace, now. Other than that accidental kiss the first night, Bree had no hope of any other feelings.

And she would not try to find out. She wouldn't push Jorie. She wouldn't flirt with her, hint at past sexual experiences, wink at her over a glass of wine. She wouldn't devote her every thought and every spare minute to letting Jorie know she was thinking about her. About her, her dreams, her interests, her likes, her wants. She wouldn't do that this time. Mea was as nice as Pam.

She couldn't go on feeling like this, but she had no hope of anything changing.

The violin case was only five or so feet away. It never stopped calling, pleading.

She had the case open on the bed before she admitted she had lost the battle again, swinging the instrument to her left shoulder without thinking, and catching up the bow with her right hand. Stupid...stupid...

Stupid Pain, because she still forgot. She wanted to smash the violin against the wall, trample on its broken pieces and just be done with it. Done. The moment passed and she gritted her teeth, moving the violin to her right shoulder, using her right hand to wrap her left around the bow.

Bach swelled in her, Goldberg Variations. She could hear every sterling note in her head. Her left hand twitched — it remembered. Coiled around the instrument's neck, her right hand did nothing. How could she begin again when her head was already crashing with the remembered passion of music she had breathed out through her fingertips?

She made her the fingers of her right hand press the strings. It still felt wrong. Her left arm bowed clumsily. The resulting A note drifted flat, the B that followed was no better. She stopped, tuned, and began again.

She played her shaky scales, sounding like a wobbly seven-year-old with her first workbook. Her right hand forgot how to make E-flat. The bow clattered to the floor and Bree swayed, too dizzy to retrieve it.

Don't be so hard on yourself.

Aunt Lani was gone and her ancestors were silent. Part of her longed for her mother's voice, but to hear it would shatter her senses. The violin would not speak for her ever again. No practice was any better than the last. Her right hand would never know a steady A or find E-flat without thinking about it first.

No Jorie now, or hope of her. No music.

She felt vast, filled to the edges with emptiness. She fell into an echoing cistern and the only sound was that of her own agonized breathing.

She put the violin in its case and carried it with her to the car. She left no note.

"Miss Starling, welcome!"

Bree returned the hearty handshake of the San Francisco Symphony Orchestra's musical director. "Sabrina, please, maestro."

"If you'll make it Kurt."

"Well now that that's all settled." She turned to the assembled orchestra and nodded.

"I, and the entire orchestra and staff, are delighted to have you with us for the first time. We are all honored to open our annual series with you."

"I'm glad it all worked out. I've been here two days and I can sincerely say San Francisco is one of the most beautiful cities in the world."

There was a round of pleased tapping of bows on music stands. The maestro introduced her to the first chairs of each section. She was used to the openly envious stares of the other violinists. The Stradivarius always had that effect.

Kurt Master-Fielding was a perfectionist with bouts of improvisation. Once he was convinced that Bree had mastered the piece — and it had been a long while since Bree had felt she was still on approval as the featured soloist — he was willing to structure his interpretation of the extended solos to suit Bree's. Of course they both liked the Paganini transcriptions of the Mozart concerto enough to fight about it. He shouted at her and she shouted back and the synergy was one of the best Bree had experienced in her life.

San Francisco seemed wonderful for other reasons, including the open presence of the gay community. She had often shied away from discussions about sexuality only because she preferred to talk about music. But a large contingent of symphony supporters were gay men and she found their panache endearing. In the back of her mind she began to consider moving out of L.A. for the cleaner skies and friendlier community of San Francisco. Maybe San Francisco was where the woman who could finally push Jorie out of her heart lived. Regardless, the late summer weather was more often fair and warm than the fog she had expected. The skies were actually blue.

When she met Diana she hardly noticed her.

That would stay with her for a long time. She took note of Pam, a short-haired sandy blond who looked as if she pedaled fifty miles daily. Pam was introduced as one of the largest donors to the symphony that year, her check specifically in support of bringing Sabrina Starling at last to the San Francisco Symphony. She seemed about Bree's age, which was several decades younger than the typical large donor.

"It was time that an open lesbian was the featured performer to start the season." Pam whisked a glass off a passing tray. "That and I like free champagne."

Bree laughed. "Thank you for your support, then. And the

170

champagne." The cocktail party to let major donors mingle with the guest performer and other key members of the symphony was turning out to be one of the better of its kind. She was aware that a forty-something redhead with a blond-tipped brush cut was giving her obviously inviting looks, but groupies had lost some of their appeal over the years. She wanted a little more than that. Not that she knew the first thing about finding it.

"Where is she? Oh, there." Pam waved over a short brunette about Pam's age and took her hand. "Miss Starling — "

"Bree, please."

Pam grinned. "I'm honored, really. Bree, then. This is my partner, Diana."

Bree had shaken Diana's hand and not really noticed how lovely she was. What she did notice was how Pam's vivacity seemed to triple when Diana was near. At one point the two women snuggled together for a quick kiss and Bree thought, first, that it was sweet, and then that times had changed. Not one person in the room seemed to care that two women were openly smooching. It was refreshing.

She liked San Francisco.

Two weeks of rehearsals concluded their preparations, capping the two months of solo practice Bree had undertaken on her own. She'd also been working on a recording which had been done in Toronto just before she needed to come to San Francisco.

The performing part of her was tired. She'd been cooped up. She needed to think about something besides music, and Pam's invitation to a dinner party in her honor was a welcome diversion. It was a real treat, feeling companionable with people associated with the symphony. She'd gone to so many dinners with people for whom she felt very little connection.

The night before the opening performance, Bree took an enormous bundle of fresh heart-shaped anthuriums and a favorite Napa Valley red wine to the Presidio Heights home Pam and Diana shared.

"How beautiful," Pam exclaimed.

"They're native to Hawaii, and they remind me of home."

"Come see what the stock market built," Pam invited. She led Bree to the kitchen where she found two tall vases for the flowers. "It feels just like Monopoly money sometimes. The bubble will burst at some point." She set the flowers out on the buffet, then led Bree upstairs to her study. "I thought a Mary Cassat would be a more lasting investment. And nicer to look at than stock certificates."

"It is lovely," Bree agreed. The simple landscape in soaked greens and grays reminded her of Aunt Lani's work. "And this is an O'Keeffe?"

"I prefer women artists, why not?"

"I admire you putting your money where your sisters are. I should do more of that myself. Can I ask your advice some time?" None of her homes felt like one. Maybe a painting, something precious, would change that. It occurred to her then she'd been stupid not to have commissioned something from Aunt Lani. She had several small pieces, and the long-ago gift of tapestry squares. Something big would be beautiful and bring a feeling of home to wherever it was she lived. She could probably go through her friend, Hamu, so Aunt Lani wouldn't know it was for her until after the contract for full price was signed.

"I'd love to — I mean, I can't afford *everything* I want. There's another Cassat coming up in a week at Sotheby's. Later let's pop online and take a look at it. And I'll show you some shots of my other passion, hot air ballooning."

Pam's enthusiasm was engaging and Bree felt thoroughly charmed. When they returned to the large main room where the other guests were gathered she felt more like a valued friend than an honored guest.

The catered dinner was lovely and the exclusive companionship of lesbians, most in couples, was something she'd never really experienced before. What social time she had was usually with other musicians.

Among the single women was the redhead from the cocktail party, Stacy. She still sent obvious signals to Bree, sometimes so blatant that Bree caught Diana smiling to herself.

That was when she looked more carefully at Diana, and then Diana realized she was looking. It was only a glance, but Bree was left thinking that Pam was a lucky woman.

Over after-dinner wine, Stacy proposed a toast to Diana and Pam, who had just celebrated their eighteenth anniversary.

"Without you guys, none of us would ever think that forever was real. Anyone who looks at you can tell that each of you finds your heart's dream in the other, still." She raised her glass. "I know I whine about the patriarchal construct of monogamy and how it ruins the dating pool, but from the bottom of my heart, I envy you both."

Glasses clinked and everyone sipped, while Diana and Pam momentarily seemed to be in a glow all their own. It was a fanciful thought, Bree acknowledged. But she agreed with Stacy on the envy part. It could have been her and Jorie counting the years. They'd never have them now.

She finished the glass of wine, not liking the cold feeling in the pit of her stomach.

She lingered for a while longer, enjoying the conversation, but when the clock struck midnight she announced she needed to be a pumpkin on the eve of a performance.

"Leaving alone?" Diana came downstairs with Bree's coat and bag.

"Yes. Tonight at least."

Diana's green eyes had a definite twinkle. "Stacy and Pam were an item before I came along."

Stacy's voice floated out of the main room. "I still can't get you guys to say yes to a three-way. Eighteen years of begging for nothing. One little three-way. What could it hurt?"

A sparkle of laughter flowed out of the room and Bree decided that while Stacy had a fun sense of humor she didn't want Diana thinking of her as an easy conquest.

That was when what Diana thought of her — as a woman, a lesbian and *not* a musician — began to matter.

The day of the concert was like any other. Bree followed her unshakable performance day routine. She went for a long, brisk walk and ate lightly. She practiced only the simplest scales, then took a preventative dose of anti-inflammatories. Carpal tunnel had bothered her since that first bout, but careful attention to the symptoms had kept it at bay. San Francisco's only drawback was the cool, damp fog that sometimes came in at sunset. Her wrist didn't care for it at all.

She attended early rehearsal and had a last quiet conversation with Kurt before going back to her hotel to dress and clear her mind. On the way up to her room she reminded the concierge of her seven-ten request for a cab.

For San Francisco she had chosen a backless gown of deep purple that Markham's image consultants had declared her best color. Her loose hair brushed the small of her back when she moved, a sensation that simultaneously tingled and calmed.

She was met at the stage door by the maestro, who kissed her hand. "Don't repeat this to anyone, but you are the loveliest woman to ever grace our stage."

"Flatterer." Bree let him hand her over to an experienced backstage volunteer who happily supplied her with chilled water. Her request for a bowl of ice and hand warmers had been met, and she spent five minutes dunking her left hand in the ice to ease the low-level ache. The discomfort wasn't enough to affect her performance, but there was no point in ignoring it either.

The hand warmers she used during the opening selection, a brief Ives sonata she could hear even though the green room was insulated. She had to hand it to Kurt, he didn't pander to his donors with nothing but the easiest music. Ives wasn't for the weak-at-heart. Even the Mozart — a composer that usually shored up donations — wasn't a common selection. Was it Cleveland where the program had consisted of a selection from Sleeping Beauty, the Rachmaninoff violin concerto, Mozart's little concerto and a medley of Sousa marches? Tonight's program was anything but saccharine.

Her mind was deep in the opening strains of the Mozart when they called for her. She shed her coat to the volunteer, feeling the cool air on her back. She lifted her violin from the case, extracted the bow and left the green room for the wings.

The audience was buzzing as the musicians tuned. Kurt bowed, took her hand, and they went on stage together.

Applause had always given her an instant adrenaline surge. As she always did, she thought of Jorie for a split second because the power surge inside her was so close to what she felt when she thought about her. Then she kissed the Stradivarius between the pegs and signaled the first violin for his tuning notes.

He listened carefully as she played them back and nodded.

There was the rustle of near silence as Bree closed her eyes for a moment. Then she nodded to Kurt and watched the baton rise, pause and fall.

She preferred performing alone, but the magic of a full symphony was undeniable. From the least experienced novice, assigned to odd bits of percussion, to the seasoned professionals that made up the core of the orchestra, they all focused their exclusive energy on following the point of the maestro's baton. Intensity upon intensity built the doorway for Bree to make her entrance, her violin soaring out with the support of the woodwinds. Her body moved — she'd never unlearned it — and her hands felt alive with fire.

Midway through the final movement she was aware that Kurt was grinning at her. She tossed her hair over her shoulder with a near laugh and launched into the last, dazzling cadenza.

Her fingers slipped on the strings.

Hot with embarrassment, she thought at first she'd simply forgotten to keep them dry with the cloth between the violin and her shoulder. She struggled to recover, then searing pain lanced up her left arm. Her bow clattered to the floor.

She nearly dropped the violin as she staggered. She was going to throw up. Kurt had frozen. There was a collective round gasp from the audience and then the first violinist was taking the Stradivarius out of her grasp — protecting her baby — while Bree fought with all her strength to stay on her feet.

She didn't remember the burly security guard carrying her off the stage to the green room, but the picture was on the Reuters entertainment page before the next morning.

She did throw up when she tried to lift her wrist, the pain coming so sharply that nausea overwhelmed her. She heard someone say food poisoning, but she knew it was carpal tunnel. It had never been this bad.

It took her a moment to recognize Pam and Diana pushing their way through the crowd gathered in the green room.

"I just need my pain medication — it's CTS." She tried to catch her breath. "It's never felt like this before."

"Like you can keep anything down," Pam said. "Emergency room. We'll take you."

She tried to protest, and had only the vaguest recollection of the ride to the hospital with her head in Diana's lap.

She read the following morning that the badly shaken orchestra resumed the night's performance after the intermission and her condition was rumored to be caused by severe food poisoning.

She tossed the paper to one side, already sick of the hospital room. Her arm was immobilized and once the intravenous painkiller took effect she stopped vomiting. Pam and Diana had lingered for quite a while, offering any assistance possible.

A few hours after she talked to Markham, flowers from him were delivered, then a steady stream from a variety of sources that astonished her. Conductors she'd worked with, other musicians, and even some from Momi in Hawaii. Word traveled fast in the information age. Great, every orchestra who wanted to book her would want a physical report — that is, if they wanted to risk working with someone unstable.

She was asking the nurses to leave the cards and take the flowers any place else — the fragrance was giving her a headache — when the specialists arrived. There were three of them, one from the hospital, one on call on behalf of the symphony, and one sent by Markham. They examined her x-rays, conferred and finally asked her a few questions about the warning signs — few — and the extremity of the pain — severe.

There was another conference and Markham's consultant seemed to carry the day. He was about to pronounce his decision when Bree spoke up.

"Two months complete rest, a regimen of exercise and anti-inflammatories."

He looked taken aback, then graced her with a distant smile. "Very good, doctor. One minor adjustment — four months complete rest."

The other doctors nodded.

Bree swallowed hard. The two-month hiatus had been difficult enough to get through. She wasn't going to go running home this time to let Jorie want her. Maybe if she pleaded enough Aunt Lani would overcome her terror of flying and come to visit her for a change. Any city of her choice.

Four months.

"And after four months, it could be another two months if not enough of the swelling has eased. You've overdone it."

Bree swallowed hard. It didn't seem like she'd overdone it. "And if I need surgery?"

His eyes narrowed. "I wouldn't recommend it. For a keyboardist, maybe. But not for anyone who plays a stringed instrument. Keyboardists have a wide range of movement in their wrist while they play, as well as varied pressure on the keys. You hold your wrist in a single position for ten to fifteen minutes during a performance, and your fingers rarely vary how hard they press on the strings."

"Are you — do you mean to say that if this doesn't get better it may not be fixable?" Bree felt a cold, burning fear ignite in the space between her heart and her stomach.

"I think you should prepare yourself for that possibility."

"What exactly do I need to do?" Any compromise was acceptable to have her violin in her hand again.

"When I get back to my office I'll have a very precise regimen sent to you. I can't promise anything, but you don't really have a choice."

The last time there had been a promise of recovery. She was nothing without her violin. There was nothing else that mattered in her life. What if she'd brought this on herself? Maybe Professor Tolan *had* been right about her fingering technique. This was all her own fault.

She might never play again.

She felt cold all over.

A knock at the door drew Bree out of a maudlin reverie some time later. She looked up to see Diana peeking around the partially open door with a covered dish in her hand.

"Hi!" She sat up awkwardly. "Come on in."

"I thought you might be overwhelmed with flowers. I noticed you liked the cheesecake the other night."

"That looks divine and so much better for me than Jell-O™. Thanks, really, for everything you did last night." She watched Diana pull the uncomfortable hospital chair closer to the bed.

"It was the least we could do — geez, you'd think none of those people had ever seen anyone get sick before. I was a grade school teacher until about five years ago, and I guess working with kids made me blasé about bodily fluids."

"I didn't throw up on you, did I?" The thought was embarrassing, but it wasn't as if she'd had a choice.

Diana's expression told her that she had. "I hated those pants anyway." Then she burst out laughing. "I should have auctioned them off on e-Bay. Some sicko would have paid big money for them!"

Bree joined her in laughter. The entire room felt lighter and brighter with her there. The fear roiling in the pit of her stomach eased.

"So when are you blowing this popsicle stand?"

"Tomorrow, I think. They want me to have this particular drug for the next twenty-four hours. That should start the reduction in the inflammation. Plus the painkillers are nice. Morphine has its uses."

Diana was nodding. "Listen, Pam and I have an offer — hotels are such dreary places and you might not feel like traveling for a while. Would you consider staying with us? We have lots of room and you could keep to yourself if that's what you'd like. I'm a better cook than room service, that is, when I cook."

Bree was deeply moved by the offer. She was, after all, a complete stranger. It was something Aunt Lani would have done and never in her life had Bree met anyone with a heart even remotely the size of Aunt Lani's. "I don't quite know what to say."

"Yes would work." Diana's smile deepened. How did Diana make her eyes do that, Bree wondered, sparkle like sunlight on the ocean?

Feeling slightly dazzled, Bree said yes. "I'm very grateful."

"It'll be a delightful change to our routine." She proffered a card with a string of phone numbers below her name. Diana did some sort of educational art consulting. "Call me tomorrow when you know they're letting you out and I'll come get you. If you like, I could move your things from your hotel."

"I should be able to move about tomorrow. It's just my wrist. Maybe we could go there after you pick me up?"

"Okay. Whatever. I'll bring you some real food, too."

"The cheesecake was a great idea."

They smiled at each other, Bree feeling rather stupid, then Diana took her leave.

It was just that she was nice, that's all. Pam was nice too. They were a nice couple. It would be nice staying with them. All very nice and safe.

The drive south through Kealakekua was slow, but that was entirely expected. Trucks stacked with surfboards vied for parking spaces at the coffee store, banana bread bakery and several breweries. Bree might have noticed another day, but today she just wanted to get to Honaunau. When Aunt Lani was troubled she always went there, to the place where her ancestors had taken refuge with their gods.

She had felt safe with Diana and Pam, and they with her, no doubt. She felt safe with Mea and Jorie...but since she knew that *feeling* safe wasn't the same as *being* safe, she couldn't stay there anymore. She could not bear the idea that she might cause Mea an iota of doubt or pain. Pam had never suspected.

"These really are amazing." Bree turned the last page of Pam's photo album from her last hot air ballooning trip. "It seems like such an elegant way to travel."

"Not that you can go anywhere much. But up is enough. I've been thinking about moving up to helium. You stay up for four days instead of four hours."

"How do you find the time?" Bree stretched. She had loved looking at Pam's photos. Pam was enthusiastic about so many things.

"Easy enough — we know when the major festivals are and we refuse to schedule any work during those times. Thank god for the

179

information age, huh? We work only when we want to. My company isn't a startup anymore. I suppose the same is true for you."

"I hadn't thought of it that way because I want to work all the time."

"I can see that." Pam put the album away and shut off the reading lamp over her desk. "I suppose if my work was what gave me joy in life I'd do it all the time. But I'd much rather do Diana."

"Hey!" From the doorway, Diana sounded indignant. "Be careful the impression you're giving of who does who, missy!"

"She talks the talk, but you know the saying."

Bree tried to look as if she did, but apparently failed.

"Femme on the streets, pillow queen between the sheets."

"You'll pay for that," Diana protested.

"Pay me later." Pam smirked, then bolted across the room to tickle Diana until Diana gave up. Diana did not seem to mind the kiss that settled the argument.

They were openly affectionate around her and somehow it made Bree feel uncomfortable, like she was seeing something so special it had to be private. Eighteen years seemed very like forever. The occasional sleepless night led her to overhear enough to be certain that whatever Lesbian Bed Death was, it hadn't arrived at this house. Sometimes when she was trying to sleep she would hear the echo of Diana's cry in her memory, rising and falling.

Pam was certainly nice enough, but...Bree didn't want to finish that thought.

Finished with thoroughly kissing Diana, Pam turned back to Bree. "Are you up for Stacy's poker game?"

"Yeah. It sounds like fun." She'd have to fend Stacy off again. Pain would be a good enough reason, she supposed.

"And we're going to be late." Diana held out her watch-clad wrist. "I swear you two get completely lost when you're in this room."

"It's comfortable," Bree said. "I don't think in any of the places I live I have a study this nice." Starting with soft-as-butter leather chairs, Bree found Pam's study addictive.

Pam had a taxi take them across town. "We both like to drink at the poker game, even if it's mostly beer. Safer this way."

"Makes sense to me." Bree gazed out of the window like a tourist.

Diana loved to walk and they'd seen a number of neighborhoods in the city on foot. Around every corner there seemed to be yet another sparkling vista of lights spilling like waterfalls into the bay. "This is such a beautiful city."

She was still considering where she might like to settle if she moved. Pam and Diana were friends now, and that alone was something she placed a high value on.

Stacy's home was in the Castro, up the hill from the landmark theater. The house itself was narrow and tall, reminding Bree of row houses in London. The entryway and a small formal sitting room took up the first floor, and Stacy led them up a flight of stairs to a room devoted solely to a large screen television, seating and a spacious desk. The next floor was obviously for entertaining with two tables, a dozen leather chairs, and a glass-and-mirrors bar along one wall. A spinet piano was under the far window and the remaining wall was lined with shelves displaying both books and what appeared to be an extensive collection of goddess figurines. Bree assumed that the floors above must be bedrooms.

She knew the other two women from dinner at Pam's house, Mandy and her girlfriend Carol. Well prompted by Pam, she produced a five-dollar bill, which was the price of admission at the poker table.

"Let's push the tables together so we can have room for snacks," Stacy suggested. As soon as everything was arranged, the game was on.

Bree didn't know anything about poker so she anted her penny chip and sat back to watch. Stacy liked five-card stud, a pronouncement that made everyone snicker.

When it was Diana's turn to the call, she shuffled. "I think I'd like Dyke."

"Wouldn't we all?" Stacy got up to get another beer from the tap. "Course you're well known for only having just the one for eighteen years."

Pam put her arm around Diana. "And what's wrong with that?"

"Boring, that's what." Stacy threw an olive at Pam, who caught it and popped it into her mouth.

"You wish you were so lucky."

Stacy shrugged and her expression softened. "Okay, sometimes I wish I were."

Diana looked into Pam's eyes with a pleased smile.

"Cough. Cough, cough." Carol drummed her fingers on the table. "Poker? Any time soon?"

With a sigh Diana gave her attention to the table. "The name of the game is Dyke."

"You're going to have to explain it to me very slowly," Bree said.

Stacy sauntered back to the table. "Somehow I think you'll pick it up quickly."

Flipping cards across the table, Diana drawled, "Sixes and nines are wild. Straights don't count and two ladies, naturally, take the pot. Tie broken by a PC split."

"I can't follow all that," Bree admitted.

Stacy, sitting next to her, promptly said, "I'll be happy to advise."

Bree found herself with Stacy half in her lap and learning the ins and outs of a seven-card stud layout. When they took a break to load up on more snacks, Bree headed for the sideboard.

Pam reached for a plate and called over her shoulder, "Honey, you want me to bring you something?"

"Sure, thanks." Diana stretched and headed toward the bar.

"Serving you is what I live for." She picked out three strawberries, skipped the honeydew melon, and dropped several chunks of pineapple on the plate. All white cheese, two meatballs with most of the sauce drained off and a handful of chips with salsa completed her effort.

"All you need is a cherry on top." Bree helped herself to some pretzels and microwave popcorn. Diana's cooking was starting to show in her waistline.

"She doesn't like cherries." Pam's serious focus on the plate faded into a smile. "Sorry, you were joking, right?"

"Yes, though I didn't know that about cherries."

"There aren't many foods my girl doesn't like, but that's one of them."

Stacy appeared on Bree's other side. "Speaking of things people don't like, you don't care for beer, do you?" She had Bree's first glass, still half full, in her hand.

"You know, *pia* is almost the state drink in Hawaii, but it's never been my taste."

"Tell me what you like." Stacy winked.

"Thanks, babe," Diana murmured to Pam as Pam handed her the completed plate. She smooched Pam on the cheek.

Pam went in for a deeper kiss and Bree looked away. She said to Stacy, on an impulse, "A scotch would be good if you have it."

"Single malt?"

"That would be even better."

"You got it, baby."

She watched Stacy head to the bar, then turned to catch Diana looking at her speculatively. She rolled her eyes but Diana didn't respond.

The scotch tasted wonderful and a short time later Bree felt quite tipsy. In the middle of a hand she started to giggle. "I'm sorry, I think — oh my. I forgot I was taking pain pills. I'm not sure scotch was a good idea."

Diana offered some cheese. "You've had nothing but carbs tonight. This will help."

"I think I'll sit out a couple of hands." She waited a few minutes, then decided more cheese was a good idea.

She took a little plate to the spinet. Her mouth full, she carefully wiped her fingertips, and lifted the keyboard cover.

The instrument was in tune. Before she knew it she was picking out "Ahe Honi" with her right hand. She missed her violin.

She might never play it again. She thought about home.

"So," Stacy was saying, "the first time I ever brought anyone out I was just amazed. She was so pathetically grateful for everything I did. Like no guy had ever figured out she had a clitoris."

Bree hummed the vocalist's melody as she settled into playing the right-hand part of the piece. A lot of violinists also played the piano, but she had never taken anything but the violin seriously. She murmured the words about the sweet island breeze that blew kisses to the waiting lover.

183

What if my wrist doesn't get better?

She didn't want to think about that. Not right now.

"I've never been anyone's first." Diana was pushing back from the table. "The two women before Pam were both experienced."

"Not that I didn't have to teach her plenty." Pam swatted Diana on the butt, then wrapped an arm around her waist as she tried to go by. "Besides, none of them knew she had a hankering for Jolt cola and donuts."

"I just said I did to keep you dropping by after school was out."

"You liked it and you know it."

Diana smoothed Pam's cheek. "Well, all those years you were slaving twenty-four seven, it seemed like the only time I could count on seeing you was when you brought me Jolt and donuts after school."

"Oh god, was I ever that young? I used to manage on two hours sleep for weeks."

"Tell me about it." Diana kissed Pam tenderly on the lips.

Stacy loudly cleared her throat. "The question is to you, Pam."

When she could, Pam said, "Oh. Okay, I've never brought anyone out either, so no story."

"What about you, Bree?" Stacy was stretching. Obviously it was break time. She drifted toward the piano.

"What was the question?" Bree still felt tipsy, but the feeling was easing.

"How you ever brought anyone out?"

"I guess so. Once." Jorie. Had she brought Jorie out? They'd brought each other out that first night. Then Jorie had gone back in. Maybe, technically, Jorie had brought Bree out. What a strange way to think about it.

"So?"

"What? I'm not going to kiss and tell."

Stacy leaned on the end of the piano. "All you did was kiss her? That doesn't count."

Mandy, with Carol lingering close behind her, flanked Stacy. "I have to say it's not something I want to do again."

Carol slapped her on the arm. "Oh I'm glad to hear that, honey."

"The sex was lousy. I did her and she went to sleep."

There was a burst of laughter. Bree could pick out which tones were Diana's.

Bree ended the piece. "I can understand that. I must say I prefer experience. Being someone's first, well, you know how that goes. She wanted everything and I got nothing." That wasn't a fair way to characterize what had happened that first night with Jorie. She felt a pang in her shoulder blades and knew it didn't feel right to joke about it.

"Play something else." Stacy joined Bree on the piano bench, her red leather pants whispering against Bree's linen slacks.

Stacy couldn't know that it hurt to think about music. "It's not my instrument."

"You're a one-instrument woman?"

"That's me."

"How...focused." Stacy put her hand on Bree's thigh.

Bree wanted to shift away, but there was no space left on the bench. She glanced over her shoulder, wondering if she could signal Diana to rescue her.

Diana was in an obviously ardent clinch with Pam. Pam's hands cupped her ass and their bodies seemed to Bree to be limned in a crimson glow. She felt a strange pang and had no words for it.

"Don't mind them," Stacy said. "They're as hot for each other as they were the day they met."

What did it matter to her? Diana was Pam's lover.

Pam was nice, but without Diana she'd be nothing.

The traitorous thought was enough to make her turn back to the piano. Pam had been so generous, but it wouldn't go away. Diana was a loving, compassionate woman, sexy, smart and adventurous.

Mandy's voice broke into her thoughts. "...So she's got her hand on my ass and says, what's the matter, are you shy?"

"Well, were you?" Stacy was egging Mandy on, to Carol's obvious discomfort.

"I had warned her, don't start with me, you might win!"

Bree fell completely out of the conversation as she played some of Jorie's Rachmaninoff. She rarely made herself think about Jorie, but she needed to now. She was suddenly so afraid. What if she could never play again?

"...The whole point of having an inner bitch is not having to make nice with anyone. I told him to fuck off."

"...I always thought a menstrual hut was a good idea, actually. The chocolate and ibuprofen would be free, and brought to you by the charred remains of all who crossed you on the first day of your period."

They drifted back to the game while Bree played. The memories of Jorie came and went, as did the fear that could paralyze her. She could pick out Diana's laugh easily. Something about her...was it as simple as her smile? She could sometimes flirt and not realize it. She was definitely spoken for, Bree reminded herself. There was Pam. And that little thing called love between them. Eighteen years, and look at all Pam had achieved with Diana's love. Pam had nothing to be afraid of.

"...Then she looked right at me and said four plus two equals seven for extremely large values of two. All I wanted was the butter."

Thinking about Diana was pointless. It was just being close to her, that was all. Pam had more appointments out of the house, while Diana and she had spent all that time walking together. If she'd spent all that time with Pam she might be finding Pam attractive instead. It was just being in close quarters.

She fought back the desire to cry. She wouldn't give in to a fear that could have no basis. She would find her violin's voice again. These feelings were all just the alcohol talking.

"...An arrogance of elitists. Sounds like that fund-raiser I went to last week."

"A bounty of boobs. Doesn't that sound right?"

"What about a pain of assholes?"

"I work with an asshole."

"A clench of clits?" There was a clamor of agreement.

"I've got one — a lick of lesbians!"

Bree had the sobering thought that maybe it was time to move out from under the same roof as Diana. It would be the prudent thing to do, given that Diana had such a kissable mouth and tender hands.

Stop, she told herself. Stop, now. What was she doing?

"Feeling better?" Diana was suddenly by the piano.

Bree couldn't look at her. "Much."

Diana had a half-full wineglass in her hand and she gave Bree a conspiratorial wink. "So what do you think about Stacy now?"

"She's very nice." Bree didn't mean to sound so coy. Her heart was pounding erratically.

"And she has designs on you."

"I think she has designs on everyone."

"Not always. She has standards. You're definitely her type."

"Am I?" Bree swallowed a mouthful of cheese and cleared her throat. "How so?"

"Attractive. Self-assured. She seems to prefer long hair and women who are..." Bree tried not to blush as Diana assessed her. "Shapely."

"Is that a euphemism for overweight? Because my hips just keep — "

"Not at all. Oh, don't tell me you're on a diet."

"Have I eaten like I'm on a diet?"

"Well, no. Pam is so picky about what she eats it's been nice to cook for someone who likes food."

Diana sounded a little annoyed with Pam, a note Bree hadn't heard before. "I like food. It obviously likes me because it hangs around."

"I think you're perfect. I mean that dress you wore for the concert would be pointless on someone with no hips. It looked terrific."

Taken aback by the sincerity of Diana's praise, Bree could only look at her. Was Diana flushed? "Thank you. I'll have all the chocolate I like, then."

Diana smiled, then looked at Bree through her lashes. "You know that's not what I meant. Anyway, Stacy and Pam were an anomaly, actually. Stacy almost never goes for the boyish type whereas in my limited experience I seem drawn to it."

See, Bree told herself. You're not even her type. "I'm not sure I have a preferred type." She tried not to think of Jorie's tall, slender body. Other lovers were shorter, wider, bigger, younger, older. None of them, except for Lila, resembled Jorie in any way. "I keep my options open."

"Then you might like Stacy. Pam says she can be flipped."

"Really?" Bree wondered what the heck that meant. She had missed out on some key lessons of lesbian lingo. What a surprise.

"Honey?" Pam was tossing a chip into the center of the table. "Are you in this hand?"

"Sure."

"I think I can play again. Well, at least I can watch."

After a couple more hands she joined in again, losing every time, but enjoying the company. When she lost her last chip she honored the house rules that allowed no one to lose more than five bucks in a night. "I'm done. But it was fun."

"I'll ante for you," Stacy offered. "I think I'm the one with most of your money."

"I'm fine," Bree told Stacy.

"But this could be your big hand. I know, penny chip for a kiss."

Diana laughed. "Bree could make more with kisses than she'll ever win at poker."

The general agreement left Bree blushing from the deserved aspersions cast on her poker abilities and the blatant compliment from Diana. "You guys are laying it on a little thick."

Stacy snorted. "I think we'd all pay a penny for a kiss from the — what did that reviewer say? The dynamic and ravishing Miss Starling — "

"Please," Bree said. "I hate that. It's supposed to be about the music, not my appearance."

"You could have fooled me." Carol tossed her penny chip into the center of the table. "That dress you wore for the performance was hardly an accident."

"That dress was a felony," Stacy said fervently.

Bree hoped the extent of her blush was somewhat hidden by her olive skin. "Okay, you got me. Dresses like that are free publicity. An image consultant chose it. I guess I can't deny that if it appeals to people I'll wear it. Though I'd play the same in sweats."

"And you like to wear it, right? What's more lovely than a beautiful femme?"

Pam interjected, "That wasn't subtle, even for you, Stacy."

"It's hard to be subtle in the presence of such overwhelming beauty."

Stacy winked again. "Come on, guys. A penny for a kiss. After all, Bree is out of work."

Carol looked outraged. "That really isn't a good idea, Stacy."

"Oh, I don't know," Mandy said. "We could all say we kissed someone famous."

Before she thought better of it, Bree admitted, "It's not like there isn't already a long list."

Pam choked on her beer while Stacy hooted. Diana looked surprised, then there was another flash of emotion Bree couldn't identify.

"I refuse to sell my kisses," Bree said firmly. "And that's that." She even managed a joke. "If I can't ever play again maybe I'll change my mind."

"Probably for the best." Diana's expression was hidden by her wineglass, but when she set it down Bree couldn't tear her gaze away. Her muddled brain didn't know how to process that look.

She felt naked, suddenly, because Diana was studying her far too closely.

A short time later Pam rose. "I think I'm ready to call it a night." She bent to kiss Diana tenderly behind the ear. Bree heard her murmur, "What about you, babe?"

She didn't know if anyone else noticed the shiver that flowed over Diana's body. Her nipples were suddenly noticeable through her blouse. "Sure, honey. Now's a good time."

"Love birds. You guys are impossible." Stacy stood up, and then everyone was getting up. "I'm surprised Bree gets any sleep the way you two go on."

"I'm not saying a word," Bree said. Her mind was still misfiring. Recalling Diana's voice in the night made her feel a little dizzy.

"You don't have to leave with us," Pam said. "I'm just a little tired."

"Right." Stacy's dry voice came from directly behind Bree.

Was Pam asking her to leave them alone for a while? It was the least she could do. Then she pictured Pam with Diana. For the first time the idea hurt.

Pam helped Diana with her coat and then caressed her shoulders.

Diana's hands closed over Pam's. There was no mistaking the gesture or the shine in Diana's eyes.

I want her to look at me like that.

Pam was in so many ways just an ordinary woman, but when Diana looked at her she became extraordinary. The love of a woman like that could make anyone feel special. It would fill her empty places, Bree thought. She wouldn't fear anything with the love of a woman like Diana.

She felt Stacy's arms around her waist. "Stay for a while longer."

"Okay," Bree said. Diana watched Stacy nuzzle her neck. She turned away with Pam. "I'd love to."

Carol and Mandy left shortly thereafter, and it was only a few minutes later, entwined on the sofa across from the poker table that buttons and zippers slid open after a languid series of kisses.

Stacy freed Bree's breasts with a quick sigh. "From the moment I saw you I have to admit I was dreaming about this."

Bree clasped Stacy's hands to her breasts. *Why am I doing this?* Bree didn't want to look too hard for answers. She didn't want Stacy, but she needed her.

"I'm afraid I'm going to hurt your wrist," Stacy said.

"I'll keep it out of the way."

"I really want you." Stacy bit her ear. "I've been known to forget to be gentle when I get in this mood."

Her shiver was unfeigned. "I'm not made of glass."

"Okay, baby. But tell me if I'm too rough. I just — you've been making me crazy."

Bree kissed Stacy firmly. The way she felt about Diana wasn't right. If Stacy could wipe some of that away, it would be better tomorrow. Back to nice and safe.

She felt like clay in Stacy's hands, molded, kneaded and shaped to fit. With her legs wrapped around Stacy, she remembered that night in L.A. with Jorie. Stacy was like Jorie had been then, direct, hard and in charge.

190

"You want me to fuck you, don't you, baby?"

"Yes." Bree wanted it now, anything to get Jorie out of her head, to replace that night in L.A. with any other memory.

Stacy stretched Bree's arms over her head, holding them down while she kissed Bree's mouth. "Keep them there."

With a shudder, Bree agreed. Stacy kissed her way down Bree's body, teasing with the suggestion of her tongue between Bree's legs. Then she came back for another kiss and Bree felt a sure hand parting her thighs. Stacy had one arm around her waist, while her hand explored Bree's wet. Pinned into place, Bree surged against Stacy's hand.

It's just sex, she told herself. It doesn't mean anything. She needed it to forget, and it felt good. It was as close to music as she could get. She yearned for her violin, and although it was temporary, no one understood how much it hurt to go day after day without it.

What if I never play again?

Stacy's fingers found soft and receptive places, teased her there, then took her more deeply. Bree kissed Stacy's throat, urging her to more, harder. She needed to forget so much.

Later, Stacy took her upstairs to her bedroom and the night was a blur of whispered questions and her needy answers. What more was there to do than say yes?

It wouldn't be dark for another two hours and Bree hoped, since it was summer, that the Forest Service hadn't closed Puʻuhonua o Honaunau yet. The winding road that led from the highway through coffee fields and past the Painted Church was traveled enough that Bree had to concentrate on driving.

She'd used Stacy to get Jorie out of her head, to help her resist Diana's unconscious allure.

It hadn't worked.

Nothing had ever worked. There was no way to forget anything, to get some peace from her mistakes, to stop hurting other people because she was hurting so much.

She didn't yet think about why she was going to a place of refuge. She knew that Aunt Lani wasn't there. Did Aunt Lani know now about that night with Stacy? Could she see that Bree had known there was no such thing as just sex, but had tried to have it anyway?

She just wanted to stop thinking, to stop reliving every tormented moment. She took a pain pill finally, because her wrist screamed at her whenever she turned the wheel. A short while later she took another. And then another.

CHAPTER ELEVEN

"I thought you grew up in Hawaii!"

"I did." Bree wheeled around the next corner, accelerated hard and passed two slower-moving vans.

Diana clutched the dashboard. "You didn't learn to drive like this in Hawaii."

"No. I learned one way in Hawaii and another way in Beijing on an exchange program. It helps to have a car with guts." Diana's Saab was a pleasure to handle.

"I am so impressed. One-handed you're a better driver than I am with both. Next right." Diana leaned into the turn. "If you do other things the way you drive, Stacy had a fun night."

Bree hoped her laugh sounded lighthearted. "You'd have to ask her."

"Maybe I will. I can't thank you enough for doing this. I'd have never made it otherwise. I can't believe I double-booked myself."

"It's my pleasure. It's the least I can do."

Bree screeched to a halt in front of the school. Diana was already opening the door. "Meet you back here in fifty minutes, okay?"

"Thank you," Diana called over her shoulder. She ran lightly across the central playground, in spite of the large case of materials she carried.

Bree would have liked to follow Diana to class and watch her explaining color and light to six-year-olds, but the urban school had no parking at all in the small lot. She couldn't imagine the enormous patience it must take to teach small children while helping them have fun. Diana was devoted to her teaching, though, and Pam's Internet stock brokerage firm allowed Diana to freelance as an art teacher, which hardly compensated for more than her materials.

She was lucky with the parking gods two blocks over and walked up the street to the ubiquitous Internet café. Another reason to live in San Francisco: she'd yet to have a bad cup of coffee. Bree acquired a simple espresso and used the time to check her e-mail as she sipped. After forty minutes she acquired Diana's preferred double-shot mocha, iced, added chocolate sprinkles and a packet of Equal and headed back to the school.

"This is great, thank you. God, what a day." Diana drank deeply from the frothy concoction. "I will be so glad when Trinity is back from her trip. It's nice that college students will work for credit and commute passes, but when it comes to living up to the schedule you get what you pay for."

Bree laughed. "It almost sounded like you were going say 'kids today, the world is coming to an end.'"

"Do you ever look at young people and ask yourself if you were ever that young?"

"It does seem hard to believe." Bree thought about the roller rink, the hip huggers, Marcia Brady hair and thinking that pop music had reached its badass pinnacle with "Smokin' in the Boys Room." She found herself thinking about Jorie skating to "Something in the Way

She Moves." "I know I was never that tragically hip. I was hardly bitchin'."

"I would have liked to know you then," Diana said, after she stopped laughing. "Bitchin' or not."

"God, I was dull. I don't think you'd have liked me. Nobody did. Not really." She hadn't meant that to sound so hurt.

"Well, I suppose a lot of kids wouldn't think they could compete with your gift. And you did have a gift that drove you."

Had Jorie felt she couldn't compete? Duh, she thought. Of course she did. "Well that's ironic, I guess. As kids, nobody wanted to compete with the violin. I've had a few lovers who wanted to, um...distract me while I was playing."

"And did they?"

"I let them."

"Of course you did." Diana closed her eyes and took a deep, relaxing breath. "You permitted it. They didn't actually come between you and your violin."

Bree studied Diana's profile, then cracked what she hoped was a cocky grin. "I never tried that position. I wouldn't want the violin to get damaged."

"Please. You are wicked."

Bree turned into the driveway. "Destination reached, madam."

"Thank you, James." Diana dug her supply cases out of the trunk. "I don't know what I'd do without you."

She found the money to give the ranger for the entrance fee into the park. She took another pill at the water fountain, then walked in her bare feet through the tall, thatched houses representing the Hawaiian way of life before Captain Cook found the islands. The low cots of the chief and royal family were covered with beautiful samples of *kapa* weaving.

She'd seen it all before. She crossed the white sand to the beach, skirting the water to get to the sanctuary where defeated warriors came to recover. It was late enough in the day that tourists were few.

She gazed out at the sea, while the rising *makani* whipped her hair around her shoulders. *Aunt Lani*, where are you?

Her shoulder blades were cold. The sanctuary had nothing to tell her.

Her footsteps traced the Forest Service path among the high palms to the wall that separated the beauty and plenty of the village and sheltered beach from a rough area of rocks with a battered stretch of sand and little shade. It was the place *Makawela* were sent, the outcasts, those who violated *kapu*.

The place frightened her. There were no ghosts here, she told herself. There were only ancestors to worry about.

She staggered a little as the latest pain pill made her want to go limp, and retraced her steps to the beach with difficulty. She sat down in the sand and let the evening sun beat across her face and shoulders. She'd be sunburned before too long, but she no longer cared.

When she waded into the water, past the signs that prohibited swimming, she felt a profound sense of conclusion. She forgot about the contract she had signed with Dr. Sheridan not to do this. The cooling comfort of the ocean closed over her shoulders.

This was the only way to stop remembering.

When Diana made a major proposal to San Francisco public school administrators, wanting them to hire more art students for nominal fees to teach basic concepts of color and art design in grade schools, Bree proofread all her materials. She pretended to be the audience as Diana rehearsed. Pam was available to sit in on the last one, all the while saying she knew Diana would be fine.

Bree surprised Diana after the presentation with a bouquet of flowers and lunch at her favorite Nicaraguan restaurant in the Mission.

When Pam went out of town for several days, Bree made sure Diana's hot water was on in the morning for her tea, and she occupied their evenings with old movies Diana had mentioned liking as a child. Diana liked Coke floats, too.

One night Diana confessed to having not a clue about modern

music, so Bree steeled herself to listen to what she couldn't play, and interpreted a short Stockhausen piece for her. She described and hummed the choices the musician was given within the piece, allowing for it to always be different. Diana's questions were insightful and the following week they had another music lesson and the week after another. They were conversations Bree never thought she could have had with Jorie, not that she had ever tried.

Pam's days were more routine; she either commuted down to Silicon Valley or she didn't. Diana had a more varied schedule and sometimes she needed a little TLC. You have the time, Bree told herself, and being there for her is repayment for the many meals she cooks for you.

A sunny afternoon in early October, Bree offered to help Diana in the kitchen. "I can't use the knives, but I'm not a complete klutz."

"Your Aunt Lani sounds like a multi-talented woman. Here, you can wash the veggies for the curry."

Bree happily dumped the potatoes and carrots into the sink. "She's really amazing. I read statistics about how so many kids are just not wanted, and I still can't believe she took me in, just because she grew up with my mother."

She reached up to turn off the water and found Diana pushing the handle over to hot. Their fingertips brushed and Diana pulled her hand back.

"I'd like to meet her some day." Diana crossed the room to the pantry while Bree adjusted the water temperature.

"I've been thinking about sending her a computer, something all set up with Internet and e-mail. Penny has one but it's in her room and I bet Aunt Lani would use one if she thought it wasn't getting in Penny's way."

"I bet Pam would help. She's all over that stuff."

"Aren't there supposed to be green beans?"

"Oh, they're still in the fridge."

Bree headed left around the center island to the refrigerator. Diana emerged from the pantry, nearly bumping into Bree. She backed up and went the other way round the island.

Bree let the air from the refrigerator cool her hot cheeks. The apron wrapped tightly around Diana's waist made the fullness of her breasts more pronounced.

She snapped beans and tried to talk about home as naturally as she could, fighting the fantasies that Diana roused in her. Nothing on under the apron...that would do for a start. She pushed the delectable image away. "Want some coffee?"

"Sure, thanks."

Bree set the full cup down on the counter next to where Diana was kneading some sort of dough. She turned away while her fingers had still not completely let go of the handle and it tipped, sloshing coffee onto the counter. It puddled and rushed toward the pristine white dough.

"What an idiot!" Bree grabbed the roll of paper towels and blotted up the racing coffee, then realized that some was dripping off the counter onto the floor. She dropped to her knees to sop it up. "There, I think that's all..."

She glanced up at Diana and could not even breathe in.

Diana was a married woman and Bree didn't know much about relationships, but Diana had no business looking down at her that way. Bree liked it, all the gods, she wanted Diana to go on looking at her like that.

Diana stepped back and then turned to the pantry. Bree got up, her head swimming.

Her back to Bree, Diana said, "My hands are floury and I need roses. I mean rosemary."

Bree went the long way around the kitchen island to fetch it. She set it on the counter, standing close enough to smell Diana's perfume.

"I think you've helped all you can." Diana glanced at Bree, then gave her attention to the mixture she was kneading between her hands.

The glance had been long enough for Bree to realize that Diana's smile didn't reach her eyes. She watched the pulse beating below Diana's ear, then forced herself to take one step back, then another.

"I'll go for a walk then."

"Sounds good."

"Yeah."

"Okay."

Bree reached the top of the first hill and used her cell phone to make a date with Stacy.

"Everyone should go to one once." Pam's emphatic pronouncement brought a sleepy smile to Bree's face.

Morning coffee was slowly bringing her to life, but Pam's enthusiasm for her most loved activity — after Diana, she was always quick to say — was infectious. "Would I get to have a ride?"

"You bet. It makes you feel like a kid, even from the ground."

"The balloons," Diana added, "they're like sky jewelry. When the sun is finally all the way up it's like someone hung hundreds and hundreds of earrings in all that blue."

Bree frowned. "What do you mean, when the sun is finally all the way up?"

"We light up before dawn. It's the best time to rise. It takes less hot air."

"And you do this for eight or nine days in a row?"

Pam was bouncing with enthusiasm. "Sure. Plus getting there is a three-day bus ride each way with all our gear. Roadside diners, loud music, trying to pee in a moving vehicle — all the fun stuff. Wait until you see the rig. I get volunteers for chase crew. The company runs a sales competition and the winners get a ballooning holiday. The company kicks in a little, but I pay for most of it. Much as I owe to the company and stock market, I don't want their name on my balloon."

"But you make the chase crew work." Diana sipped her coffee. "Come with us," she said to Bree. "It's an unbelievable amount of fun."

Bree found herself agreeing, helpless to resist. Diana insisted. Pam insisted. It *did* sound like fun, but didn't Diana worry if it was safe to travel in close quarters like that? Where would Bree run if she found herself completely flustered by Diana the way she had been in the kitchen?

She knew she was playing with fire, but every time she thought of leaving she felt a flash from Diana that kept her there.

Pam didn't seem to notice. It seemed both a reason not to worry and a justification. On the one hand, that Pam wasn't alarmed meant there was nothing to worry about. On the other, what kind of lover was Pam that she didn't notice Diana giving another woman signals?

But were they signals? Couldn't they just be the looks of a well-known friend? It wasn't as if Bree would know the difference. Lovers she'd had, but friends were virtually unknown.

The Balloon Bullet was a converted bus sporting the most fabulous custom paint job Bree had ever seen, depicting Pam's balloon over a fantastic landscape of desert and rainforest. The back bore the slogan, "Ballooning isn't a matter of life and death. It's far more important than that."

The inside was sumptuous, with tables and couches designed to make long hours comfortable. A large refrigerator sported every conceivable non-alcoholic drink and a multitude of snacks. Pam and two volunteers took turns driving and Bree was amazed at how quickly the California landscape flew by.

By night they were almost to Arizona and everyone enjoyed a frolic in the motel's indoor pool. Bree wasn't sure she was actually going to swim until she saw Diana in a bikini. She jumped in the water, afraid her expression would give her away.

A slow but steady one-armed backstroke took her diagonally across the pool. You're acting like a lovesick puppy, she chided herself. She's a married woman. Pam's your friend. You have to stop. You will stop.

She tired quickly and had to give it a rest. "It's the altitude," she muttered to Pam.

"If you say so," Pam teased. She handed Bree a canned soda. "I wouldn't have said you had chicken arms."

"I do not!" Bree assumed a weightlifters pose and extended her right arm. "Feel that."

Pam squeezed, hard. "Very nice."

"I should think so. I do keep up the exercises. If I don't it'll all be gone if I play again."

"If?" Pam opened her mouth, but Bree interrupted.

"When. I meant when of course."

Looking concerned, Pam glanced at Bree's wrist. "They gave you a good prognosis, right?"

"Yes, of course. I'll be fine." She didn't know why it was important for Pam not to know how worried she was inside.

"I really hope you are. I know you'll leave us at some point, but I'll miss you."

Was that feeling guilt? Whatever it was, it churned her stomach into a queasy mass.

A wolf whistle distracted Pam and Bree was spared an answer. She turned to see Diana climbing the pool steps, her body streaming water from every curve. Rising from the sea, Bree thought.

"Knock it off." Pam's sharp tone stopped Bree from even attempting to mimic the appreciative whistle.

The whistle had come from one of three men on the other side of the pool. They were all feigning innocence.

"I appreciate the compliment at my age." Diana dropped onto the lounger in front of Pam. "Nobody meant anything."

"I hope not." Pam pulled Diana back into her arms. "That's the trouble with leaving the Bay Area. It's a different world out here. I like a city where the men only whistle at other men."

"We're safe, baby." Diana snuggled her wet hair into Pam's chest. "I'm nothing but safe with you."

Bree could only think that without seeming the least bit weak or helpless, Diana could make a woman feel like a supreme being. With Diana wrapped in her arms Pam's eyes closed almost as if she would cry for happiness.

Her room was next to theirs and in the night Bree was tortured with the rising and falling music of Diana's passion.

They rolled into Albuquerque at dusk the third day. Bree was exhausted from her struggle to always be where Diana wasn't. If Diana went forward, Bree moved to the rear. If Diana sat on the left couch, Bree found a reason to move to the kitchen area.

In spite of her efforts, they were standing too close together when a bump jostled them all nearly off their feet. Bree caught herself on the counter, sparing her bad hand just in time, and found Diana stumbling into her side. It was pure instinct to steady Diana by throwing an arm around her waist.

"Okay?" Bree could have cried out for how pliant Diana seemed against her.

"Yes." Diana didn't move.

"Sure?" Let her go, Bree told herself. Pam could look back. She couldn't make her arm obey her.

Diana nodded and looked away, leaving Bree to stare at the graceful throat. Her chest seemed to heave, then she stepped back abruptly, fighting the pressure of Bree's arm. Her voice was quieter than a whisper, but Bree still heard her over the engine and creaking cupboards. "Please."

Bree let her go. She did not know how many times she would be able to do that without the struggle showing in her face.

They checked into a hotel arranged nearly a year in advance. The following morning, at five a.m., Bree joined the other groggy members of the party — only Pam seemed thoroughly awake — for the first ascension.

The balloon was withdrawn from an impossibly tiny storage case. Diana and Pam directed everyone in the careful unfolding process to spread it on the soft grass of the fiesta field. A large industrial fan began the job of pumping cold air into the flat balloon.

Pam's balloon was a rainbow pattern of colors draped over black. Once it was more than half inflated with cold air, Pam began firing the propane burners to heat it inside. Bree was astonished when it began to rise off the ground. All around her balloons in brilliant hues and outrageous shapes were lifting from the ground to wave tautly over their baskets. It seemed like no time until Pam's was straining the tiedowns.

Whistles chirped in the morning air as the balloons rose in waves, timed by black-and-white-clad officials everyone called zebras. Their uniformed backs bore the slogan, "Get it up, get it hot, get it out of here."

Two volunteers — one the sales champ — went up with Pam, who kept in touch via radio. In less than an hour hundreds of balloons had lifted, and it was exactly how Diana had described it. Brightly colored jewels hung in the sky everywhere. Cows, pigs, an ATM machine, a carousel, Cinderella's castle, even an unlikely cluster of chili peppers all floated above her.

Looking at it *did* make Bree feel like a kid again, as astonished as she had been by that first waterfall. She rarely had time in her life to simply stand still and let beauty come to her. She realized then that part of what she felt for Diana was like that. Beauty coming into life.

"Time to chase," Diana announced. They all piled into the rented truck, and Bree found herself in the cab squished next to Diana, who drove with abandon to catch up to Pam. The city of Albuquerque was used to the fiesta balloonists landing in their backyards, fields, trailer parks and even in the Rio Grande.

"It's called a Splash and Dash," Diana explained. "You get real low and your passengers jump out. Sometimes the balloon doesn't always rise afterward. Let me tell you, it takes forever to dry out the inside of a balloon."

Bree bounced against Diana and tried to ignore the fact that to make more room in the front for Bree and the rather burly volunteer, Diana had extended her arm along the back of the seat.

Pam radioed that she was losing altitude and couldn't find an updraft. She gave her navigational readings and Diana had Bree punch them into a map program that pinpointed Pam's position. They arrived at the open field about two minutes before Pam landed. Everyone whooped as she bounced, then used their combined weight to stop the basket so that the balloon would neatly fall beyond it.

"What a great flight," Pam exclaimed. "You have to come up tomorrow, babe."

Diana kissed Pam thoroughly. "I'm always glad when you come down safely."

Diana turned away, but Pam grabbed her. "For that kind of greeting, I always will." Their kiss made Bree lower her gaze. Once she had found it private, something not for her eyes. But now it was a different emotion, an unpleasant one. It felt as if all Pam ever saw in Diana was sex.

Her shoulder blades itched, but Bree had grown more adept at ignoring the whisperings of her ancestors. Of course she was different from Pam. She saw all of Diana, especially her quick mind and vivacious personality. Pam hardly seemed to deserve such an incredible woman.

The pangs of disloyalty which thoughts like that had first caused were getting more faint as each day went by.

The pattern of days was pleasant once Bree resigned herself to getting up so early. She had to explain to the room service people what a double-shot espresso really was, but once they got that right getting up was easier. The people in Albuquerque were as friendly as Bree had ever experienced as a traveler. It was hardly cosmopolitan, but something about the city was charming.

Her first ride in the balloon was astounding. There was only the sound of the wind and the occasional blast from the burners. Diana pulled Bree to her side of the basket, one arm around her waist.

"I love this view," she said over the snapping wind. "I could live here if they learned to make decent coffee." Her thoughts echoed Bree's so closely that she squeezed Diana back. Abruptly she realized she wanted to kiss her, badly. Pam was right behind them.

Diana moved away and didn't look at Bree again for a while. Pam demonstrated the Albuquerque "box" which drew the balloonists here, and to Bree's amazement for the next two hours, by shifting up and down in altitude, they never went more than a quarter-mile from the spot where they had lifted.

They were all out of sorts when it rained, grounding everyone the next day. They explored museums and a craft market. Diana liked metal sculpture, but came running to find Bree when she stumbled onto a booth of beautiful handwoven fabrics.

"Wouldn't your aunt like some of these?"

Bree gave her a warm smile. "Definitely, thank you! That was so thoughtful of you." She bought a number of different fabrics in small quantities and arranged to have them sent.

By the end of the day, Pam admitted she was coming down with a cold.

"If I get a lot of rest maybe I'll kick it early." Pam morosely regarded her mostly uneaten dinner.

"You really should." Diana stroked Pam's hair. "If it gets into your sinuses and ears you can't fly."

"Yeah. Okay. Drugs and sleep. You don't have to babysit me. Why don't you and Bree go to a movie or something?"

Diana hesitated. Over Pam's head she gave Bree a look that was enigmatic but nevertheless very unsettling. "Are you sure?"

Pam nuzzled her head into Diana's shoulder. "Just put me to bed and go have fun."

Bree met up with Diana a short while later in the hotel lobby. "Do you want to see a movie?"

Bree shrugged. "I wouldn't mind just going to a bar and having a drink." She grinned. "I haven't needed anything stronger than ibuprofen for weeks now and a nice scotch sounds lovely. An early night would do me good, too."

"Okay. Well, we can do that here, no need to drive out. I'm afraid that if the rain doesn't let up the field will be too wet. At least Pam will have another day to get better. It's such a drag."

They settled into a booth away from a cluster of people excitedly watching a baseball game on the big TV. To Bree's surprise Diana ordered a bourbon — she'd never seen Diana indulge in anything stronger than wine.

They clinked their glasses and sipped in silence.

"I've been meaning to tell you." Bree felt awkward. "But I'm not exactly gifted with words."

"I hadn't noticed." Diana swirled the amber liquid in the heavy crystal glass.

"I feel helpless without my violin. Anyway, I so appreciate your hospitality and generosity. You guys have been just wonderful to me."

"It's our pleasure, Bree. You're so much fun to be around." Diana was giving the bourbon whirlpool all of her attention.

"Really? I feel like a shark with a sore nose most of the time."

Diana laughed and finally looked up. "That's what I mean. You can be so whimsical sometimes."

"It's just a phrase from home."

"Tell me about the island of Hawaii. Pam and I have been to Oahu and Honolulu."

Bree sat up with the air of having great secrets to tell. "Then you haven't seen the most beautiful island of all, the big one. The others have their strong points, but Hawaii is so varied. There's even an entire cowboy culture in the high valleys where cattle are raised. The song of the paniolo is very similar to what I imagine is a cowboy's music in these parts." She finished her drink as she described the things she loved about the island, and finished a second while she was still talking.

Diana kept up with her in drinks while asking questions. Bree found herself describing Aunt Lani and Jorie as a girl, the way that Dee had sold her violin and Aunt Lani had helped her find her voice again.

"It must be killing you." Diana's speech was slightly slurred. "To be without it."

Tears abruptly stung in her eyes. Maybe Diana did understand, a little. "It does hurt when I think about it. There's a chance that it might not be better after all this waiting." She hadn't wanted Pam to know, but she could bear Diana knowing. But talking about it might make it true.

"Don't think about that," Diana said quickly. "You'll face that if you have to, but meantime, don't borrow trouble."

"I was only with Stacy because I was lonely," Bree blurted out.

If Diana thought it was a strange thing to say she didn't look it. Instead she stared into her glass again. "I can understand that. Besides, it's not like you're in a relationship and neither is she. Nobody gets hurt."

"I envy you and Pam. I've never been able to find that with anyone."

Diana's expression softened and she looked up. "She's pretty wonderful, isn't she? She's so modest, but that company would have never amounted to anything without her. I loved teaching, you know, but we both admit that not having to work has changed our lives completely. We can obsess about each other and things we love to do, like being here."

What couldn't someone do with a woman like Diana to love her? Bree returned to that thought again and again. Diana was so generous, so loving. Diana would make all things possible. Bad things wouldn't happen with a woman like Diana to help.

They talked about any topic that came to mind, and Bree learned about Diana's childhood in the San Fernando Valley where she'd met Pam in college.

"You must have been a great teacher."

"I still am, thank you." Diana signaled for another drink. "I loved classroom teaching, but sometimes it was incredibly frustrating — budgets and cutbacks and lack of materials. Teaching experiential art for grade schools at a price they can afford is like a dream come true. All the fun of teaching and none of the politics."

It was after eleven when Bree realized how tired she was. Tired and drunk. The four scotches had gone to her head. "We should get some sleep," she finally suggested, though sleepy as she was, she could have talked all night.

They were both unsteady on the way to the elevator. Bree was gratified to make it to her room, the nearest, without stumbling. "Thanks for the talk. It was better than a movie."

"You're welcome. Oh — mmm, I meant to look outside before we left downstairs. If it's still raining I'm calling off the lift."

"Come on in." Bree unlocked her door and Diana followed her inside. She opened the curtains to see that drops were still sheeting down the glass. "I think we're all sleeping in."

"Well, that's something. Can I use your phone?"

Bree went to the bathroom while Diana left messages for the chase crew to sleep in. They'd all meet for a late breakfast at ten in the hotel coffee shop.

"Thanks, I didn't want to wake up Pam, who'd fuss. I can safely tell her it's a done deal. Can I use the bathroom?"

While Diana was in the bathroom, Bree got into a sleep shirt and flannel boxers. Diana had seen them before but never in Bree's bedroom.

Diana noticed immediately. "You're ready for bed."

"Yes, I am." Bree didn't move from next to the bed. She wanted to say more. She wanted the words to find life.

Diana gazed at her for a long, long minute. "Then I'll go."

Bree hurried to get the door for her.

For the space of a heartbeat Diana didn't move when the door was open.

If she'd left then Bree might never have stayed with them through Christmas, but instead, for an instant, Diana leaned toward her, her eyes troubled.

Bree closed the distance, so close she could feel the warmth of Diana's quickly exhaled breath on her neck. Diana didn't back away. Another heartbeat, then Bree kissed Diana gently on the lips.

Diana reacted as if stung. "I don't — I'm drunk, Bree."

"So am I. I'm sorry — that was inappropriate. It was just the alcohol talking."

"Okay." Diana slipped into the corridor. Bree watched her make her way to the next door.

Diana glanced back then, and that brief look made Bree tremble. How married could Diana be if she looked at another woman that way?

When Pam asked if she wanted to stay through the holidays, Bree said yes.

Winter arrived slowly in San Francisco, but when it did show up, it was with a lashing rainstorm that downed power lines and blew over trees. Diana was on foot to a class she was teaching in the far flung Richmond district. Bree persevered the traffic and weather to arrive at the right time to pick Diana up. She even had a hot double shot mocha waiting.

When Diana had a bad headcold, Bree undertook the cooking with mixed results. She tried. The fish stew even turned out, though she'd had to call Aunt Lani six times for help.

Pam took off on a two-hundred-mile bicycle ride for charity, and Bree kept Diana company at the check points.

Pam helped Bree buy and configure a cute little computer to send to Aunt Lani, Internet-ready and loaded with a DSL modem. Their first e-mail was a delight for both of them. Diana was the one who was there to share the moment with a quick hug. Like all their contact, it went on too long and so Bree didn't leave. She knew she should, but she couldn't.

It was Pam's idea to go the mountains for Christmas.

Was it fate's intervention that kept her behind for two days, sending Bree and Diana to the cabin ahead of her? Maybe, Bree thought, but what kind of lover was Pam that she let business keep her from holiday plans that Diana had accepted with such eagerness?

If fate had been kind, Aunt Lani would have accepted Pam and Diana's sincere invitation to spend the holidays with them as well. But she wouldn't fly and that was that.

Fate wanted Bree to be alone with Diana, Bree told herself. It was meant to be. She ignored any burning in her shoulder blades as she considered what she might say and might do. Her ancestors were ignorant island dwellers who didn't understand Bree's life. She woke every morning with her arms around her pillow, wishing it were Diana.

She could make someone fall in love with her. She was so tired of being good. She could make Jorie love her. No — she pushed that thought away as the winter landscape of the rugged Sierra Nevada swept by.

This wasn't about Jorie. It wasn't about her secret worry about her wrist still hurting after all this time. It was about Diana and finally being in control of who and how she loved.

They stopped for groceries before they picked up the key to the cabin, then crunched through the snow laden with bags and suitcases. Bree wasn't as much help as Diana, so she settled for unpacking groceries.

"Which bedroom do you want?"

"You guys should have the one with the private bath. For that special couple time."

Diana flushed. "We can do that anywhere."

"I don't doubt it." Bree gave her a teasing glance.

Diana disappeared into the master bedroom. "Okay, we'll take this one. If you're sure you don't mind."

"Makes sense to me. I think you should have left me at home, though. Really, you must be tired of me hanging around."

"Don't be ridiculous." Diana still looked flushed when she reappeared. "I know that eventually you're going to have to go and I'll — I'll miss you."

Telling herself to tread gently, because Diana looked like a deer that would run at any moment, Bree said softly, "I didn't know you cared."

"Of course we do." Diana opened the refrigerator, then closed it, still empty-handed. "You're a special person, Bree. I can't believe that no woman out there hasn't managed to snag you. I should start setting you up with every single woman I know."

"They might be able to catch my body, but it's not often that anything else gets caught."

"Is that a warning?" Diana put her hands to her cheeks. "I can't believe I said that. Never mind. I can be a flirt sometimes."

Bree shifted so her back was to the counter and she could look directly into Diana's eyes. "I said that it's not often, but I didn't say it never happens. Sometimes...sometimes it does, even when I know it shouldn't."

"It shouldn't," Diana whispered. "It really shouldn't."

Bree nodded, trying to appear resigned. "I know. You're a charming, very sexy woman, but that's all I'm allowed to say. I probably shouldn't even say that. Just don't ever sell yourself short."

Diana was trembling. "Do I say thank you? I need some fresh air. I'll be back in a bit."

Bree watched Diana hurry down the steps to the driveway, then tread more carefully across the snow-crusted grass. It would be dark soon. She hoped she wasn't gone long.

Ma'ele'ele, her ancestors murmured. Wake up from your numbness, they urged her. *Lolelua*, unstable, fickle. *'Epa* they added, traitor. Bree turned them away. They couldn't possibly understand how she yearned for someone who loved her, who needed her. She needed Diana's strength, her vitality. Diana could protect her from anything.

Her wrist throbbed slightly from the strain of carrying even the lightest weight grocery bags. It might never be better, she reminded herself. She needed Diana.

Kolohe, evil. Love couldn't be evil, Bree protested. If Diana didn't love her she would say no, always. If Diana really loved Pam she would never be tempted. *Haʻihaʻi*, they called her, a pursuer of what didn't wish to be caught.

She heard bars from the turtle lullaby, very faintly, and told herself it was just an errant memory. After all these years her mother's voice was lost, and it had nothing to tell her anyway. Her ancestors' voices rose again.

Kolohe, they warned. *Kolohe*.

She'd made Diana's favorite tea in the next little while, and explored the wood-burning stove, which was set with a ready-to-go fire. When the front door finally opened again, she was sitting on the pillows near the stove, sipping tea.

Diana stomped snow out of her boots, then shed them and her coat at the door.

"Make yourself some tea. The water is probably still hot."

A few minutes later, Diana joined her on the pillows. They sipped in silence, then she said, "We have to talk about it."

"About what?"

Diana gave her a narrow look. "You know. This isn't all in my head."

"Sorry." Bree put down her cup. "I can't help the way I feel."

"The things you say are nice to hear, but you have to stop. I don't play around, Bree."

"I know."

"Then why — why are you...why do you say things like you said earlier? Letting me know that you..."

"That I find you fascinating and desirable? You're incredibly sexy, Diana."

"I'd rather you didn't talk that way." She turned her head so Bree couldn't see her expression. "I know at first I flirted with you. I thought it was safe. I never expected...to feel like this. You have to stop."

"I know. But I'm too old to want to hold it in. You should know, but I don't expect anything from you."

"Don't you?"

"No. All the gods know I want you." Bree let her voice fall deep into her chest. "I know we would be good together."

"Please."

"I know you'll never say yes."

Diana was silent for so long that Bree reached over to brush her hair back over her shoulder. Diana leaned away from the touch, but not so far that the strands didn't brush over Bree's fingertips.

Her voice shaking, Diana finally said, "I didn't expect to feel this way either. I thought you were fun, then attractive, then...when I realized you were going with Stacy, I couldn't stop thinking about what you did with her. I love Pam. I love everything about her."

"That's it, then."

"That's it."

They made a simple dinner and ate largely in silence. They read by the fire as they often did in the evening, though Bree found it hard to absorb anything. She was aware of every movement Diana made.

They agreed to turn in early to be better rested for the morning. Diana planned to ski.

Remembering that Diana always sought out a glass of water before going to sleep, Bree lingered in the kitchen making a cup of herbal tea. Diana had seen the sleep shirt and boxers so many times it wasn't as if they'd be alluring.

Diana appeared shortly thereafter. She filled a glass and headed back toward the master bedroom. "See you in the morning."

"Diana."

She turned. Bree looked at her with a faint smile. "Nothing. Pleasant dreams."

She was closing the door when Bree said more loudly, "You don't have to lock the door."

Diana didn't look back as she said, "It never crossed my mind." She closed the door.

Bree couldn't sleep. Her ancestors wouldn't leave her alone now, and they crowded into her drowsy mind. She was allowed to love someone, she told them angrily. Especially if that person loved her back, and Diana did.

After several hours of tossing and turning, she decided on a glass of milk. She was surprised to see Diana huddled near a revived fire.

Diana's back stiffened as Bree approached. "I'm okay. I couldn't sleep."

"Neither could I. Would you like anything?"

"No, I'm fine."

Bree heard a sniff. "You're not okay."

"I am. I'm just..."

Bree sank down on the pillow next to Diana, careful not to touch her. "Darling, I'm so sorry. I don't mean to upset you."

Diana raised her tear-streaked face toward her and for one final moment, Bree knew she could have pulled away and left Diana in peace. "I've never even been tempted, Bree, never before. There's only been Pam. Everything has always been Pam for me. She's the only person I've ever wanted."

"Until me." Bree leaned toward Diana, her lips parted.

A gasped "Yes" was enough. Bree did not hear that Diana's moan was also filled with pain. She didn't see the tears in Diana's eyes. All she cared about was that kiss and the knowledge that Diana wanted her.

A woman like this could make her life complete, she thought. If the worst...if she couldn't...Diana would be there.

The heat between her shoulder blades faded as she pulled Diana more firmly into her arms. She had Yes and there was no stopping now.

Diana's hands fluttered along Bree's back, coming to a rest finally in Bree's hair. Bree's fingers tightened their grip and she was no longer kissing Diana, she was being kissed. She was wanted for what she was: a desirable woman, something of sufficient value that Diana would give up...

"Bree, stop, please."

She squashed that thought as she pushed Diana gently down on the pillows. "I can't bear this. Don't kiss me and then tell me to stop."

"I can't believe the way you make me feel." Diana cupped Bree's jaw and slowly drew her head down. "I have no right to do this."

"It's just about tonight. I won't ask for more. I know — you have a life. I have a life. I'll go back to mine."

"Does it work that way?" Diana's fingers were warm on Bree's cheek. "I don't think — a night won't be enough, god help me. Kiss me."

Bree kissed her again, losing herself in the welcome of Diana's mouth. Diana moved under her with a sensual abandon that negated the half-sobs that escaped her. Firelight danced across her face, then her bare breasts.

"I've wanted you so much," Bree whispered. "When I realized you might...I couldn't believe you could care for me."

"I do." Diana's hands were in Bree's hair. "I didn't know how much until I saw you with Stacy. Then I couldn't stop thinking about you and her. I know what she's like — Pam told me that much."

"I was trying to forget about you," Bree admitted. With a hiss of indrawn breath she grazed her teeth over one full nipple. "About this."

"Oh...please."

Was Diana asking her to stop? Maybe she was. But her body moved and Bree took Diana's nipple into her mouth, holding it gently between her teeth. Diana's fingers were stroking Bree's scalp with increasing pressure. Her thin robe was falling open even more, and Bree could hardly breathe.

"God, you are so beautiful." She had thought she could find more words, but there weren't any. Diana was music, could be her music, a different kind of instrument to tune and learn.

She kissed Diana's thighs and slowly stroked through her with a gentle finger. She was wanted, and then she tasted. Diana was pure light, a clasping eagerness, a crying spiral of want.

Her mouth was full of Diana and her life was complete. She had Diana's love. Diana surged against her, calling her name, and Bree answered her need, sliding into her and listening carefully to the song of Diana's response. She had done this so many times in her mind, and she'd been right about what Diana craved.

Her own breathing was still ragged in her ears when she felt Diana's hands pulling her boxers down. She rolled over and Diana was on top of her, parting her legs with her knees.

"I've wanted this," she said hoarsely. "I don't care about tomorrow."

Her hand touched Bree, who couldn't hold back her moan. "Please," she pleaded, as Diana had. "I love you."

She believed it when she said it. She needed Diana to believe it, too.

"I love you, Bree." Diana's voice broke and her touch grew more firm. "I can't believe this is happening. God help me."

Bree reached down to take Diana's hand in her own. She shaped it, then guided Diana's fingers into her. "Please, like that."

Diana made a noise that Bree couldn't interpret and then she was hard inside of Bree, her mouth finding Bree's breasts. "I don't believe this..."

Bree lifted her hips and curled upward enough to kiss Diana's mouth. The kiss broke when the pleasure of Diana's fingers was too much to stand, too fevered to deny. She wrapped her good arm around Diana's neck and held on, answering Diana's fingers, then her mouth, with every response she could give.

They moved to Bree's bedroom and rolled through the dark, restraint fading into the past.

CHAPTER TWELVE

"It's so easy to hold you," Diana had murmured, curled in Bree's arms.

It was easy to let the cool ocean water claim her. Bree ignored the shooting pain in her wrist as she swam toward the open sea. It was hard to breathe over the pain, but she didn't care about breathing now. She was sleepy.

"It's so easy." Diana rolled over in Bree's arms. "I wish time could stand still."

"It doesn't work that way." Bree kissed her softly. She had made her dreams and reality the same. She could stay here for the rest of her life. "Let's spend all day in bed."

"That sounds like a good idea." Diana's body was supple against Bree.

"I love you," Bree whispered. She was covered in Diana's scent, and her mouth was bruised from the kisses that had lasted most of the night. Diana was as sensual as Bree had thought she would be. The night had been full of love and tenderness, ferocity and eagerness. She coiled her hand in Diana's hair, loving the sensation of it.

"I don't know what it means. I — love you, Bree. You make parts of me I didn't know existed come alive."

"No one has ever made me feel the way you do." Bree's mouth sought the hollow of Diana's throat. Complete...she was complete now.

"When Pam gets here we'll tell her the truth."

There was an expectant quiet after Diana's words. She had made a statement, but it was a question, too. It needed an answer.

The answer was poised on Bree's lips. She tried to speak. Yes, fine, of course, okay — anything. But the words would not come.

I love her, Bree thought. I love this woman. I won't need...anything else now. I love her.

She heard the warning of violas, then. She almost turned her head to listen. The violin always gave the obvious theme, she knew that, so it was usually left to the violas to remind the ear that the theme wasn't always what it seemed.

There was a rattling of timpani, and sweep of harp.

I love this woman, Bree told herself again. And with the crashing cacophony of truth, the music she'd been ignoring because it hurt too much to listen and not play, that music told her she was lying to herself.

Jorie...no, she thought. Not Jorie. Not now. I can't think about her now. Diana erases Jorie forever. She has to. I can have Diana again, she told herself vehemently, right now, the way I never had Jorie the same way twice. I can kiss Diana and she will say she loves me again, the way Jorie never said it. She didn't need Jorie's love now.

All the gods, Bree thought. All the gods, what have I done?

"Bree?"

"I'm sorry...I was...my wrist..." Another lie. Her heart pounded in her ears.

"Did it get strained? I'd never forgive myself." Diana sat up, the sheets pooling around her waist. "You were so..." She flushed. "I completely forgot."

Bree felt nauseated. She had thought she'd feel never broken, never hurt if she had Diana's love. Instead, she was lying the way she'd never needed to before.

"Are you okay? Can I get you some water? Your pills?"

"No, I don't need anything." She swung her legs over the side of the bed, wondering if she was going to be sick. You can't give me what I need, she had almost added.

Diana doesn't have the power to heal you, Bree thought desperately. She never did, so what have you done? For the sake of what? She would have never...you seduced her...Pam has no idea.

'Epa, her ancestors hissed. Traitor.

Want was not love. Need was not love. Lust was not love. Diana had had love, all that could be true and real. Sharp as fire, her shoulder blades burned. All the gods, what had she done?

She never knew if it was her silence or her expression that told Diana the truth. Diana reached for her and Bree shrank from her touch. She'd fouled Diana enough.

"What's wrong? Say something." Diana's expression was both wary and alarmed. "You need to say something."

Kolohe, evil.

"It was just sex to you, wasn't it?" Diana was backing away. "I was just something to pass the time."

It sounded too much like truth for Bree to bear it. "It was more than that." All the gods, it had to be.

"But you don't want me to tell Pam. You don't want...me. Except in bed." Her gaze turned inward. "Pam will never forgive me. I'm never going to forgive myself."

"I've never done this before, Diana — "

"Could have fooled me. Because you reeled me in like a pro." Her bitterness broke over Bree's numb disbelief. "Every day I wanted to

218

tell you to go away. But Pam liked you. How could I tell her why I needed you to go? That you looked at me in a way I'd forgotten even existed? In a way that should have made me feel cheap but instead made me feel like, like a goddess?"

She threw back her head to gaze unrelentingly into Bree's eyes. "If all you wanted was sex, why didn't you just stay with Stacy? Why couldn't you leave me alone? What do you want from me?"

Nothing, Bree wanted to say. She had thought Diana would change the person she was, but nothing was fixed. All that had changed was her realization of what she had done. Pam didn't deserve this. Pam and Diana were meant to be together. Envy, greed, frustrated fears — none of those were Pam and Diana's problems.

Boredom? A challenge? Conquest? What kind of woman was she? It was an old-fashioned word, virtue, but one of the things that had drawn her to Diana was just that. And she'd destroyed it.

Lecherous, thieving snake, she raged to herself. You've had her and now you don't want her anymore? What did you think you were playing with? She's not some groupie, and was never, ever interested in a single night.

Her happiness was not yours to shatter. She didn't encourage you. All you had to do was go and none of this would have happened.

Diana was crying now. "How could I be so weak?"

Bree didn't see the slap coming but she deserved it. *What had she done?*

Diana stumbled to the other bedroom and Bree heard the lock click into place.

Her cheek stung for a moment, then she was just numb, empty and so cold.

As the water became deeper its chill intensified. Bree barely kept her nose above the swells, drifting now, hoping she was far enough out not to have to swim anymore. She was sleepy and shivering, empty and cold. The memories hadn't stopped. She could feel the sting of Diana's hand on her face. Diana hated her. Which was right.

She was *Makawela*, an outcast. She'd stolen something precious, used it and then tossed it away. Untrustworthy, evil, unbalanced, she was doomed to wander on the rocks forever. The gods would not want her. She would be no one's ancestor.

Jorie had been scared. She'd needed time and understanding. Instead, Bree had chosen not to listen. It was easier to leave than stay.

Lila had toyed with her and it had hurt. Jorie wasn't Lila.

The next trip was always ahead of her. She could never linger past breakfast, all those mornings waking up with different women. She was never there to accept a second date. Sex, breakfast and on to the next city, the next performance. The compulsion to express herself through the violin was so strong she had never seen the price she and everyone around her paid. She hadn't wanted to see it.

Aunt Lani had said that what she did with her body didn't matter, but how she treated her *'ohana* did. When Jorie had made even the faintest overture of friendship, Bree had rejected her. It was easier to be unhappy than risk being at peace.

Diana...she hadn't listened to Diana either. She might have never said no, but her tears had tried to say it. She'd asked Bree to stop, to leave her alone. She remembered Diana and Pam at the poker game, adoring each other, caring nothing about showing it to the world. That love was shattered by Bree's casual evil.

Guilt felt like stones in her pockets.

What had she done to Aunt Lani in the service of art? Aunt Lani had the heart of a whale, the joy of a dolphin, the compassion of the all-forgiving sea.

Was that why she couldn't say goodbye to Aunt Lani? Aunt Lani hadn't deserved Bree's avoidance of Jorie. It didn't matter that Aunt Lani understood. It hadn't been fair.

Every step toward a caring heart and a good life had been paved by Aunt Lani. Aunt Lani's kindness and commitment had been endless — *look what you've done with it.*

The violin wasn't the only gift she'd been given. It was just the one she'd paid attention to and when it was taken away she had nothing else to rely on.

Her soul was ash.

Diana's tear-streaked face flashed before her. Pam's stricken cry of confusion filled her ears.

She spluttered on a mouthful of salt water, then coughed violently as a wave broke over her head.

Bree didn't hear the car in the driveway. She'd sat for several hours in the bed, surrounded by the smell of what had been a night of Diana's love. Diana hadn't held anything back. Bree tortured herself with the memory of everything they'd done, stabbing the guilt into her heart, over and over.

It wasn't until Pam stood in the doorway, later that day, that she faced the coming storm. There was no escaping it.

"Heya," Pam said easily. "I got away early. Is my girl still skiing? I want to surprise her."

"No, she's — "

"Pam." Diana appeared in her bedroom doorway. "I need to talk to you."

Bree wanted to scream at Diana not to tell her. Let Diana hate her, but if she said nothing she could keep Pam. *Pam loves you, you fool, she loves you, and you never stopped loving her.* She wanted to leave now, ahead of the storm. Another city, another concert — and then she remembered that she couldn't escape to her violin. She had lost everything. "Don't."

Diana's look felt like a knife. "You don't get it, do you? You don't understand anything about love. She'll know anyway."

"Know what?" Pam's expression was clouding, as if she knew already but the truth was too terrible to take in.

"I slept with Bree. Last night." Diana sounded utterly cold.

Pam's mouth moved but Bree couldn't hear the words.

"It's my fault." She didn't even know if she spoke. She meant to. Pam had to believe it.

Diana burst into hysterical sobbing, falling to her knees. Neither she nor Pam moved.

"What are you telling me? Are you leaving me?"

221

"It was a mistake. Please forgive me, please."

Pam shook her head, then abruptly snapped her gaze to Bree. "How could you? I thought you were my — how could you do this?"

"I don't know." Bree wiped away the tears of tension that spilled down her cheeks.

"You fucked my girlfriend and all you can say is that you don't know why?"

"It was all me." Bree found the truth. "She never set out to do anything. I did it."

"All she had to do was say no!"

"I didn't give her the chance. Pam, I did it."

Pam's face twisted into a rigor of anger. "I can't believe I invited you into my home. What kind of evil bitch are you?"

"I thought I loved her."

Pam raised an arm, her entire body trembling. Poised to strike, she took a deep breath, then her arm dropped limply to her side. "How could you do that and not even love her?"

She whirled in place, hurling words at Diana in a scream. "She didn't even love you! Why did you do it?"

"Please, I don't know. You deserve to hate me, forgive me, baby, please."

"Oh god, don't." Pam stormed to the front door. "I can't look at either of you."

They were both ships on rocks Bree had brought into their lives, shattered and bleeding. "I didn't let her say no. I kept after her. I took her friendship and made her think it was more. Blame me, Pam, not her." It had to be mendable. She had to be able to fix it. How could she have broken something so precious? Even if Pam got over it their relationship would never be the same.

Kolohe, her ancestors reminded her.

The door slammed violently behind Pam and Bree knew she had to make Pam listen, somehow.

She winced at the snow soaking through her socks. Pam was opening the door to her car when Bree reached her.

"Beat me up, hate me, I did this. She'd have never looked at me twice if I hadn't done everything I could to make her. You have to believe me. She'd have never — "

"Shut up!" Pam slid into the driver's seat without looking back. She reached for the door.

Bree stretched her hand out to grasp Pam's shoulder.

Like she had the cabin door, Pam yanked the car door shut with all her strength.

Bree drew back with a cry, but she wasn't quick enough, and the brace wasn't designed to protect her wrist from the crush of metal designed to meld seamlessly with the frame of the car.

She shrieked in agony and only then did Pam look back.

Pam screamed something as Bree toppled into the snow. None of the words made sense.

She could only hear the stinging curses of her ancestors before they went silent. In the calmness of shock, the world going to gray static, she agreed.

She deserved this.

Bree coughed up more water, then felt something brush by her foot. She looked down to see *honumaoli*, the grandmother of the sea, swimming gracefully toward land. Her enormous shell was marked with the scars of a long life, but she moved like an angel through the water. The lullaby washed over her and she knew it was her mother's voice, once forgotten but so needed now. *Flying honu take me away, to where my true love will always be.*

She tried to spit salt out of her mouth. Her arms felt like lead. She was so tired.

She could hear a distant whisper through the fog of the pills and her limitless anguish. *Milimili keiki, milimili keiki...*precious one, beloved child. It was as if mother turtle sang to her as she glided by. *Come home, keiki.*

She knew how to swim too well, she realized. Muscle memory kept her afloat and would until she passed out. But now she was too tired to fight the incoming tide. She floated after the gliding vision, gently riding the surf until her knees scraped rocks. She stumbled out of the water to collapse on the sand.

She deserved her pain. She couldn't tell anyone why. What she'd done to Diana, and to Pam, had no forgiveness. There was no redemption, no fixing it.

Dr. Sheridan — and everyone else — thought Bree's despair was about the violin.

It was, it was, but so much more. No music, and her guilt, all of it. Her arrogance of playing games with someone's heart. Everything she'd said, everything she'd done had all been calculated to seduce Diana as if she was a prize. She hadn't done it for love, even, but for loneliness and fear. If she lost the violin she needed to replace it with something, and that object had been Diana.

She'd wept for months, it seemed, crying through her first appointments with the therapist Markham insisted she see. Dr. Sheridan offered theories about grief, about profound loss, but she didn't know anything about being filled to ecstasy with the power of music, the irresistible call of the violin. She couldn't begin to comprehend what it felt like to have your voice ripped out of you and *deserving* to lose such a gift. Bree signed the No Suicide contract but the thought was never far from her mind.

She refused Aunt Lani's offer to come to her in Los Angeles, lying and lying and lying that she was getting better.

Despondent — that diagnosis was a laugh. She refused the antidepressants because she had no business feeling better. She lost track of what day it was, then what month it was. If she was lucky, she sometimes forgot what year it was. The past, any past before Diana, was the only place where the pain was remotely bearable.

Two surgeries and another year of learning words for different kinds of pain left her no better than when Pam had screeched into the nearest emergency room. After the second surgery, which increased rather than reduced the scar tissue, she'd refused all further offerings of hope. She would not see anyone in Vienna, nobody in London. All the gods, not even the promise of a cure would make her return to San Francisco.

She'd been happy there, with Diana and Pam as her friends.

She'd smashed her friendship with Diana to pieces, and destroyed the pure magic of Diana and Pam. She'd tried once to contact Pam, to try again to explain that Diana wasn't to blame, but the answering machine was the only voice she ever heard. Pam's clipped words did not offer to accept a message for Diana.

She had no idea where Diana had gone.

Playing games with other people's hearts — she deserved every wave of agony she would suffer for the rest of her life.

Why couldn't she end it? She wanted the pain to stop. Life was pain. Life was suffering. Better to let the music fade away now.

The sand was hot as it gave up the heat of the day.

Come home, keiki.

She dragged herself up off the sand, barely taking the time to brush it from her face. Some tourists were looking at her surreptitiously.

Her legs felt like rubber. Pills, she thought, reaching into her pocket. A couple more and maybe she wouldn't have pain at all. Nevermore, quoth the *manu*. The pill bottle was full of water. She might have more in the car.

Come home, keiki.

I have no home, Aunt Lani. I have no music, no love, no soul.

Her eyes could hardly focus enough to get the key in the lock. Belatedly, she realized she was on the wrong side of the car. She was in Hawaii, not London. She got out again, but stumbled, thudding to the asphalt. Her sharp cry sounded very far away.

Even though the asphalt was warm, she was shivering. She used her good hand to pull herself up to her knees. That was when she saw the violin case.

She flipped the latches and took the violin out, holding it by its delicate neck.

It was only a practice violin. She'd only had it for years. It was only filled with countless hours of her devotion, the exercise of the gift she'd been born with. A gift from the gods, she realized now, was double-edged. Play the violin and be filled with music and empty of so much else.

Holding the violin gave it voice. It whispered its lies. Play me and you will be fine. *Play me and she will love you. Play me and they will forgive you. Play me...*

She stumbled over the soft, white sand, violin in her right hand, bow clutched clumsily in her left. She stood near the sanctuary, where the ocean was smooth and gentle.

Violin to chin. Bow on string.

Her right hand had nothing to remember. Her left twitched with the agony of memory.

Even in the sacred place, wanting desperately for something to change, to get better or worse — anything but living day to day in such pain — she could find no grace or elegance.

To the rocks then, to be *Makewela*. To live without simplicity or ease. To suffer for every moment of life while pain was allowed to blaze symphonies into her helpless mind. To be an outcast from her ancestors.

To never see Jorie again. If she had the violin she could be near Jorie and resist her feelings. Without it she was weak. Diana hadn't even wanted her at the first, and Bree had still managed to ruin her life. Part of Jorie still wanted Bree and there was no way Bree could resist temptation now. She had become so weak and foolish, thinking she could find happiness at Pam's expense. She would not do to Mea what she'd done to Pam.

The rough rocks of the place of outcasts bit into her feet when she left the trail. Lumps of black, frozen 'a'a, sharp and glassy, scraped her heels. When she fell she saved the violin from damage, and knew she'd cut her thigh.

On that small stretch of tormented sand, where forbidden ones tried to survive until forgiveness was possible, Bree tried for the last time. Violin to shoulder, bow to strings — ignore the pain, she told herself. You deserve to suffer.

You have to live with what you've done.

Come home, keiki.

There is nothing you can't do, Bree...

Yes, she wanted to scream. *Now there is. I can't do this!*

Words were impossible.

She swayed on her feet, aware dimly that blood was running down her leg. A wave pounded the sand, sending spray into the air. Her cut burned and she thought she heard the violin scream.

It was full of lies. She couldn't believe them.

Something had to change. She could not stay here.

The lotus flower had had none of her grief.

She stood in the surf, ignoring the relentless sting of salt water on her abraded feet and torn leg. It was so insignificant that she called it the Meaningless Pain.

She forced the bow under the strings where they were lifted highest over the sounding box, and centered it. She kissed the violin between the tuning pegs. Wading deeper, she waited for a large swell to set the violin on its journey.

Goodbye Aunt Lani, goodbye Jorie, goodbye music. Good-bye all that she loved. All that was left was the pain and the aching void she could not seem to escape.

She regained the shore as the violin drifted away. If her grief went with it she didn't feel it. If guilt was diminished she had no proof of it.

Goodbye ecstasy, goodbye passion, goodbye grace.

Whatever was left meant nothing.

She stood there as the sun streaked the ocean with gold. She wanted to go back into the water and this time let go. This time she would end the pain.

It would be too easy, her guilt reminded her. She deserved to live and suffer.

She deserved the life she had earned.

"My God, Bree! What happened?" Jorie was frozen in the act of putting away a coffee cup.

"I fell, that's all." Bree knew she looked like something dead the tide had spit up.

"You're bleeding." Mea picked up a tea towel. "You need to get this cleaned up."

"I'm okay. I'll take a shower before I do anything else."

"Penny, get the first aid kit, okay?" Jorie didn't seem to hear Bree's protest when she brushed her fingers over Bree's thigh.

Bree jerked herself away from the contact. She couldn't stay.

She stumbled to the bathroom, locking the door behind her. The shower might have been hot, but she didn't really feel it. Sand streamed off her body as she shed her clothes and the water at her feet ran pink into the drain.

She used an old towel to staunch the blood as she dressed. The pain pills were wearing off and her aching legs and arms were beginning to scream almost as loud as her wrist.

"Bree, you've got to let me bandage that." Jorie stood in the doorway, a white kit in her hand. "I think it needs stitches."

"I'll be fine." She pulled her suitcase from under the bed and tossed in a handful of clothes. "I have to go."

"What? It's after nine o'clock. Go where?"

"I can get a helicopter to Honolulu. From there anywhere." But she knew where she was going.

"You're crazy."

Was that abrasive sound her bitter laugh? "You understand at last."

"Bree, you don't have to — "

"Yes, I do!" Bree knew that Jorie didn't deserve to be shouted at, but she couldn't help herself. "And you know why!"

"I don't understand."

"That's the whole fucking point, Jorie. It's always been the point. We've never understood each other. I can't stay now. I'm not strong enough to stay."

Jorie crossed the room quickly. "You can't leave like this."

Bree pushed her away before Jorie could embrace her. "I'm not a rock." She saw Mea in the doorway now. In the faintest of whispers she let the truth finally come into being. "I've never stopped loving you. I'm leaving because I'll hurt you or her if I stay. This is my problem, not yours. It's always been my problem."

"We can work it out — "

"How?"

When Jorie didn't answer, Bree went back to filling the suitcase.

She heard Mea murmur something to Jorie but what didn't matter. Penny was the only one who cried when she left.

The sun was rising in Los Angeles. Her leg had finally stopped bleeding, but her entire body was stiff when Bree struggled up the jetway.

She hadn't been able to sleep on the flight, or eat, or even think. All colors were shades of gray. The music in the terminal sounded like static.

She gave the cab driver the address. He was pleased with the length of the drive, but Bree hardly cared.

Brown sky today, though that might have been her exhausted eyes painting the landscape in sepia and hopelessness. All the gods, she hated this feeling, though she deserved it. The cistern of despair was huge and she could feel herself falling into it again.

"This it?"

Bree started out of her daze. The hour's drive hadn't registered any more than the flight had. "Yes."

She left her suitcase on the path as she stumbled to the front door. It took both hands to steady herself enough to ring the bell.

She rang it again after a few seconds, then the curtain in the nearby window flickered. She heard a lock turning. Please, she thought. I made it this far.

Dr. Sheridan gazed at her in deep concern.

"I need to — to..." Her legs gave way under her and the last thing she remembered was the swirling arc of the hopeless sky.

How does that make you feel?
Like I want to die, she answered. There was only truth left in her.
How does that make you feel?
Like I killed her and Pam, killed what they were together.

229

How does that make you feel?
Like I want to shove that stupid question down your fucking throat.
Why are you angry?
Because I had everything and I threw it away.
You didn't throw the violin away. You were hurt.
I threw away Aunt Lani's love. I never let Jorie in. I robbed myself of watching Penny grow up. I ran from every woman I ever touched. Those were the things that really mattered.
If you could play right now, would you still think you had lost everything?
You don't understand. I don't even understand. The violin played me. I could never say no.
How does that make you feel?
If it hadn't been so beautiful, so welcome to so many people, I would have felt cursed.
How does that make you feel?
I crave it, every minute of every hour.
How does that make you feel?
Like I want to die.
How does that make you feel?
Like I want to shove that stupid question down your fucking throat...

Bree tugged her suit sleeve down to hide the scars on her left wrist. Dr. Sheridan constantly reminded her that while it felt like she would never get used to it, eventually she would. She smoothed her skirt and smiled at the young woman behind the desk.

"How can I help you?"

"I don't have an appointment, but I think she'll see me. I'm willing to wait for even just a few minutes between appointments." Bree proffered her card.

The woman's eyes widened when she read the name. "Well...I can check. But I can't promise anything."

"I'll wait. May I?" She indicated one of the chairs flanking the desk.

"Of course." Bree waited patiently until the woman glanced at her phone display, then went into the office behind her. She returned in short order, her expression guarded. "She'll see you now."

Bree hoped the receptionist didn't see the shudder that ran through her. She hadn't told Dr. Sheridan she was going to do this, but her ancestors wouldn't let her be.

Wiwoʻole, they hummed.

She stood in the doorway a moment, then stepped through. Only when the door was closed behind her did the woman at the desk look up.

Pam had always been thin, but to Bree she looked emaciated now. In a couple of months it would be two years.

"I can't believe you have the nerve to come here."

She saw Pam's gaze flick to her wrist and was glad she'd covered it. "I'm not here to ask for forgiveness."

"Good thing because there isn't any. Why are you doing this?"

Bree crossed the large office, but stopped when Pam abruptly stood up. "You're the one with the power to mend things. You're the only one who can."

Pam looked again at her wrist. "I'm not a doctor — "

"I don't care about that." Tears started in her eyes because it wasn't quite the truth yet. But Dr. Sheridan said Bree was not far from the final stage of her grief, acceptance. All the gods, that was annoying, being a textbook case.

"I don't believe you."

"I'm learning, literally, to live with it. It was an accident. That's not why I'm here."

"You have about thirty seconds before I have you tossed out on your ass. I don't care who you are. Or were."

It was meant to hurt, but Bree could let it go. "She was more than your lover, Pam."

"She betrayed me."

"She had help. A lot of help from me. I ignored every way she tried to tell me no."

"Did she ever say it? I know she didn't — she told me she didn't. And she expected me to forgive her."

Pam's anger was so close to the surface, even after all this time, that

Bree felt the heat of it. "You can forgive."

"Never."

Bree spread her hands. "Do you like the way you feel, Pam? Will anyone ever make you feel the way she did? I know she hurt you, and I did, too. It can't be like it never broke, but it can be mended. And it's all up to you."

"Have you talked to her?" The question seemed to force itself from between Pam's lips.

"No." It was the truth. Bree felt a flicker of hope. Pam and Diana's love for each other had been deep and real. "But I know where she is. And I know when she'll be there."

Pam sank down into her chair with a quiet moan. "I don't want to stop being mad at her."

"I know. Because if you did you'd realize that she hurt you about as badly as she could, but it didn't kill all the love."

"Stop."

"An hour. I can have you there and back in an hour. You can decide if you want to talk to her."

"I can't."

"She looks just like you do, Pam. Like she's walking around with half of herself gone."

"I can't."

"If not today, I'll come back tomorrow. I'll come back the day after. Tell me when, unless you really want to go on feeling this way. I know how you hurt."

Pam's eyes flashed with anger. "You can't possibly know, not after what you did."

Bree pulled her sleeve so the surgical scars were visible. "Since I was four I was in love with the violin. It was an all-consuming passion, a desperate addiction and I never minded because it was so beautiful, what we created. I never let anything in my life mean more. It meant more than breathing."

Pam's eyes had filled with tears. "I never meant for that to happen."

"I know. It was an accident. I'm trying to say that I'm learning to go on living with it." Bree took a shaky, deep breath. "There are days when I can't think for the memories of music in my head. But I'm learning. I'm trying. The thing is, as much as this has cost me, I know that I cost you so much...more."

The tear trickling down Pam's cheek matched Bree's own. "I can't do this. It still hurts too much. It's going to hurt forever."

"She loved you. Even when she said yes — for one short moment of weakness that I exploited into a few hours — she was thinking about you. She looks horrible, Pam. Even if you can go on feeling the way you do, can you let her go on that way? You're the one with all the power here. You're the only one who can help her."

Pam sank into her chair again, her head in her hands. "I trusted you. I liked you. I should have seen what you were doing and fought for her." Tears splashed onto the desk.

Bree dashed away her own tears. "I was an invisible evil. You had no reason to see me there."

"Where is she?"

"Not far. Come with me."

Pam dried her eyes. "I don't go ballooning anymore, either. You took everything away."

Bree circled Pam's desk and went to one knee next to her. "Nothing I can ever say or do will make up for the pain I've cost you. I know that. It is harder to live with that than it is my wrist. If you come with me now you will never have to look at me again no matter what it is you decide to do."

After a brief conversation with her assistant, Pam left the building with Bree. The drive was short and silent.

Bree knew the place to park in the school lot that faced Diana's door. "The bell will ring in four minutes."

"How did you find her?"

"I assumed if she wasn't with you she went back to teaching."

"Of course she would. I should have known." Pam sniffed. "I didn't look. She took half of the money out of the household account, left me a note and then nothing. Her name is still on everything but the

233

only thing I had the energy to fix was the answering machine. You both left me frozen."

The prolonged ringing of the school bell broke the silence of the next few minutes. Classroom doors opened and children streamed toward waiting buses and cars.

Pam's agonized gasp told Bree all she needed to know. "My god. Oh, my poor baby."

She didn't think that Pam even cared that it was her shoulder she cried into. Bree gave her a moment, then handed her a tissue. "I told you — she looks like hell. Just like you do. Neither of you can move on, if that's what you want to do. You can't stay like this. I know what I'm talking about. Something has to change."

"I can't just walk up to her. Not after all this time."

Bree reached into the back seat. "You can. You have presents."

"What?" Pam blew her nose as she looked at Bree.

"I couldn't find Jolt anywhere, but maybe this will do. But those are the right donuts, aren't they?"

Pam looked at the six-pack and box. "Fuck you for knowing she would like this."

"I had all the time in the world to give her. You were busy living a life with her."

"I'm never going to thank you. And I never want to see you again."

"I know."

Pam got out of the car, then abruptly reached in for the soda and donuts. She slammed the car door, then, and walked away.

Bree watched her hesitate in the classroom doorway. After a few seconds, the soda and donuts fell to the floor and she disappeared inside.

Three minutes later, when Pam didn't reappear, Bree backed out of the parking space. She was willing to bet that Diana would give Pam a lift home. Maybe they couldn't mend it enough to be together. But now maybe they could move on.

How does that make you feel?

Happy, and I don't deserve to be, Bree thought to herself. She didn't deserve anything but pain.

CHAPTER THIRTEEN

Time does not heal all wounds. Even if her ancestors had sung it to her, Bree would never believe it. Time allowed her to grow bigger than the hurts she carried inside and out, but the scars would always be there.

She could carry a light bag in her left hand now, and it was just one of the ways Bree knew this trip home would be different. A wedding was much more pleasant to contemplate than a funeral.

It had been three years since she'd staggered back to L.A., and yet the mountains and sky hadn't changed. A year of therapy, then a year of wandering, trying to feel as if she could settle someplace and start a new life. It hadn't worked. She couldn't settle into something new while she was surrounded with the old.

Another year then, to tidy up her life, sell condos, arrange the gift of her notes and papers to her old conservatory and settle herself in L.A. where at least she could see the ocean. The last year had finally eased some of the ache. Markham had pestered her with lecture opportunities all along. She'd finally given in just to have *something* to do.

Three years, she thought. The land and sea were forever beautiful. She'd been away from them too long. This was home. She'd settle here if it weren't for still loving Jorie.

She helped the skycap find her bags — no violin case to ignore this time, but instead a large box with her wedding gift and the awkward case that contained the electronic keyboard she used for composing. When she let herself, she found a small measure of pleasure in composition. Her ear always heard the keyboard as violin and it never sounded like she knew it ought to. But her left hand could manage the keys decently enough. It helped to think of it as a creative effort, not real music. It no longer hurt so much to breathe any kind of music in.

She drove south along the Queen Kaahumanu Highway, the windows down and the radio tuned to Two Guys in the Afternoon. The words to the Hawaiian version of "The Twelve Days of Christmas" came back to her with ease.

She sang her way through Kona, resisting the urge to drive like Beijing when it slowed. No reason to stop along the way. This trip she carried regrets and grief, yes, but she was no longer pursued by demon memory.

She was realistic, though, and had insisted she stay at a hotel instead of the house. Even after she'd finally told Dr. Sheridan everything, even three years later, after enough tears to drown out a volcano, her feelings about Jorie hadn't changed. She had never made it to acceptance about Jorie.

So she'd said, in that brief conversation with Jorie, that there was too much going on for a houseguest. After she checked in, she aimed her arrival at the church to be just in time for the rehearsal where she was joining Jorie and two of Penny's best friends as maids of honor.

She saw Jorie before Jorie saw her, and told herself it would not always be so hard to breathe. It cost her a pang to smile at Jorie, then she reminded herself it would get easier. The hubbub of the rehearsal was a good cover. A few words and they were separated by necessity. Hamu was trying to get everyone into places. Bree had barely enough time to hug Momi.

Riki looked like all his dreams were coming true when he gazed at Penny. Bree had a good feeling about their marriage, even if they were both barely nineteen.

"Come back to the house for rehearsal dinner, Aunt Bree. You're not too tired," Penny insisted. "Tell me how you are and everything. I mean you said in your e-mails, but I want to hear all about it."

Bree laughed. They paused on the steps as people sorted out who was riding with whom. "You just want to hear about me meeting Boyz Without Gunz."

Penny laughed. "Okay, maybe I do. But you have to wait until I find Amelia — she is a fanatic about them."

Bree ended up with Penny, Riki and his younger sister in her car. "Okay, so I was just there to arrange a strings section overlay on this one song. It does help to have an agent who sees possibilities better than you do. It's not what I would have thought of as something I could do."

"So what were they like?" Amelia bounced in the seat next to her. Penny was cuddled with Riki in the back seat, listening.

"Pretty ordinary, actually. Drinking coffee and the drummer was having a hot dog. The lead singer — Mark — "

Amelia squealed.

"Mark was sort of in charge. I think he knows the most about music." Mark was the only one in the band who'd attended music school.

She dropped her voice to approximate a sleepy Grunge baritone. "So. Glad you could help us out. Totally dug your Mozart-Paganini."

Penny chortled.

"Then," Bree went on, "he looks at my wrist." She held it aloft so the three of them could see the scars from the final surgery. "And this is what he says." She cleared her throat. "Brutal, man."

She joined them in laughter. In a way, the young man's succinct assessment had been exactly what she needed to hear. The session had turned out to be both intriguing and rewarding, just as Markham had promised. Damn him anyway. All the gods, she hated other people being right about what she needed.

"Hey, that's so cool!" Penny took Bree's wrist and turned it so she could see the underside. "Turtles swimming."

Riki seemed equally impressed. "That must have hurt like anything."

Bree shrugged and pulled her hand gently away. It was awkward to drive with her hand pulled over her shoulder. "There's pain and there's pain. I didn't feel it much."

Dr. Sheridan had approved of the tattoo. Bree thought she might go back and have the design finished all the way around her wrist. The artist had integrated the scars into the outline of the shell in places. In some ways it made her wrist something she had chosen.

She turned into the driveway and the headlights played over the kitchen window. Someone was there. Jorie, maybe? Mea slicing oranges? The thought of them hurt, but it no longer incapacitated her.

Again, it was helpful to have a lot of people around. She chatted with Momi and made herself useful finding serving spoons and fetching ice from the freezer in the garage. She consciously let the moments blur. After a while it would be easier to stay in the moment and accept the ache of what she would never have.

She was helping Jorie find a platter when it sank in that she hadn't seen Mea. Not at the rehearsal — but then she'd thought perhaps Mea had had a class — and not here.

Her heart missed a beat.

No, she thought. I won't wish for anything. Jorie doesn't deserve it and neither does Mea.

The dinner was a happy affair. Best men and maids of honor went to great lengths to embarrass both bride and groom with stories of peccadilloes that made both mothers and Riki's father lose their eyebrows into their hairlines.

"Aren't you glad you didn't know about the naked snorkeling?" Bree gave Jorie a bright, teasing smile.

"I'm stunned. But you know, Mom didn't catch me at half the stuff

I did. I thought she was just not being very observant. And I obviously did no better!"

Under the cover of the laughter, Bree muttered, "Lani would have never known you-know-what if you hadn't told her."

"She'd have known," Jorie admitted. "My own choices gave me some blind spots about Penny's."

Bree nodded and wondered how to ask about Mea. But there didn't seem an easy way to bring her up. With the house rearranged for the large dinner party and the reception tomorrow, she couldn't spot any obvious signs of Mea not living there anymore. Her glance into the bedroom was equally uninformative.

She would not hope.

She stayed to do dishes and clean up with the older crowd while the young people dashed off in cars for bachelor and bachelorette parties. Without realizing it until the door was closed, the rest of party had drifted to their cars as well and she was abruptly alone with Jorie.

She hadn't meant that to happen. "It's one a.m. on my body clock," she announced. "I'd better get some serious sleep or I'll be useless tomorrow." Mea's absence was obvious now, but she couldn't ask.

Jorie ran a weary hand through her hair. Though tired, she looked pleased. She imitated Penny's chirp. "Let's have a wedding at Christmas break, Mom. You can finish grading your papers early." She groaned. "What was I thinking?"

"That with any luck she's only going to get married once."

"Oh please. I couldn't do this twice. If there is a next time it's a ticket to Vegas."

"I don't think there will be a next time for them. They got it right early."

They stared at each other when their smiles faded.

"You look good," Jorie said. "Better. Your hair's growing out."

"Thanks. I feel better."

"Aren't you going to ask? Or did you ask someone else?"

"I didn't want to pry."

"San Diego. There was a sudden opening in the med center there and she took it."

"Just like that? But you two seemed so — "

"I know." Jorie didn't seem heartbroken, just sad. "I need some air. Walk up the hill with me?"

She shouldn't. Bree knew she shouldn't. The hill had too many memories.

Of course she went.

Jorie led the way, her sandals nearly silent in the moonlight. She gained the fallen tree first and sat down, her head tipped back to look at the stars.

Bree joined her, stretching her legs out in front of her with what she hoped was convincing nonchalance.

"She made the right choice," Jorie said. "I did love her."

"I know you did." That's why I left, Bree wanted to say. Her heart was pounding with confusion.

"I loved Brian, too. Well, he was a guy and it was always easier to be casual with guys. Like they didn't really touch the right places inside me. I thought I loved the lying rat bastard, too."

"May he rot in hell," Bree intoned. She recognized that smothering Diana in attention was like the tactics Penny's father had used on Jorie. She didn't feel good about that.

"Yeah. I thought I loved the first woman I slept with after Brian. It wasn't Mea."

Bree tried to hide her surprise. All the gods, not that she was judging Jorie in any way. "I hadn't realized there was someone before her."

"A couple of someones. I tried to be casual about it. Sort of like I had treated guys. But it always meant so much more with women. I couldn't play with women's hearts. And then Mea came along and she was so nice. And we got along so well. I did love her, but not enough. I wanted to."

Bree's heart rate continued to escalate. The moonlight was playing tricks. When Jorie turned her head to look at Bree, gaze directly into her eyes, Bree thought Jorie was going to kiss her.

No, she thought. I won't go through it again. Her reflexive fear of the greatest pain she knew — not having Jorie's love — made her draw back.

Moonlight shimmered in Jorie's eyes. "You don't have to say

anything, Bree. You can leave if you want and I'll never bring it up again. But I have to say this. I've tried so many times. I tried to admit that when we said we were doing it because we were friends that I didn't feel the least bit friendly. You never heard me. I didn't think you wanted to."

Bree could hardly breathe. "You might be right. It was easier to leave than it was to stay."

Jorie's lips curved in the glimmer of a smile. "I thought I loved other people. Part of me did. But they could never be you. They could never measure up to you. After you left, I told Mea the truth. That even though you had never wanted me in your life, that I could never possibly compete with the other demands on your energy, that you'd say you loved me then push me away, I loved you with the best part of my heart."

Jorie's gaze flicked to Bree's wrist, then came back to her face. "I was afraid when I was young, and still afraid later when I saw how you'd changed. I couldn't compete with all those women, and not with the violin. I never wished that on you!" Jorie leaned forward, abruptly intense. "I never wanted your career to end. I thought I'd have to live with it, that's all. And find what happiness I could. But now..."

"Everything's changed." Bree abruptly felt flooded with her anger and grief. She shook the emotion away. She had to, or she'd screw up what Jorie was offering. The future mattered so much more than the past.

"I don't want to be friends, Bree." Jorie put her hand over Bree's. "I want to try to be more. Because we might get it right this time."

Bree wanted to say that she'd always loved Jorie, which was true. But her mind was spinning with all the music she'd ever thought described Jorie and she realized none of it was right.

She looked into Jorie's eyes and saw things she knew. There were as many things she did not know, too.

She studied Jorie's face while her heart pounded in erratic double-time. She let herself feel and consider a future made up of Jorie. She dreamed a new mansion for them, one based on love, not fevered adolescent longings or irrational adult pride. Instead of a castle in the air, it looked more like this island, this house, this hillside.

There was no reason to be afraid of it anymore. She hoped no one ever asked her what she would choose if she could have the violin back, but only if she gave up a life with Jorie. It was not a question she could resolve now, if ever.

But that choice was no longer before her.

She touched Jorie's face. She stopped thinking about what would happen the next time she and Jorie were alone together. This time was what mattered.

If she was willing to set aside her arrogance and fears, this time could last forever.

"I don't deserve this." Bree brushed her fingertips over Jorie's hair. "I don't deserve you."

"I know." Jorie grinned at her and the reflected moonlight from her laughing eyes pierced Bree's heart to the very core. She looked twenty again, the way she always looked twenty. "*Hupo haole*, you've been an idiot."

MAYBE NEXT TIME by Karin Kallmaker. 256 pp. Sabrina Starling always believed in maybe next time...until now.   ISBN 1-931513-26-0 $12.95

WHEN GOOD GIRLS GO BAD: A Motor City Thriller by Therese Szymanski. 230 pp. Brett, Randi, and Allie join forces to stop a serial killer.
ISBN 1-931513-11-2 $12.95

A DAY TOO LONG: A Helen Black Mystery by Pat Welch. 328 pp. This time Helen's fate is in her own hands.   ISBN 1-931513-22-8 $12.95

THE RED LINE OF YARMALD by Diana Rivers. 256 pp. The Hadra's only hope lies in a magical red line...Climactic sequel to *Clouds of War*.
ISBN 1-931513-23-6 $12.95

OUTSIDE THE FLOCK by Jackie Calhoun. 224 pp. Jo embraces her new love and life.   ISBN 1-931513-13-9 $12.95

LEGACY OF LOVE by Marianne K. Martin. 224 pp. Read the whole Sage Bristo story.   ISBN 1-931513-15-5 $12.95

STREET RULES: A Detective Franco Mystery by Baxter Clare. 304 pp. Gritty, fast-paced mystery with compelling Detective L.A. Franco
ISBN 1-931513-14-7 $12.95

RECOGNITION FACTOR: 4th Denise Cleever Thriller by Claire McNab. 176 pp. Denise Cleever tracks a notorious terrorist to America.
ISBN 1-931513-24-4 $12.95

NORA AND LIZ by Nancy Garden. 296 pp. Lesbian romance by the author of Annie on My Mind.   ISBN 1931513-20-1 $12.95

MIDAS TOUCH by Frankie J. Jones. 208 pp. Sandra had everything but love.
ISBN 1-931513-21-X $12.95

BEYOND ALL REASON by Peggy J. Herring. 240 pp. A romance hotter than Texas.   ISBN 1-9513-25-2 $12.95

ACCIDENTAL MURDER: 14th Detective Inspector Carol Ashton Mystery by Claire McNab. 208 pp.Carol Ashton tracks an elusive killer.
ISBN 1-931513-16-3 $12.95

SEEDS OF FIRE:Tunnel of Light Trilogy, Book 2 by Karin Kallmaker writing as Laura Adams. 274 pp. Intriguing sequel to Sleight of Hand.
ISBN 1-931513-19-8 $12.95

DRIFTING AT THE BOTTOM OF THE WORLD by Auden Bailey. 288 pp. Beautifully written first novel set inAntarctica. ISBN 1-931513-17-1 $12.95

CLOUDS OF WAR by Diana Rivers. 288 pp. Women unite to defend Zelindar!
ISBN 1-931513-12-0 $12.95

DEATHS OF JOCASTA: 2nd Micky Knight Mystery by J.M. Redmann. 408 pp. Sexy and intriguing Lambda Literary Award-nominated mystery.
ISBN 1-931513-10-4 $12.95

LOVE IN THE BALANCE by Marianne K. Martin. 256 pp. The classic lesbian love story, back in print! ISBN 1-931513-08-2 $12.95

THE COMFORT OF STRANGERS by Peggy J. Herring. 272 pp. Lela's work was her passion...until now. ISBN 1-931513-09-0 $12.95

CHICKEN by Paula Martinac. 208 pp. Lynn finds that the only thing harder than being in a lesbian relationship is ending one.
ISBN 1-931513-07-4 $11.95

TAMARACK CREEK by Jackie Calhoun. 208 pp. An intriguing story of love and danger. ISBN 1-931513-06-6 $11.95

DEATH BY THE RIVERSIDE: 1st Micky Knight Mystery by J.M. Redmann. 320 pp. Finally back in print, the book that launched the Lambda Literary Award-winning Micky Knight mystery series. ISBN 1-931513-05-8 $11.95

EIGHTH DAY: A Cassidy James Mystery by Kate Calloway. 272 pp. In the eighth installment of the Cassidy James mystery series, Cassidy goes undercover at a camp for troubled teens. ISBN 1-931513-04-X $11.95

MIRRORS by Marianne K. Martin. 208 pp. Jean Carson and Shayna Bradley fight for a future together. ISBN 1-931513-02-3 $11.95

THE ULTIMATE EXIT STRATEGY: A Virginia Kelly Mystery by Nikki Baker. 240 pp. The long-awaited return of the wickedly observant Virginia Kelly.
ISBN 1-931513-03-1 $11.95

FOREVER AND THE NIGHT by Laura DeHart Young. 224 pp. Desire and passion ignite the frozen Arctic in this exciting sequel to the classic romantic adventure Love on the Line. ISBN 0-931513-00-7 $11.95

WINGED ISIS by Jean Stewart. 240 pp. The long-awaited sequel to Warriors of Isis and the fourth in the exciting Isis series. ISBN 1-931513-01-5 $11.95

ROOM FOR LOVE by Frankie J. Jones. 192 pp. Jo and Beth must overcome the past in order to have a future together. ISBN 0-9677753-9-6 $11.95

THE QUESTION OF SABOTAGE by Bonnie J. Morris. 144 pp. A charming, sexy tale of romance, intrigue, andcoming of age.
ISBN 0-9677753-8-8 $11.95

SLEIGHT OF HAND by Karin Kallmaker writing as Laura Adams. 256 pp. A journey of passion, heartbreak and triumph that reunites two women for a final chance at their destiny. ISBN 0-9677753-7-X $11.95

MOVING TARGETS: A Helen Black Mystery by Pat Welch. 240 pp. Helen must decide if getting to the bottom of a mystery is worth hitting bottom. ISBN 0-9677753-6-1 $11.95

CALM BEFORE THE STORM by Peggy J. Herring. 208 pp. Colonel Robicheaux retires from the military and comes out of the closet. ISBN 0-9677753-1-0 $12.95

OFF SEASON by Jackie Calhoun. 208 pp. Pam threatens Jenny and Rita's fledgling relationship. ISBN 0-9677753-0-2 $11.95

WHEN EVIL CHANGES FACE: A Motor City Thriller by Therese Szymanski. 240 pp. Brett Higgins is back in another heart-pounding thriller. ISBN 0-9677753-3-7 $11.95

BOLD COAST LOVE by Diana Tremain Braund. 208 pp. Jackie Claymont fights for her reputation and the right to love the woman she chooses. ISBN 0-9677753-2-9 $11.95

THE WILD ONE by Lyn Denison. 176 pp. Rachel never expected that Quinn's wild yearnings would change her lifeforever. ISBN 0-9677753-4-5 $12.95

SWEET FIRE by Saxon Bennett. 224 pp. Welcome to Heroy—the town with the most lesbians per capita than any other place on the planet! ISBN 0-9677753-5-3 $11.95